blocked

lisa n. paul

Cover design by Regina Wamba of Mae I Design
Formatting by JT Formatting

First Edition: February 2015
Library of Congress Cataloging-in-Publication Data

Paul, Lisa N.
Super Dandy Publishing
Blocked – 1st ed
ISBN-13: 978-0-9892465-5-2 | ISBN-10: 0989246558

To those of you who have started over.
Be it in love, career, family, or self—you're an incredible mentor
and a thriving survivor.
To those of you still wondering if you can do it…
You CAN. Believing in yourself is the only way to ever really
become unBlocked.

CHAPTER
FIFTEEN

(No, Really You Haven't Missed Anything…
Here's A Glimpse of What's to Come)

ER GREEN EYES shimmered, revealing mutual desire as she lifted the glass of merlot to her full lips, parting them to take another small sip. Christ, those lips, so soft and sweet…Decker could practically taste them as he tried to convince himself to look away from what shouldn't have been such an ethereal sight. But it seemed as though everything April Maddox did was sexy as hell and erotic as sin. He couldn't fool himself into thinking otherwise; therefore, why bother missing any part of her beautiful show? With his gaze focused squarely on the delectable vision next to him, he inhaled—there was no ignoring the erection pulsing behind the zipper in his slacks. Everything the woman said or did affected him, and he'd venture to guess she was not clueless to her role in his torture. No, he could see the hunger in her eyes, the mutual ache of sexual desire. She was wanton. As the glass touched her mouth and the deep burgundy liquid ran up the tapered bowl of the wineglass, caressing her glossy painted lips, Decker's mind automatically fixated on apples. When he claimed her lips after dinner, would they still taste like the apple gloss he'd enjoyed earlier that evening? Or would the sweet grapes of the wine touch his tongue and flavor their kiss? Not that it mattered, as long as he got to own her mouth for a few minutes, got to taste the essence of the woman who was quickly changing the very foundation on which he'd built his life. She could taste like wood filler, and he'd relish it. A man could easily become addicted to those lips, as well as those mind-bending kisses—lord knows he had, and it'd only been two real dates. Well, this was their third...

"Decker?" Just the sound of his name in her honey-smooth voice had his heart beating faster and his length hardening to an aching throb. "Deck, is everything okay?" April lowered her glass to the table, shifting her lithe body smoothly in the U-shaped booth.

As they turned toward each other, his knee gently brushed her leg, and he watched her questioning gaze descend slowly from his eyes to where his hands gripped his upper thighs, his thumbs all but digging into the cotton of his perfectly pressed pants. April's perusal paused briefly, the minute she noticed what was practically impossible for him to hide. The audible catch of her breath as it held for a beat, and the slight flush that kissed her cheeks a fraction of a second before she licked her lips, and brought her steamy green gaze back to his face, nearly set him ablaze. Yeah, everything would be just fine once he finally got her alone and beneath him. His body vibrated with need for the incredible woman beside him. It had been so long... so long since he'd felt this way. Had he ever truly felt like this before?

"You look...stiff, Deck." Her shy smile was now charged with a vixen-like confidence he'd never seen on her before.

That look made him want to sweep the dishes from their table—to hell with the mess or the prying eyes of the other diners—spread her out before him like a main course, and finally see if her whole body tasted as sweet as her damn lips. When she placed her small hand over his and began tracing tiny circles with her index finger over his sensitized flesh, Decker was pulled from a lustful haze and into the moment. April Maddox knew exactly what she was saying, knew just how her gentle touches were affecting him.

"I've heard massage can help with *that* sort of problem." Her gaze flitted to his lap then back to his eyes before a smirk curled the ends of her upturned mouth. The innuendo played openly on her beautiful face.

Lifting both of their hands from his thigh, he twisted his wrist to bring her palm to his lips. Decker breathed in her warm, fruity smell then placed a kiss on the soft skin. "You're a funny lady, you know that?"

He could barely contain the laughter in his voice, and truth was he didn't want to. He liked April as a person; her humor, intellect, and warmth set her apart from so many of the other women he'd dated. When his libido wasn't sucking the blood from his brain and depositing it directly into his balls, he could tell the feeling was mutual.

"Yes, I'm freaking hilarious." Her brow arched. "In

fact, I may be one of the funniest people I know," she confirmed, a smile stretching across her face as the deep dimples in both cheeks winked, practically begging him to touch them, taunting him to kiss them.

Extending his arm, he cupped her face, stroking the divot in her right cheek. Silk... her skin felt silken beneath his touch, and as the backs of his fingers traveled down her neck, reveling in the supple skin, electricity jolted through his body.

"April Maddox, *you* definitely are amusing, but you're so much more. You're smart, sweet, and... well..." his gaze traveled from her face to the scooped neckline where the swells of her breasts subtly formed the perfect amount of cleavage. "Let's face it, you're fucking gorgeous."

Watching her chest rise and fall with her shallow breaths as his words resonated sparked a fire in his gut. As her cheeks flushed, his blood heated. Her scent flooded his nostrils as he breathed in slowly while recomposing himself in the leather booth. The instant her pink tongue slid over her plump bottom lip, Decker knew all attempts at being suave were lost. He was lost. *Take her home*, he told himself. *Charlie will never find out*, he promised his troubled conscience then took the leap he'd wanted to take for months.

Slipping his thumb under her chin and tilting it back, Decker stared into her hooded eyes. "I can't stop thinking about your mouth, the way it tastes, the things you say—I want you, April. I need you in a way that makes no sense." Desire clawed its way up his chest, demanding its release.

"But right now, I don't give a shit about making sense…"

"Decker." April sighed, her voice low and husky as her chartreuse eyes practically glowed with anticipation. She leaned forward and pressed her lips to his.

Her moaned agreement had his heart pounding double time as he did his best to keep his cool exterior from melting onto the leather booth. She pulled her plush bottom lip between her teeth, and for a brief second, the world faded away. He heard nothing, saw nothing but those lips.

As if she sensed his momentary loss of time and space, April gently stroked his jaw until his eyes once again made contact with hers. "And I've wanted you since the first second I saw you at the gym." Her lips curved. "Any man who can bench-press that much weight and not make those silly grunting noises is someone I pay attention to." Her dimples sunk deeper. "It didn't hurt that you were easy on the eyes and compassionate to boot. When that older woman tripped and fell getting off the treadmill, you helped her up and got her ice for her ankle. You were so kind and gentle with her. Kind of like a superhero that day, Decker Brand."

"Are you saying I'm not a superhero every day, Ms. Maddox?" Dimples, again… it was like playing Skee-Ball and scoring in the coveted top ring. No matter how many times you win, you always feel like a champ. Seeing April's dimples and knowing they were aimed at him… yeah, totally fucking winning.

With one hand placing whisper soft touches on his throbbing cock, April lifted the cloth napkin from her lap and laid it gently on the table. "Do you wanna get out of here? I can show you how super I think you are." Her wide eyes showed she was just as surprised by her brazen actions as he was.

After three dates, hours spent at the gym, and countless dirty chats and texts, maybe April Maddox was dying to get her hands all over him like he was her. Maybe she, too, wanted to feel the length of him pressing into her as they came together for the first time. *Fuck, I want her.*

Decker lifted his hand and signaled for the check.

W ITH THE CHECK paid at lightning speed, Decker placed his large hand on the small of April's back and led her to the restaurant door. The heat from his palm sent tingles up her spine and moisture between her thighs.

Oh my God. Is this really happening? Holy shit, this is finally happening! Like one of her preteen students instead of a grown woman, her thoughts flipped-flopped from excited to nervous, from giddy to curious. Had she made the right moves? Brazen had never been her way, but the years she'd spent tucked away inside herself hadn't brought her happiness either. So at the advice of her friends and siblings, she decided to leap outside of her comfort zone and reach for what she wanted. And she wanted Decker Brand. Due to circumstances beyond their control, their timing seemed to veer on the opposite end of opportune.

There was no questioning the desire they shared—Christ, she felt as though she could drown in its depth—but her past had taught her a bitch of a lesson, and it wasn't one she'd ever care to repeat. Therefore, she'd taken the tortoise's route instead of the hare's. Slow and steady kept her safe, but left her horny as all hell. However that would be remedied shortly, because she intended to hop her ass to the finish line no matter what, and she couldn't wait to collect her reward.

Walking through the small parking lot with his arm draped protectively around her waist sent small jolts of anticipation zipping through her already hyper-aware body. Everything about the man to her left was imprinted into her memory—the way his tall, hard frame gave balance to her knees that just barely kept her upright, his scent, a spicy blend of cedar, pine, and Decker, hung ever so lightly in the spring air, just enough to make her mouth water and her heart race. The man was a sensory feast, and she suffered from insatiable hunger.

They stopped in front of her car. They'd agreed to meet at the restaurant because she still felt more comfortable having her own transportation.

"I'll drive slowly so you can follow me back to my place." April's skin bloomed with goose bumps as Decker's thumb glided up and down her arm as he spoke. "But just in case, please enter my address into your GPS." Decker shifted closer, his mouth mere inches from her ear. "I don't wanna lose you tonight, April." Yep, those seven words had her blood pulsing through her veins while eagerness clenched at her core as she tapped in his address.

"Are you sure you want to take this back to your place, Deck? I mean, I've never been there before and… what if Charlie finds out?" She saw a quick flash of something pass over his face. If it was guilt or the thrill of getting caught, April had no idea. But as quickly as the look had come, it was gone.

Decker opened her car door and waited until she was tucked and buckled safely into her seat before speaking. His brow arched as his chocolate eyes glittered. "It's late, April. Charlie's been sleeping for a while." His lips curled up in the half grin that April had named his *gotcha* smirk as his voice dropped to a gravelly pitch. "As much as I look forward to hearing how you sound when you're screaming my name as you come"—he winked—"tonight, we're gonna have to go on touch instead."

"Ahh, so kind of like mime sex," April teased, squeezing her thighs together. Everything the man said sparked her libido, and she was one flare away from detonation.

Her heart sped up, pounding wildly into her ribs as Decker's brown eyes blackened at her comment. Their relationship flourished due to their easy banter and similar sense of humor, but as he licked his lips and leaned into her car, the only thing that occupied her mind was getting his mouth closer to her own. She didn't have long to wait. Decker tipped her chin up and crushed his lips to hers. His tongue breached the seam of her lips and demanded entrance into her mouth. Her breathless whimper seemed to rev up the fire between them as their bodies fused as one. He nipped her bottom lip before ending their scorching kiss, his forehead pressed gently to hers as she breathed in his warm sweet breath.

"Fuck, April. Let's get out of here before I strip you down and take you in the backseat of your car like a horny teenager."

Lust struck and aroused, April grazed her fingers over Decker's stubbled jaw. She loved the way his brown eyes were practically black with desire—desire for her, and no one else.

PROLOGUE

Four Years Ago

April

I'M SORRY, SNUGGLE-BUNNY, I am." The words left Ben Spears's mouth, but repent wasn't at all the emotion April sensed oozing from her husband as he shrugged with blatant indifference. "I just can't do this..." He gestured his hands back and forth from his body to hers. "This whole thing between you and me anymore. I need to be happy." Condescension dripped from his tone. "And you should want that for me." Ben tossed the rolled pairs of socks from his drawer into his suitcase in a basketball-like fashion. His eyes lit up with accomplishment each time a pair made it into the open case. Packing had always been a little game to him. And there, in that moment, even after he'd dropped a proverbial grenade on his wife, blowing their life apart, he still took time to *score* points with each pair of socks.

"Wait, let me get this straight." April rubbed her

trembling hands over her rounded belly. An action which had previously brought surges of excitement about their future now provided her with unwavering purpose. At thirty-six weeks pregnant, their unborn baby was the only reason she hadn't gone all Lorena Bobbit on her lying, cheating, son-of-a-bitch husband who, sadly enough, had also been the love of her life since her sophomore year in high school. Her one and only love and she his, or so she'd thought until fifteen minutes prior, when she came home from work early with a headache and found him packing his things.

"Four points." Ben pumped his fist as two more pairs of socks landed in the suitcase.

"Ben." While trying to control the quiver in her voice, April was unsuccessful in reining in the volume. "I don't understand. You're telling me you've been having an affair?"

"Yes." Another two points celebrated as Ben kept his back turned from April.

"And this *woman*…" April could barely grit out the word seeing as her mind had already conjured the female into a monster, nothing more than two tits, a hole (maybe two holes), and a heartbeat. "You…cheated on me with her back when we were in college?" April rubbed at the moving form in her belly. Judging by the placement, it was probably their baby's elbow. Yep, their child wasn't even born yet and already knew that its daddy was an asshole. Great, just great.

"Yes, April." Ben faced her and nodded. "Yes to everything. I'm in love with her, and I think I always have been. When she came to work at my firm eight months ago, I realized that those feelings never went away." Not waiting for a response, Ben turned his back and walked into the closet to gather his suits.

Shock filled April like water flooding a sinking boat. After all, she *was* sinking. Her life was being torn apart right before her eyes, and she was completely out of control. Grasping for answers like a life preserver, she threw out questions, hoping the answers would help in some way. She'd settle for anything that would clue her in on what the hell was going on.

"Eight months?" April shrieked. "So around the time we got pregnant, you started fucking another woman? And it never occurred to you to tell me?"

Ben's silence spoke volumes. April tugged at her hair clip, releasing the silky strands from the prison they'd been trapped in all day. Her head had gone from an ache to a migraine, and her stomach was beginning to churn. Their baby continued to shift in her belly, a reminder that it wasn't just *her* Ben was leaving but *them*.

"So you're now leaving me and *our* baby to be with her because you"—she threw her hands in the air to surround the next words in quotes—"'just can't do this anymore'?" She inhaled slowly, attempting to slow her pounding heart. The obstetrician had warned her during her last appointment, an appointment that, ironically enough, Ben had missed due to work, that an elevated blood pressure was bad for the baby. April continued to pull in deep breaths, putting her baby's safety before her own heartbreak. *She* would put her child first...always.

"No, I'm leaving you to be with her because I. Don't. Love. You... I love her." Ben answered from inside the walk-in. "Sorry, snuggle-bunny."

She flinched at the once-adored nickname as he pivoted.

His easy glance rested on hers. His narrow shoulders shrugged nonchalantly as if he were apologizing for forgetting to bring home milk—something he often did. "We just weren't the fairytale I thought we'd be. It isn't *all* your fault."

She couldn't contain the gasp that left her mouth as his words sliced through her. Ben stepped out into the bedroom, hands filled with clothes. His gaze flittered past hers and quickly snapped back, zeroing in on her face. Maybe it was her rounded eyes, her tightly drawn-in lips, or her clenched fists. Possibly it was the way her nostrils flared or her uncharacteristic silence that screamed in the dead air, but whatever it was clearly made Ben Spears uncomfortable, and when Ben got uncomfortable, he began to ramble.

"Um, April, snuggle-bunny, there's no need to lose your head over this." Ben's brows arched, nearly reaching his hairline. "I'm sure you and the kid will be fine. That's one of the reasons I waited this long to tell you. I wanted to make sure the kid was fine before I left. Now you won't be alone after I'm gone. I've got it all planned."

April felt her jaw drop. Was he kidding? There was no way this was the man she'd spent the past eight years of her life with.

"We'll work out child support. You know I'm good

for the money, right?"

She stood silently, staring at her husband and watching his lips move as bullshit spewed from his mouth. It was obvious that her silence was making him nervous, but in that moment, she didn't give a damn how he felt.

He continued to ramble. "Sooo, I'll just send a monthly check and stay out of your way. I can go be happy with Becky, and you and the kid can... you know, do your thing." He quickly turned and entered the bathroom to pack his toiletries.

He's good for the money? Do our thing? April screamed in her head as emotions cycled through her mind. *He was supposed to be a good husband and a good father. We made vows stating that we would spend our lives doing our thing together. What the hell just happened?* She refused to crumble in front of him, the person who was walking out on her and their baby. No, apparently it was just her baby. The little life inside of her was no more than a nuisance to a man who was nothing more than a stranger. She'd obviously missed the signs that her husband was an unfaithful shit. While she could make a valid point that her lack of observation was due to pregnancy hormones, she wondered just how long she'd been living with blinders on.

The hammer that had been pounding in her skull when she arrived home was now accompanied by a drill and a buzz saw, while waves of nausea inched acid up the back of her throat. Her throat tightened by the second as sadness took hold, forcing shallow breaths and causing her eyes to sting. Inhaling slowly through her nose, April forced oxygen into her burning lungs. She closed her tear-filled eyes and exhaled, releasing carbon dioxide and a promise that she would not cry. No way would she show him any sort of weakness when he was clearly displaying no heartache at all. So instead, she held herself together and grabbed onto the only emotion that would keep the sadness away until he left: anger.

With her hands caressing her belly, she waddled over and stood before the floor-to-ceiling bookcases. Each of the wooden panels displayed collections that she and Ben had each spent years acquiring. In the left case were her beautiful paperback books, each one signed by its author and in perfect condition. On the shelves to the right were Ben's fucked-up, creepy bobblehead dolls from every sport, movie, and event he'd ever attended. Goddamn things had been freaking her out for years. She swore the little bastards nodded at her every time she got undressed, and the larger her breasts became during her pregnancy, the more their little heads bounced. She clenched her teeth, grabbed the first doll, and quickly went to work.

"What the fuck, April?" The bitter question came from a very unhappy Ben some time later.

Standing amongst a pile of de-bobbled dolls, April lifted her gaze to her husband's surprised stare. She'd become quite efficient at the decapitation process while Ben was in the bathroom packing. She'd overheard him having a not-so-quiet, not-so-sullen phone conversation with his new girlfriend. April was appalled when she heard Ben report that *he* thought the encounter with his wife went *pretty smooth*. But when he told good ol' Becky how he was looking forward to spending the night with her wrapped in his arms, well, that was when the bobbleheads really started flying.

Ben crouched down, picking up the remains of his beloved Princess Leia figurine. "I loved this one." His eyes glistened with unshed tears. "I can't believe you would do this to me, April."

April stared at her husband. Words evaded her. Was he insane? Had aliens invaded his body? That fucking doll was reducing him to tears but leaving his wife and unborn child meant nothing? Uncertain if it was pure rage or pregnancy hormones, April once again found herself pulling in cleansing breaths.

"Hmm." A sardonic smile pulled at her lips. "Well at least I didn't lose *my* head over this." She pointed at the broken toys. "They did. Now get your shit and get the fuck out of my house." In that moment, her baby kicked hard, as if it too agreed with April's rage. "And, Ben, if you ever call me snuggle-bunny again, your dolls won't be the only things to lose their head."

She took pleasure in the look of dejection on Ben's face as he tried to gather his precious dolls. Brushing past him, she walked gracefully—well, as gracefully as a pregnant woman in her ninth month could—and stopped when she reached the bathroom door.

"Get out," she screamed, her voice cracking like thunder in the quiet room, startling Ben and causing him to drop the possessions in his arms. The sound of plastic heads falling to the hardwood floor was almost musical and his panicked face was comical.

The man grabbed his bags and scurried out of the room like the rat he turned out to be. Once April heard the garage door close, she allowed the tears to fall freely, along with her dreams of her perfect little family.

Decker

DECKER BRAND SAT stiffly on the granite bench that faced his wife's gravestone. The coolness of the stone sent a shiver through his clothes and into his skin. Sleeping peacefully in a stroller by his side was their daughter, his sweet angel—blissfully oblivious to her surroundings. At almost two years old, little Charlotte missed her mother, but after the first few months, when she'd begged for her momma and cried herself to sleep, his little girl seemed to be adjusting to her new normal. What was it people always said about kids? They're resilient? Decker shrugged. While he didn't necessarily agree with that theory, he *did* know that kids did what they *had* to in order to get by. His gaze landed back on the shiny black marble.

"My God, Olivia," Decker said, his voice barely above a whisper. "I can't believe it's been a year. We miss you."

He leaned over and caressed the stone as ripples of nausea and waves of guilt sliced through his gut. Guilt for how they'd been and the way he felt. Remorse for all of the things he could have done differently and hadn't. And deep regret that his little girl would grow up without her mother. He looked at the sky as a fresh burden washed over him, and he prayed for peace. He needed to let go of the blame that weighed him down. Logically, he knew the accident wasn't his fault, but the marriage—well, he sure as hell wasn't blameless there. And for that, his heart hurt every single day.

Staring at Olivia's headstone, memories from that horrific afternoon slammed into him. She had been angry with him, and she had been for quite some time. But instead of discussing her feelings the way he'd urged her to do many times, her behavior defaulted into passive-aggressive tantrums and finally a text message tirade. Her last words were branded in his mind and on his phone.

Charlotte sighed softly in her sleep. The sweet sound quickly brought Decker out of the past as he watched his baby girl fall quiet once again.

A year had gone by in a flash, his daughter keeping him on his toes and on the go. But when the house was quiet at night as he got ready for bed, Decker let his mind wander. He allowed himself to think about Olivia and how things had been back when they first met. When they saw what they thought they wanted in each other as they fell in love with the illusion of love.

After all, it hadn't been that many years before when the woman who'd shared his last name had been exactly what he thought he should have. Someone laid-back and intelligent instead of a dim-witted, over-eager woman looking to get her hands on either his money or his dick.

While he'd been happy to share both, it eventually got mundane, and he started looking for more.

When he was first introduced to Olivia Colver, he'd been having drinks at the country club where she and his brother were members. Not being a country club kind of man, he'd never met her before, and he was entranced by her beauty, her shrewdness, and her refined demeanor. She was the opposite of what he'd been unsuccessfully dating and exactly what he thought the business side of him should appreciate. He wanted her, and he could tell by the way she flirted with her pretty smiles and tiny giggles that the feelings were mutual, so he pursued her with little resistance and savored the catch. His desire was so strong that he ignored the glaring warning signs and the flashing lights screaming that there were large differences between them. Over time, the very things that had attracted him to Olivia and her to him were the things that wedged them apart.

He'd been on a new job site the day of Olivia's accident. His company, Brand Construction, had once been a small business founded by his grandfather and grown by his father into a large group; now one of the biggest companies in the Philadelphia area and one that was known for giving back to the community when it could. Decker and his younger brother, Ford, were its sole owners. While there wasn't a job too big or small within Brand Construction (BC) that Decker or his brother couldn't do, they each had their preferences of what made them happy. Ford excelled behind the desk, crunching numbers, assembling business deals, obtaining building permits, and schmoozing with the right people. That left Decker doing what he loved, what he was passionate about—building.

Decker's father had taught him, as a young boy, about wood-working, electrical wiring, and drafting. There were even weekends when he got the opportunity to join his father on a job and learn from the man who was his hero. Those were some of Decker's happiest childhood memories and where his love of the trade truly began, a love that ran bone deep, one that he treasured with his soul. Something Olivia refused to understand. Something she refused to accept.

While Decker practically thrummed with pride and excitement over landing a huge account, the Robertson Project, one that several of the top construction companies in and around the city had been bidding on, Olivia disapproved of the entire project. In fact, she was livid when she learned that BC had offered to do the entire job for the cost of materials and not a penny more.

"That is no way to run a business, Decker," she chided coolly. "Your father must be rolling in his grave."

The words she'd used to cut him barely stung, as she had obviously never met his father. Had she, she would've known how truly proud the man would've been to see his sons continuing to give so generously.

Olivia came from wealth. She was fine wine, pressed suits, and ballroom dancing, but it was the social status and public opinion that she thrived on. Therefore, the thing that bothered Olivia most, the thing that made her ever-present mask of calmness finally begin to crack, was the fact that Decker himself would be the foreman of the job.

He would be overseeing the entire project from start to finish, and he would be working side-by-side with his men—his version of heaven—rather than sitting comfortably behind a desk or out on the golf course. In Olivia's eyes, public perception of him would be that of a common worker and not the wealthy business owner he actually was.

He and Olivia had been arguing. More like Olivia expressed her strong dislike of certain things, and if Decker didn't concede to his wife's wishes, she would freeze him out both emotionally and physically. Having grown up in a loving and nurturing home and seeing the way his parents communicated with each other when they disagreed, Decker tried to compromise with Olivia when the situation needed it, but she was not just a strong woman—she was stubborn. Her desire to be *right* far outweighed her ability to see how unhappy they were becoming as a couple.

Had Olivia not been pregnant when BC landed the coveted Robertson Project, a facility that would house a multitude of resources to help soldiers reintegrate back into society, Decker wasn't certain they would have stayed together. From that point on, Decker decided which battles to wage and which were best to cede. He loved his wife the best way he could by tucking away pieces of himself and giving her only what she wanted to see. He chose a life with her and their baby, Charlie, or Charlotte, as Olivia demanded their daughter be called, and he knew he'd remain loyal to both his woman and his little girl for the rest of his life.

When the building was finally out of the planning

phase and ready to be built, Decker could no longer stay locked behind his desk. The day his brother knocked on his office door changed his life forever.

"Deck, we need to talk." Those words, combined with Ford's serious tone, never boded well.

Without looking up from his computer screen, Decker silently waved his brother in and waited for him to take a seat. "What's up?" Decker asked through a yawn.

He'd been up several times during the night with Charlotte. Olivia refused to do any middle-of-the-night feedings, stating her sleep was what allowed her to retain her patience during the day while Decker was at work and she was *stuck* at home with their child. While he would never complain and would proudly walk through fire for his daughter, his frustration with his wife grew exponentially. After all, Olivia had a nanny watching the baby for four hours a day so she could have "me time." They had housekeepers, someone who pre-cooked meals, and a laundry service, and when he got home from work, Olivia passed Charlotte off to him, saying that she was exhausted and it was "Daddy time." Decker hadn't had more than a few hours of sleep on any given night in almost a year, yet his wife never seemed to stop complaining.

"Look, Deck," Ford's voice shook Decker from his reverie and brought him back to the here and now. "I know you know this, but I'm gonna say it anyway. They break ground on Monday."

Decker's eyes lifted to meet his brother's. Of course he knew when they broke ground. This project meant the world to him, them. "Yeah, I know."

"You wanted this job, bro. You lobbied for it, you procured the funds, you found the perfect site... this is your heart, Deck. You need your hands on this job with your men."

Decker looked at his brother, and he could see the sincerity in his eyes. Ford was a dependable friend, a tough-as-nails business partner, a compassionate man, and a loyal brother. There was no doubt what he was saying was coming from the heart and was completely true.

"Ford"—Decker rubbed his heavy eyes—"you know it isn't that easy. She'll be pissed as hell if I run this job. It's gonna get a ton of publicity."

His brother closed his eyes, scrubbed his hands over his face, and pulled in a deep breath, holding it for a second before exhaling slowly. "For fuck's sake, Deck, when the hell isn't she pissed?" Ford opened his eyes and leaned forward in his chair, his palms flattened on Decker's desk. "She's been slowly draining the life out of you since the day you met her, but you loved her, so I've kept my fucking mouth shut. But honestly, I can't do it anymore."

Decker waited in silence while Ford carefully measured his words. It was something his little brother was known for in both their business and personal lives. The man never spoke without weighing how his words would affect the outcome of a situation.

"I know she's your wife. Okay, I get it. But what I don't understand is why your marriage is all about what Olivia wants, what Olivia needs, and what makes Olivia happy. What about you?"

"You're right." Bile rose in Decker's stomach as he conceded quietly. "I want to do this job, Ford, I need it." Decker ran his fingers through his hair. "I feel like I'm fucking suffocating sitting here behind this desk. No offense, I know you love this business side, but I need to get my fucking hands dirty, man." As if a weight had been lifted off his chest, Decker breathed deep. Come Monday morning, he was finally rejoining his crew and taking control of some part of his life. "I'll contact Troy today and let him know that I'll be stepping in as foreman. I'll move him to a different site where he'll not only be in charge but he'll have the opportunity for overtime. The guy will be thrilled." Ford's eyes mirrored his own excitement, and for a moment, he swore he saw his father in his younger brother's smile.

"You do realize that this is gonna go over like a lead balloon at the Macy's Thanksgiving Day Parade, right?" Ford quipped as he motioned toward the picture of Olivia and Charlotte on Decker's desk.

"Yeah, Ford, I know. But honestly, she and I are gonna need to discuss it tonight. Because you're right, our marriage has been all about her for way too long. Things need to change before it's too late."

The following week, while wiping the sweat from his brow, Decker marveled at how finally getting the opportunity to work in the field had brought some semblance of peace back into his mind, if not his marriage. Little did he know how short-lived the euphoria would be.

His phone vibrated in his pocket. Sliding a soiled thumb across the screen, he answered his wife's call.

"Hey, Olivia, what's up?"

"Decker."

It amazed him how one word in her icy tone could tighten his entire frame.

"There's media coverage at the site today." It wasn't a question as much as an accusation and he refused to get into another argument with her.

"Yeah... so what?" He didn't bother hiding his annoyance.

"So what?" she shrieked. "Do you have any idea how many people will be watching the news? I saw the teaser, Decker, and there you were. You looked filthy. Like... like... a bum all covered in dirt and grime. You pay people to do that kind of grunt work, you don't do it yourself. What will people think of us or our family if they see you working like a low-class nothing?"

They will think I'm a great business man who isn't afraid to get his hands dirty. He bit that thought back, knowing damn well the words would be wasted on a woman who didn't care to hear logic. Pinching the bridge of his nose between his thumb and middle finger, Decker spoke. "Olivia, we've discussed this, and frankly, I don't have the time or the desire to go over it again. I want to do this job. I *need* to do it. I'm doing it for us, our family. Now, I have to get back to work. See you when I get home." Decker's disgust and frustration were cresting to a point they'd never reached before, and he knew he needed to end the call before he said something he'd later regret.

"Absolutely not, Decker Brand." Her chastising tone was a new addition to her demeaning repertoire. It gave her the simple shove from passive aggressive right into nasty aggressive. "I am coming down there with a proper suit for you to wear. If you think I'm going to allow you to be interviewed in ripped jeans and a dusty tee shirt, then you are sadly mistaken. I'll be there in twenty minutes." Olivia ended the call before Decker got the chance to speak another word.

His phone buzzed, indicating a text message only seconds later—

O: *Make sure your hands are clean you don't want dirt on your suit.*

What the fuck? Anger thrummed through Decker's body as he tapped out his response.

D: *Do not come here, Olivia, I mean it.*

O: *On my way, be ready and clean*

D: *If ur driving don't text. It's dangerous. Go home to our daughter, Liv.*

O: *YOU DO NOT TELL ME WHAT TO DO, DECKER!!*

O: *Clean up! People respect money not dirt*

Decker's head spun as his frustration hit levels never before reached. He pumped his fingers into a fist to avoid tapping out a response to what sounded like Olivia's descent into lunacy, but he refused to encourage more texting while she drove. That was just another point of contention between the two of them, so he would have to wait until she arrived. He shook his head at the impending scene she was sure to create. There was no way he would cater to any more of her bullshit. His brother had been right—he had lost so much of himself in the three years since he and Olivia had been together. While he was willing to compromise, he realized that she was completely averse. Another text buzzed—

O: *You think people take you seriously?*

O: *You have no respect for me or for Charlotte.*

O: *She wants a powerful daddy not some man with mud under his nails and*

Decker stared at the screen, waiting for the next acrid text. Thoughts of his sweet baby girl filled his mind, releasing some of the anger that flooded his gut. He would teach his daughter not to care what someone did for a living as long as they worked honest and hard. She needed to learn that love was more important than status. In that moment, he wished that he'd followed his own parents' example.

More than thirty minutes passed as Decker paced in the work trailer, gearing up for what was sure to be an enormous argument, the likes of which they'd never had before. This time, he had no intention of backing down. This time, Olivia was going to listen to what he had to say or… or he was going to do the one thing he promised himself he'd never do. He was going to break up their family and leave her. The thought alone sent a jolt of pain directly to his stomach. While he wasn't in love with his wife the way he'd once thought he was, he did care for her, and he'd promised her *forever* the day they said their vows, and he'd meant every word. Although they had a child, it was more important that Charlotte grow up surrounded by peace than in a home where the two parents eventually grew to hate one another. Decker let out a steady breath. No, he would get Olivia to understand that they could all be happy if they just compromised. The little voice in his head knew his good intentions were pipe dreams, but Decker chose to ignore that little voice once again. Instead, he left the trailer in search of his wife, who was now more than forty minutes late.

The distant sound of sirens once again pulled Decker's mind back from the past. He was no longer wandering around a bustling work site, prepping himself for the impending tongue lashing. Instead, he sat stoically in the cemetery, almost a year after the very argument that had just consumed his thoughts.

Decker slid his cell out from his coat pocket. He swiped his thumb over the screen, bringing the small device to life. Scrolling through the text messages once again, he went directly to the last few sent from Olivia. She had so much anger... so much fear. He wasn't able to see the fear back then, but now, now it was clear. She'd harbored abhorrence at the thought of not measuring up, not being good enough, and she used that fear as a weapon instead of a tool.

"I'm sorry, Olivia," Decker spoke quietly into the cool, early spring air. "I'm so sorry that you're gone, that you aren't here to see how smart our daughter is, how beautiful... I know that you and I weren't meant for each other, but it doesn't mean I didn't wish for your happiness." His eyes burned as he allowed his true feelings to come to the surface. "I wasn't *me* with you, Liv. I'm not blaming you, but I'm stating a fact. I *wasn't* me. I think it's time I start to find the man I once was so I can be the best daddy for our little girl, and so I can finally feel happy again." Decker reached over and stroked the cold stone. "I will never, ever let her forget you, Olivia. That I can promise you. Rest in peace." Decker swiped the stray tear from his cheek, stood from the bench, and pushed the baby stroller out of the cemetery.

It was time to move forward.

CHAPTER ONE

Fluffing Perfect

"ELIJAH, HONEY, WAKE up. We're here." April shifted her four-year-old son from one hip to the other. Her mouth ticked up as she looked down at her sleeping child.

"That boy sleeps so deep, an earthquake wouldn't wake him," chuckled August, April's older brother.

"I know. It's a blessing on the weekends and a bitch during the week. Poor kid goes to day care half asleep most days." April passed her son to her brother's outstretched arms and went back out to her car to gather the Christmas presents.

It was early Christmas morning, and April and both of her siblings had always kept their tradition by arriving at their parents' house before dawn to place the gifts under the tree and prepare breakfast.

"Wait." April lifted her index finger and turned her head, searching the first floor of her parents' house. "It's really quiet, Aug. Are you telling me that I actually got here before 'I'm always early' Ember?" April couldn't help the rush of excitement that flooded her when her brother nodded and grinned.

November, or Ember for short, was April's older sister, the middle child, and it seemed as though Ember had spent her entire life going out of her way to prove she was anything and everything other than the proverbial middle child, even if it meant using the full Maddox spotlight for herself. April found herself born into a competition that she didn't care to win. Her indifference made Ember even more competitive. It took years of patience for the sisters to build a functional relationship, one filled with trust, love, and a healthy dose of rivalry.

"I'm here now, brat," Ember called wedging herself through the front door her arms loaded with packages. "No, no, don't all rush at once to help me." Her smile stretched across her beautiful face as she wiggled into the house. "Seriously, Dad, August, I could really use some assistance. There are two more bags in my car."

April giggled as her father and brother rushed out in the frigid winter air to retrieve what was sure to be an overabundance of gifts that Elijah didn't need. April looked down at her beautiful son, curled up in a ball and still sleeping on the sofa. Barely a day went by that she didn't think of Ben, the bobblehead-loving jerk-off, and how he could have walked away from such a perfect little boy, but he did. And other than the original half-assed offer for financial support, which she rejected and suggested he shove where the dolls don't bobble, Ben had kept to his promise and stayed out of their lives. Sure, she'd seen him a few times over the years at the market, but just like the good husband and father he was, he pretended he didn't see her and walked in the other direction.

"April, I need a hand in here." Her mother's heavy voice traveled the short distance from the kitchen to the family room.

"Coming." April sighed, giving Eli a soft pat on his back before unfolding herself from the sofa and making her way toward her mother.

"Merry Christmas, dear."

Her mom's lips were soft against her cheek, and the familiar scent of her lotion brought back a lifetime of memories, both good and frustrating. "Merry Christmas, Mom." April stayed silent under her mom's watchful gaze. She knew what was coming next. It always came. 4,3,2,1—

"April, when's the last time you had a facial? Your skin looks dry, dear. You're only twenty-eight years old. You don't want the face of a forty-something do you? And your hair, baby. Your hair used to be so pretty. But every time I see you, it's pulled up in that mess of a bun. How are you ever going to find a man when you let yourself go?"

April sucked in a deep breath and released it ever so slowly. *It's Christmas, and she's your mother. Don't freak out. It's Christmas, and she's your mother. Don't freak out.*

"Well, Mom," April spoke, her words creeping through her clenched jaw, "thank God for me, I'm not looking to find a man. Eli and I are doing freaking great on our own." It wasn't until she felt the sharp sting of her nails in her palms that she realized both hands were clenched tightly into fists.

"Well," her mother huffed, turning her back to April and moving toward the coffeepot. "I'm just saying your life would be happier with a nice guy in it."

Don't go there, April. Let it go. Just keep your mouth shut... don't... "Really, would it, Mom? I seem to remember my life being super flipping dandy with Ben." April felt her cheeks heat as her heart thudded behind her ribs. The sarcasm was thick in her voice as she added, "Yeah, that worked out great. I was really happy back then."

"Ellen, are you kidding me? You promised you wouldn't start with her today." Jack Maddox's booming voice both startled April and comforted her. That was how it always was with her parents. While she knew she was loved by both, her mother was her biggest critic and her father her greatest champion. "You constantly ask me why she doesn't come around as much as August and November. Well, maybe if you stopped with the insults, you'd see her more."

With her dad's arms wrapped around her, April felt the things she craved the most—strength and unconditional love.

"I'm not insulting our daughter, Jack." Ellen's round eyes and pinched brows made it nearly impossible for April to stifle her giggle.

Her mother's truly shocked response to her father's anger was the only reason why April loved instead of loathed her mom. The woman actually believed her *helpful hints,* as she referred to them, were a way of loving those around her. Although Ellen was definitely harder on April than her other two children, and her negativity had gotten worse over the years. April couldn't pinpoint when it started—she only knew that she left her parents' house with a headache and a complex more often than not, hence the reason her visits became fewer and farther between. It took a strong and confident person to be associated with Ellen Maddox.

"I was merely pointing out that she could be beautiful if she put some effort into it."

"Ellen... "

"Well, I see we're all getting along perfectly in here." August chuckled, shooting April a wink. "But Eli is finally awake, and the little man is salivating over the gifts. I, of course, laid down the law and told him breakfast always comes first." August clapped his hands together. "But we should probably get started. Hate to keep the poor kid waiting on Christmas."

As if perfectly scripted, Elijah toddled into the kitchen as fast as his little legs could carry him. "Mommy, look." Hazel eyes danced with delight in a way that made April melt every time she looked at her son. His sweet green-brown eyes were one of the few reminders of Ben that didn't make her cringe. "Uncle Gust gam'me a truck before breakfast. Here, see." Her sweet boy proudly hoisted the large truck out in front of him, seeking his mom's approval.

"It's awesome, Eli." April admired the shiny metal fire truck before handing it back to her son. "I love it.

Please go put it down, and you can play with it and Uncle Law Maker, I mean August, after breakfast." From the corner of her eye, she saw her brother scrub his hands over his face. "Good to see you made those rules clear, big brother." She shook her head in mock annoyance, but only joy filled her heart. "Seriously, haven't you learned that you can't trust a four-year-old with a secret? Sad, August. Just sad."

Laugher filled the kitchen as April and her siblings prepared their famous Maddox french toast (sprinkled with toasted pecans), scrambled eggs, cinnamon rolls, bacon, and fruit for their big meal.

"Umm, Ember, you know that your job was to bring *fresh* fruit for the fruit salad, right?" August teased as he grabbed the packaged peaches from his sister's hand and held them out of reach.

April could barely contain her snort when Ember responded with an exaggerated eye roll. "Do you have any idea how hard it is to find fresh peaches in Pennsylvania this time of year? Christ, it's nearly impossible. So help me cut the rest of the fruit and can your bullshit."

"Looks like you managed to *can* for all of us," April cackled, pointing at the canned peaches.

"Wow, that was a horrible joke." Ember shook her head. "For real, not funny at all," she added. After a brief pause, the three Maddox siblings dissolved into hysterics until breakfast was ready to be served.

"OH... A GYM membership," April stared at the certificate in her hand and bit the inside of her lip, trying to keep the thoughts that flooded her mind from leaving her mouth.

After all, Eli was only a few feet away, and April was working hard to curtail her bad language after the *fuck-frenzy* that had occurred the previous month. There was nothing more embarrassing than being in the checkout line at the food market and having your four-year-old decide to put the word "fuck" before all of the items as you placed them on the belt. *Fucking* peas, *fucking* milk, *fucking* corn flakes—didn't matter how cute his little voice had sounded. No more cursing in front of Elijah.

The gift-giving portion of the morning had been wonderful. Her son was showered with more presents than any four-year-old in the history of Christmas could ever desire. Then each of the adults got the opportunity to open their packages. Everyone was happy. Both August and Ember got clothes, gift cards, and tubs of Johnson's caramel popcorn—a treat that came directly from the boardwalk in Ocean City, New Jersey. Oh, but not April. No, she got an envelope and a case of fruity energy water. Ick, she hated water that tasted like anything other than... water.

"What the fu..."

April shot her brother a warning glare.

"Fudge. What the fudge, Mom? Why did April get a crappy gym membership when Ember and I got all of this fun stuff?"

April loved how disgusted her brother was on her behalf. She would have smiled had it not been for the fact

27

that she wanted to choke her mother.

"Ellen, enough is enough." Jack hoisted himself up from the floor as his brows pinched together, his voice low and angry. "That was unkind. In fact, you're damn lucky that little guy is here right now, Ell. When they leave, you can bet your aaa…"—her father faltered, trying to replace one word for another—"abacus, that we are going to discuss this once and for all."

The color drained from Ellen's face as she looked around the room. She cleared her throat and addressed the family but looked directly at April. "First of all, that gym is far from crappy. It's the best gym with the finest equipment around. Second, I didn't just purchase the membership. I bought her private sessions with a personal trainer."

April tried to breathe, but anger and insecurity weaved through her body like a ribbon. She considered herself to be in decent shape. No, she didn't belong to a gym, but she ran miles on the track at the middle school where she taught every day after the students left but before she picked Eli up from day care. She also used the school's weight room whenever she had extra time. Damn it, she was doing the best she could. While she didn't have the perfect size-two body anymore, she was damn proud of how she juggled her job and being a single parent. Hell, she was pretty freaking satisfied with how she looked… usually.

"I didn't mean any offense," her mother started.

"What *did* you mean, Mom?" April hissed, but the instant she felt Ember's fingers weave through her own in a show of love and support, the venom slowly diluted into nothing more than irritation.

"Umm, well, I guess I just thought a woman can always stand to look a little better."

"Oh, that's interesting," April answered stiffly, "being that Ember got a big ol' tub of caramel popcorn. Yeah, she's beautiful, but I didn't realize she was fu… fluffing perfect." The knot in April's throat tightened, as did the grip of her sister's hand.

Her mother let out an exaggerated sigh. "No, dear, I just figured there are probably a lot of very nice men at such a high quality gym. I was hoping maybe you would meet someone."

April watched as something akin to uncertainty crossed over her mother's face. Pulling in a deep breath then exhaling, April looked around the room at her family. Elijah was playing in the corner, unaware of the drama going on around him, her siblings and father sat motionless, gaping between her and her mother as her mom kept her vision trained on her hands.

"Okay." April's voice was slightly above a whisper. "Well, thanks for the gift, it was… generous." She nodded as she placed the certificate back in the envelope and stood from the floor. "I'm going to get some fresh air. Please keep an eye on Eli for me." She reached over to the sofa, swiped the thick chenille blanket from the arm, and walked out the door.

T HE SQUEAKING OF the porch swing came as more of a comfort than a discontent as April creaked back and forth in the freezing cold air. "Here's a gym membership, fatso." April mimicked her mother's voice and then her own. "Oh gee, thanks, Mom, you're so fucking kind. I feel blessed. What? No facial for my old crusty skin? I'm so disappointed."

"Uh, sis, I hate to admit it, but maybe Mom was right." Her brother's mouth ticked up just a bit on the corner, showing off the cocky smirk that April loved to hate. "I mean, look at you sitting out here, talking to yourself like a loon. Maybe a hard workout and some gym friends are exactly what you need." He chuckled as he plopped himself on the swing next to her.

"Bite me, Aug." April's words held no malice. Her brother was one of her closest friends, and regardless of the teasing, he'd always come to her defense. The two siblings sat in a comfortable silence as the tired old swing creaked back and forth.

"Look, Tiny…" April's heart went soft when her brother used the nickname he'd bestowed upon her back when they were children. "I'll never understand why mom says and does the things she does, but if we're being honest, she isn't the issue here."

April's stomach clenched. She knew where this conversation was heading, and she still wasn't ready to deal with it.

"I made you a promise more than four years ago, do you remember?"

She remembered quite clearly the promise her big

brother had made. She'd hoped after all the time that had passed without him bringing it up that he'd be the one who forgot. Silently, April exhaled and pulled the blanket tighter around her shoulders, staring into familiar green eyes. *Maybe if you don't answer, he'll stop talking.* But when August squeezed her hand and began to speak, she was reminded that feigning ignorance never worked with her older siblings.

"When that son of a bitch left you, I promised you that you wouldn't spend the rest of your life alone."

"I'm not alone, Aug. I have Eli, and we're doing great." The forced brightness she infused into her voice was useless, and they both knew it, so instead of looking at him, April glared down at her own hands. Tears stung the back of her eyes as the words escaped her mouth. "I'm a great mom and a successful teacher. My son has never wanted for anything." April inhaled a shaky breath, realizing that her eyes no longer stung because the tears were no longer trapped. Brushing away the wetness, April looked up at her brother's sympathetic gaze.

"Tiny, I've never doubted your parenting for a second. Eli is the best kid ever, barring the whole Fuck-Frenzy thing." The joke cracked some of the tension between them. "But you know damn well that I wasn't talking about your son. It's time, April. You've been hiding behind Elijah and work and heartbreak for long enough. It's time to get out there and start dating again." Her brother seemed to scan her face, his brows lowered briefly before he continued. "You're really beautiful, sis, but if you sit around waiting too long, you're gonna end up look-

31

ing like old Ms. Elkridge next door—all frumpy, dumpy, cranky, and bogged down with a house full of talking birds." August cringed. "Have you been in there lately? You can't say anything without it being repeated twenty-five times. It's a fucking nuthouse."

"Well, at least she has a support system who agrees with her decisions," April deadpanned and shrugged her shoulders. "That must feel nice." She smiled at her own humor and laughed at her brother's frown. "Stop pouting, Auggy. I understand what you're saying, and while I think it was a monumentally bitchy call on Mom's part, I have heard amazing things about that gym." She watched as her brother's face lit up. "Don't get too excited. I'm *only* going to work out, not to boost the already inflated egos of the pretty boys who spend more time romancing themselves in the mirrors than they do lifting weights."

August rolled his eyes and laughed. "That's the open attitude I'm looking for, little sis. Keep that up, and the dates will be pouring in."

"Whatever." April shook her head and smiled as she leaned into her brother's strong embrace. He wasn't wrong, and she knew it. It looked like the new year was going to include a new work-out routine. That wouldn't suck at all.

CHAPTER TWO

Gallant Behavior

NO DOUBT ABOUT it, the woman was stunning in more ways than one. He watched in the mirror as the blonde's pert ass rounded with each perfectly executed squat. *Her* exercise routine was definitely a total body experience for...Decker. He had to constantly remind himself, and his dick, to pay attention to his own damn workout, because *her* leg routine nearly brought *him* to his knees. But thanks to the mirror, he could appreciate the view discreetly without looking like a complete jackass. The same could not be said for Mr. Meathead, who'd started out blatantly leering at her before upping the ante by adding touch.

The blonde had just racked her weight bar, evidently taking a break between sets, when the Schwarzenegger-wannabe swaggered up behind her and snaked his hand around her hip. *Fuck.* Decker placed his dumbbells on the ground and watched the encounter through the mirror. He noticed how her eyes went round at first but quickly narrowed as she removed her ear buds and looped them around her neck. Between the clanking of weights and the music pumping through the gym's sound system, Decker couldn't hear much of their conversation, but he couldn't misconstrue her unimpressed and extremely irritated body language. Funny how he could pick up those vibes from across the gym and the guy standing right next to her couldn't clue in. It was when she removed his leather-clad hand from her body for the second time and cocked her head to the side, her brows furrowed in what appeared to be frustration that Decker decided to intercede.

"Hey, beautiful, everything all right over here?"

Decker placed a protective hand on the sweat-slickened shoulder of the woman he'd spent weeks not-so-subtly flirting with at the gym. They'd swapped smiles, exchanged a few words here and there, and even engaged in a brief conversation the day he'd assisted an older woman who had sprained her ankle after falling off the treadmill. He'd led the injured senior to a bench so she could rest her leg while he went to get an icepack and a staff member to aid the woman further. When he returned to find the sexy blonde tending to the woman, offering a small, warm smile and her cell phone, his heartbeat kicked up a notch. Other than knowing her work-out schedule, because clearly it was the same as his, and the fact that she seemed as kind as she was beautiful, not much about their acquaintance should have made his blood pressure spike the way it did when he'd caught the gym-jerk approaching her with a smarmy smile and lust-filled eyes. No, it shouldn't have pissed him off... but it did. He knew she usually didn't notice other men's attention. In fact, other than the rare occasions when Decker spoke to her, she kept to herself, earbuds in, body in motion... and oh, what a body it was.

He knew touching her was risky, especially after seeing the disgust that marred her face when Meat Hook grabbed her. Over the years, he'd seen that same guy repeatedly hit on several women at the gym, making it clear that his skull was as thick as his muscles and left no room at all for his brain. The man never took *no* for an answer, so it would take more than words to get the point made. He just hoped the woman played along.

Decker wasn't sure what surprised him more: her reply to his question or the fact that she tightly wrapped her arm around his waist, effectively pulling him closer to her. "Everything's perfect, honey," she cooed, staring up at him with the most incredible pale green eyes he'd ever seen. "I was just telling Rocco here that while my boyfriend does appreciate my"—she glared at the moron who still hadn't figured out that he was unwanted—"what did you call them, Rocco? Oh yeah, my delectable ass cheeks, and while he does agree that a real man could spend a whole night buried between them"—she turned her stare back to Decker and smiled—"he doesn't particularly like to share them or me." April's brows lifted as she punctuated the end of her statement. "But since you're here now, maybe you could explain it better, *baby*."

"The fuck?" Decker snarled, wrapping his arm around the slender woman to bring her even closer to his body. He allowed his hand to run from her shoulder down her arm, a gesture that would appear possessive but hopefully not make her feel uncomfortable while he dealt with the trash in front of them. "Listen here, Rocco," Decker growled, staring down at the shorter man, "you think I haven't seen you struttin' around this place, trying to pick up anything that isn't nailed down?"

Rocco's cockiness clearly prevailed over his sense of preservation. "Yeah, old man, I've got skills. You jealous?"

"No, boy." Decker smirked. "I'm not jealous... just nice. I'm giving you a warning to stay away from my girl here, or you're gonna need to find *skills* that don't include smiling, cause you won't have any teeth. Got it?"

Rocco's toothy smile faltered as he lifted his hands up in a defensive pose. "Sure, dude, whatever. But you should really keep your chick on a leash, because she was throwin' out mixed signals. Shit, she was practically beggin' me to come over here and check her out."

"I was not, you bloated piece of shit."

Decker nearly lost his footing when the woman lunged forward in attempts to do who knew what to the clearly IQ-challenged idiot egging her on. He quickly firmed up his stance, keeping the angered woman tucked safely in his arms. "Tsk, tsk, Rocco. I'd walk away if I were you," Decker warned. "She doesn't like being compared to a dog, and I'd say that leash comment just crossed the line."

When Rocco laughed in response to Decker's remark, the tenacious woman spoke up once again. However, this time, to Decker's surprise, she was the perfect blend of calm, stern, and funny as hell. "Listen here, Puffy McPuff-erson," she addressed Rocco directly but stayed rooted to the spot next to Decker. "Your advances were neither so-licited nor wanted, and I can guarantfuckingtee that the other women who work out here feel the same damn way about your *Rico Suave* act. So I suggest you take your steroid-injecting, Axe-body-spray-wearing, grunt-while-you're-lifting, sorry ass out of here, or I'm gonna get you thrown out." He felt her triceps flex beneath his hold as her hands balled into fists at her sides. "Was that uncom-plicated enough for you?"

Shit, the woman was a riot of surprises, each one more breathtaking then the last, but this time, she'd literal-ly stolen his breath and his words. Trying his hardest to contain his reaction, Decker bit down on his tongue. *Bite till you bleed if you have to, man, but don't you dare let it out. Don't you dare.*

———•———

H OLY SHIT, DID *those words just come from my mouth?* April inhaled, realizing for the first time just how quiet the space around her had gotten. The solid arm that had been holding her tight just moments before was trembling, as was the body it was attached to. *What the... hell?* She tilted her head to the side and looked up at her make-believe boyfriend, whose focus was still set on Rocco. However, his face no longer showed the same overwhelming sense of acrimony it had possessed at first.

His bottom lip was gripped firmly between his teeth, the plump flesh white under the pressure of his strong bite, and his nostrils flared as if he was having difficulty regulating his breathing. When her stare finally landed on his eyes, it wasn't anger or hostility she saw boiling to the surface. Nope, judging by the fine crinkles that outlined the corners of the man's chocolate orbs, he was holding in—laughter. Just barely, it seemed, by the small snort that escaped his tightened lips, but yes, he was definitely amused.

Uncertain as to what exactly had Super-Hot-Gym-Guy so tickled; April turned her attention back to the target of her rant. Rocco stood just feet away from her with flushed cheeks and a dropped jaw. He'd taken off his leather weight-lifting gloves and was twisting them nervously in his thick hands while his wide eyes scanned the gym as if he was looking to make certain no one else had heard the tongue-lashing he'd just received. Unfortunately for him, that wasn't the case.

Two beautiful women walked up to them, stopped, and smiled at April before turning to Rocco. "Stay away from us too, Puffy."

Clearly frustrated and embarrassed, Rocco turned to leave the main work-out room and mumbled, "Bitch."

"What did you, say?" Super-Hot-Gym-Guy growled as his posture went from lax to rigid in a blink.

"Nothin', man. I didn't say nothin'." Rocco hadn't turned to face them.

"Yeah, you make sure you keep it that way. Because I only play nice once. You got it?"

April struggled to keep her own jaw from touching

the shiny laminate floor when big, loud Rocco nodded before slithering out the door. She didn't know it then, but that was the very last time she would ever see him.

Quickly shaking off the entire scene, April faced the man still standing at her side. "So now that you've defended my honor and practically felt me up, I think it's time we introduce ourselves." She extended her hand. "I'm April Maddox."

"Yeah, look, I'm really sorry about that." The man appeared to be studying her face, but he never reached for her hand.

"Wait"—April smiled—"are you sorry for defending my honor or copping a feel? Because to be honest, neither one was a hardship for me."

She realized what she'd said when the crinkles around the man's eyes reappeared and his mouth curled up in a sexy smirk. It was as if his lips alone had spoken the word, *gotcha*.

"Shit, no… no… no… that is not at all what I meant." April felt her cheeks warm with embarrassment. "What I was trying to say was it felt so good to have a man want to touch me that way…" She slapped her hand over her mouth and prayed that the words would just stop spilling out before she died of mortification.

"April—" Super-Hot-Gym-Guy started to speak.

She needed to untangle the ridiculous web she'd spun before the man walked away thinking she was a nutcase. "Please, just give me a second." She inhaled deeply, forcing air around the lump that had suddenly formed in the back of her throat. "What I meant to say was thank you.

It's been a really long time since there was someone other than family to have my back like that. We don't know each other, and still you stepped in and helped me out. That was… cool. Really cool. So thanks." *Cool*? What decade was she living in? She was a teacher in a public school. She knew cool was no longer… *cool*. She moved to retreat, hoping to leave with at least a modicum of dignity left in her arsenal when he stopped her. *Eh, who needs dignity?*

"My name's Decker Brand." He extended his long, muscled arm and waited for her to shake his hand before he continued. "And yes, I am sorry for manhandling you without your permission. That's usually not my style. However, I'm sure as shit not gonna apologize for getting between you and that asswipe. To be honest, April, I'm not sure your honor needed *my* defending. You were doing a fine job on your own, but when I saw him touch you…" April watched as his brows snapped together, anger and something else she couldn't identify etched on his ruggedly handsome face. "Hell, the second he laid his hands on you, I didn't just want to throttle his ass, I wanted to protect yours." Decker's gaze quickly left hers and landed somewhere on the ground. "How's that for embarrassing confessions?"

H E WASN'T SURE what he'd expected when he revealed his innermost thoughts. Hell, he hadn't even known he was gonna do it until the words were literally falling from his mouth, but in that moment, she seemed so open, so exposed that he felt the deep-seated need to honor her vulnerability by exposing his own. What the hell was wrong with him? He'd sworn after Olivia that he wouldn't fall victim to illusions again, but there was something in his gut that screamed this woman was genuine, and maybe it was time to start listening.

"Decker," she spoke his name lightly, a slight tease in her tone. "Both me and my ass are grateful for your gallant behavior." She punctuated her statement with a wink.

Her levity caused him to smirk, which in turn had her small grin splitting her face into a dazzling, dimpled smile. *Fuck, look at those dimples*, he thought as his cock twitched in his shorts.

"Gallant behavior? Who says gallant these days?" He chuckled, trying his best to get his mind off the sexy-as-hell divots in the sexy-as-hell blonde's face.

She threw her head back and laughed a husky sound that did absolutely nothing to slow the blood flow to his dick. "I do. I guess that's what happens when you're a middle school English teacher." She looked at him, her eyes dancing with delight. "Next time I'll say, 'Thanks for your super cool help, dude.'"

Decker chuckled. "No, I can handle the larger words, but thanks for trying, Ms. Maddox." He hesitated briefly then asked, "Or is it Mrs.?" He found himself holding his breath while he waited for her to answer the question.

She shifted her eyes to the left and paused for a second. Decker felt his heart pause too. *I knew it was too good to be true.*

"It's Ms. Maddox." She looked up at him and swallowed. "I'm divorced, and Maddox is my maiden name. I took it back the second my divorce was final."

Decker slipped his thumb under her chin, tilting it up until their eyes met. "Well, Ms. Maddox, it has been a pleasure finally meeting you properly. May I walk you to your car?"

"That would be awesome, dude."

They laughed and chatted as they walked through the parking lot.

He felt like a nervous teen when he asked for her phone number, and he wanted to pound on his chest when she gave it to him. "Here, let me text you right now so you'll have my number as well."

April opened her mouth as if to say something but instead pulled her lip between her teeth and kept silent.

"What's wrong, April? You're not gonna call me?"

She shrugged. "To be honest, no. I probably won't. At least not at first."

"What? Why?" Decker, at thirty-three years old, had done more than his fair share of dating and had been married to a woman who had made him work hard for each smile, laugh, and ounce of happiness they'd ever shared. He'd played every game, knew every trick, and saw through all sorts of bullshit, yet never once had he come across a woman who was so brutally honest.

"Look, if we're gonna be anything—even just friends

—you need to know that… well, my mother is fucking crazy." April ran her long fingers through her ponytail. "Seriously. I've spent most of my life trying to do the opposite of nearly everything she told me, but some things have stuck, and there's nothing I can do about it. One of them is not calling a boy too soon."

Decker smiled as April's face flushed. "A boy?" he asked with humor lacing his tone.

"Yes"—April nodded emphatically—"a boy. It was drilled into me and my sister that it was *bad* to call boys too soon. And I've never gotten over the fear of what would happen to me if I did."

"Dare I ask?" Decker's abdomen clenched as he tried to hold in his laughter once again. This woman was giving him his core workout for the week.

With her face as serious as he'd seen it so far, she answered. "Sure. According to my mother, if a girl calls a boy too soon, she will not only be viewed as easy, trampy, and stupid, but, and this was always the main sticking point for me and my sister, those girls would never ever reach orgasm, because the guys they chased after would know they were desperate little hussies who didn't deserve it. Therefore, no, I will not be calling you for a little while. Sorry, but I like my orgasms." She shrugged and added under her breath, "From what I can remember."

"Wow, your mother sounds like an interesting woman." Decker smiled as he watched April toss her gym bag into the back of her Acura RDX.

"You have no idea."

"All right, well, I'm certainly not one to tell a *girl* not

43

to listen to her mother." He knew he must have looked like a loon with his smile spread clear across his face, but he couldn't help it. The woman had intrigued him from the first moment he saw her, and now that they'd finally spent a few minutes together, he was as good as caught, completely beguiled by her sense of humor and quick wit. "But I can tell you I completely disagree with her theory." He shook his head slowly. "Not that it matters, because it's not gonna be an issue in this situation." Two prominent dimples flashed back at him. *Nope, not gonna be an issue at all,* he thought as he watched her climb into the driver's seat of her black SUV.

"It was nice to finally meet you, Decker Brand. To be honest, in a strange way, I kind of owe some gratitude to that asshole Rocco." With her cheeks flushing at the admission, April slid her key into the ignition and flipped on the engine.

"What do you mean gratitude?" Decker asked, genuinely confused. In fact, just hearing the guy's name on April's lips made his skin crawl.

Shrugging her shoulders, April eyed him. A bashful look crept over her features. "I don't know… I've wanted to talk to you for weeks, but you never seemed that interested. So other than our quick 'hellos,' I've pretty much stayed away."

"Are you kidding me?" He ran his fingers through his hair. Twice. Words were caught in his throat, stuck between the shock and awe. "April, you couldn't be further from the truth. There have been several times when I've wanted to approach you, but you always have your earphones in and this look of intense determination on your face... like you were at the gym to exercise and get the hell out."

Her eyes snapped to his, but she didn't say a word to either confirm or deny his observation.

Therefore, he seamlessly changed the subject. "Frankly, after seeing the way you chewed up and spit out poor, poor Rocco"—Decker curled his upper lip in disgust—"I'm glad I didn't try anything sooner. Christ, that could've been me." He let out an exaggerated shiver and enjoyed the show when April's dimples made their appearance.

"I don't think you have anything to worry about." She checked the time on her watch. "But I do need to get going. Thanks again for today, Decker. Chat soon?"

The sweet look of hopefulness in her expression, combined with the slight uncertainty that he heard in the question, made him want to howl with excitement. Instead, he calmly closed her car door and motioned for her to slide the window down.

"Yeah, I might give you a call sometime." He winked. "But don't you call me, because you never know. I could run into your mother one day, and I'd have to tell her exactly what kind of daughter she raised."

"Oh, trust me, my new friend, she already knows." April rolled her eyes and repeated, "She already knows. See ya later."

The glass partition lifted between them, and she flashed one more quick smile before driving out of the parking lot. Decker stood with the cool air chilling his sweat-soaked body and watched until the beautiful blonde's car was no longer in sight before hopping in his own Ford F-450 work truck and heading home.

CHAPTER THREE

Flirting For Fools

"IT'S DECKER," APRIL exclaimed by way of greeting as she set her satchel down in the teachers' lounge first thing the next morning.

"Who decked who?" The muted question came from April's best friend, the school librarian, Aurora Velez.

"Rori, can you please get your head out of the refrigerator?" April rolled her eyes. "I hate having conversations with your ass."

Sighing, Rori backed out of the fridge, closed the door, and popped the cap on her Sharpie marker. "April, you know I have to label all of my food. Someone keeps swiping my stuff, and I can't figure out who the hell it is." Annoyance was clear in Rori's narrowed hazel eyes. "I'm gonna find the sneaky rat who keeps stealing my Greek yogurt, and when I do, it's not gonna be pretty."

"Blech, I can guarantee that it's not me," Janie Silver, a teacher and friend to both April and Rori, announced as she glided through the door. "I can't stand Greek yogurt.

In fact, if I ever told you what that sour, goopy shit re-minded me of, you'd never eat it again, Ror."

Rori crossed the room, her lips pursed in disgust as her hands gripped her curvy hips. "Janie, you've shared your descriptive and insightful thoughts on my lunch more than once." Rori's nose scrunched up as if her olfactory senses had been assaulted. "I've tried my hardest to bleach your words from my mind. So please, I beg of you, keep all Greek yogurt descriptions to yourself and that sexy boyfriend of yours."

The women broke out into fits of giggles as other fac-ulty members began to file into the room.

"Girls," April interrupted, tapping her Mary Jane-clad foot on the ground, "do you want to hear about Decker or not?" Two pairs of wide eyes stared in April's direction as she tried to figure out the best way to recap the events that happened the previous day.

"Umm, we're waiting," Rori sang out impatiently. "Seriously, who the hell is Decker?"

"Eeep!" April could barely contain the excitement that was bubbling to the surface. "Super-Hot-Gym-Guy, his name is Decker."

"Oooh, that's a sexy name, April." Janie clasped her hands together. "I want full details later, but I promised Max I'd call him when I got to work. My car has been making a strange noise, so he worked on it last night and wanted me to call him when I got here to let him know if it was better."

"And...how is it?" Rori inquired.

A dreamy look spread over Janie's face. "It's perfect.

Absolutely perfect." She grabbed her bags and left the lounge.

"So I'm thinking she wasn't referring to the car just then."

"I think you may be right, Ror," April confirmed, her neck arched to the side as she watched Janie's form disappear through the double doors of the school exit.

"Ahem." Rori cleared her throat. "Chica, we don't have all day. You gonna give me the goods on Super-Hot...err, Decker or what?"

Her directness was one of the reasons April loved her best friend of five years. Rori was more of a soul mate than anything else. She was the kind of person who truly cared about those she allowed in her life, and April considered herself lucky to fall into that category. Her friend wasn't fake she didn't ask questions if she didn't want to hear the answers, and she was always there to listen when April needed to talk. Rori might not always tell her what she wanted to hear, but it was always what she needed to know. Hell, her friend couldn't stand Ben, and that was before he'd packed up his shit and left April and their unborn son. After he left... well, that was an entirely different and ugly story.

"Oh my God, Ror, I wish you were there yesterday. The whole thing was like a scene out of a movie." April quickly explained the scenario from start to finish, including how she'd blurted out her mother's correlation between calling boys and orgasm defection.

"You did not!" Rori cackled, wiping the tears from her eyes. "My God, April, maybe we should enroll you in

49

a flirting class or something. Oh, I know, Flirting For Fools."

April shook her head as her friend dissolved into a pool of laughter. She finally interrupted her fun when Rori began to snort. "You know, Ror, for a librarian, you sure are loud." At her comment, they both broke into a fresh round of giggles. April checked her watch. "Oh shit, I need to get to my classroom."

"I'll walk with you," Rori volunteered, and they made their way down the hall. "You know I'm gonna need all of the details, right?"

April nodded. She knew exactly where the conversation was going.

Rori continued, "Because you know… the words make a story good…"

"But the details make it great!" The friends finished in unison.

April shoved her purse in the bottom drawer of her desk before looking up at her friend's impatient face. "Don't give me that look, Ror. I would have called you with the juicy deets last night, but you know how I feel about splitting my focus when I'm with Eli. The boy only has one parent who gives a shit, and I feel bad enough that he spends most of his waking hours in day care. So when I'm with him, he gets my full attention."

April had cried every single day for months when she returned to work six weeks after giving birth to Elijah. That wasn't the way it was supposed to be. She and Ben had planned for her to take off the rest of the school year, and the summer before deciding whether or not she would return to teaching. However, with Ben gone and April too proud or, as her mother constantly said, too damn stubborn to accept Ben's guilt money, April needed to return to work as soon as her maternity leave was over.

"Once I put the little guy to bed, I graded those damn papers, which by the way"—she playfully smacked her friend's arm—"didn't I ask you to remind me not to give the students such long papers? Gah... please don't allow me to assign the usual term paper at the end of the semester. I swear I dreamed in red ink last night. Anyway, before I knew it, it was midnight. I fell asleep on my bed in my clothes. Again." April shook her head but didn't say another word.

Rori sat quietly on the edge of April's desk with her hands folded on her lap. April knew the pose well. Rori was waiting for April to voice what she *really* wanted to say, and not the other bullshit that had just spilled from her mouth. They'd played this game many times before, each of them taking turns as the attendant during the other's time of need. So April knew quite well that for as stubborn as she was, Aurora Velez had her bested by a mile. Her friend could wait her out until the gates of hell froze over and the devil himself lounged on an iceberg, licking a Popsicle.

With only five minutes until the students would start traipsing into the classroom, April let out an exasperated sigh. "I don't want to get excited over this guy, Ror. I mean, sure, he's hot as hell, and after yesterday, I can say he seems nice, but..." She hesitated. "Ben seemed great up until the day he left me."

"Pff, listen here, chica." Rori lifted her index finger, waving it as aggravation lit up her big hazel eyes. "That man, and I use the term loosely, you were married to was a despicable excuse for a husband, and that was before he left you. You thought you were so lucky to have him, but sweet friend; it was the other way around. He never deserved you. You refused to see it then. Christ, half the time I think your vision is still a bit fuzzy. But other than being a sperm donor, he wasn't a part of your pregnancy from the time the stick turned blue." April startled when Rori intertwined their fingers. "You may not believe it, but the best thing that *man* ever did was walk away."

"Rori," April warned. She hated when anyone tried to make light of the hell Ben had put her through, especially when it was her best friend. Rori knew damn well how her world had been ripped apart, and her innocent son was left without a father even though the man was still alive and well.

"No, April, listen, I was around for the devastation that was left in his wake. I remember it. But I can tell you with one hundred percent certainty that when you were married to that shithead, I never saw even a fraction of the happiness in your eyes as I've seen over the past month from just the brief interactions you've had with Super-Hot-Gym-Guy."

"Decker," April supplied quietly with a smile.

"Decker, Licker, Sucker whatever! The man *we've* been lusting over for weeks makes you smile like that, and you get excited." Rori hopped off the desk as the first bell rang. "Love you, chica," she called over her shoulder as she hurried out the door.

"Back atcha, toots."

IT'S APRIL," DECKER announced as he walked into his brother's pristine office and closed the door behind him. He yanked off his grime-encrusted gloves and plopped his filthy, denim-clad ass on the expensive leather guest chair.

Normally Ford would bitch about Decker's lack of decorum—he even referred to his older brother, and the cloud of dust that followed him during working hours, as Pigpen. But Decker could tell by the way Ford's brows were furrowed that he wasn't going to get his normal razzing.

"Umm, Deck, you feelin' okay, bro?"

Decker mocked Ford's response. "Umm, yeah, why?"

"Because look at the calendar." Ford slid the small paper tear-off day-by-day across the cherry wood. "It's fucking February, not April, you fool."

Shaking his head, Decker chuckled. "Nope, I'm pretty sure it's April." Just about the time Ford started looking really concerned Decker let him in on the joke. "The hot blonde from the gym, the one I've been telling you about, her name is April."

Ford's eyes lit up with recognition before he threw his head back and laughed. "Nice, Deck. You finally grew some balls and got her name. What did it take, a month?

Six weeks? I thought I was gonna have to send her a note on your behalf. You know, 'I like you. Do you like me? Check *yes* or *no*.'"

"Fuck you, little brother." There was no bite in either of their tones; that was how they communicated, how they played, and how they loved one another. "Don't you forget, I taught you *everything* you know about women." Decker, being five years older than Ford and very popular amongst the ladies, had in fact taught his brother many things, but the dark look that quickly passed over Ford's face, one that he'd seen several times before, made Decker wonder about the things Ford had learned long after Decker stopped teaching.

He brought the conversation back to the intended topic. "Anyway, I told you, she didn't seem the type who was open to pick-up lines and flattery."

"So what changed?" Ford rubbed at his shadowed jaw, genuine interest evident in his exhausted eyes.

"It seemed as though she was extremely turned off by douchebags in tanks tops that say *All You Can Eat* across the chest. She definitely didn't like said douche telling her in graphic detail about the ways he'd like to invade her asshole."

"Fuck me." Ford swiped his hand over his forehead.

"Yeah." Decker nodded as irritation once again reared its ugly head. "The guy was quite the charmer."

"What did you do to stop him?" Ford asked through gritted teeth, clearly as frustrated and disturbed by the situation as Decker had been.

Both Decker and his brother had been taught about

honor and respect very early in life by their parents. Their father, Ernest, a man born into conditions that could rival most horror movies before finally being adopted by the Brands, had always put in an honest, hard day's work; and still found time to be an active, positive role model for his sons, as well as a loving husband to his wife. Their mother, Robyn, was a woman they had watched work her ass off to keep BC running while tending to her sons and maintaining the household after their father had passed away. In their actions, their parents had taught them that love, determination, and hard work would earn a good name and great respect. It was an honorable gift from the Brand matriarch, for which their admiration was boundless. In fact, they appreciated and respected all women, even if they didn't always deserve it.

That had been one of the reasons Decker had found it so hard to turn his back when his marriage crumbled. Even when Olivia challenged him with hateful words and cold treatment, he refused to dishonor her, refused to stoop to a level so low. Some may have thought him a pussy, spineless even for allowing someone to treat him so badly. Decker didn't see himself that way. He was protective and vigilant with the people he cared about, and he cared deeply for her. The cold hard fact was his marital problems didn't begin and end with his wife. No, somehow during his time with Olivia, he'd lost his way, and that was something he would never allow himself to do again.

"Hello, Deck?" Ford interrupted Decker's thoughts. "Please tell me you kicked Donnie-Dumbell's ass or at least busted a few of his teeth?" Ford mumbled, "Fucking bastard. Who says shit like that to a woman?"

"Bro, I have a kid. I can't go around throwing punches at random people. What kind of example would *I* be setting?" Decker shook his head. The fact that he'd threatened to do exactly what his brother suggested clouded his mind.

"You'd be teaching your daughter that no man, big or small, has the right to touch her or hell, even talk to her like she's a piece of trash," Ford snarled.

"Relax, killer," Decker joked, attempting to lighten the mood. "You know damn well I'd never bear witness to that kind of shit and not get involved. I'm embarrassed to say that I was this close"—Decker held up his hand, spacing his thumb and index finger only a half inch apart—"to offering him my dental services when April beat me to it. The woman basically told him where he could shove his barbell." When a smile crossed Ford's face, Decker laughed. "It was priceless."

"Nice. Feisty, huh?" Ford wagged his brows. "Sounds like my kinda woman."

Even though there wasn't a doubt in Decker's mind with regards to Ford's loyalty, just hearing him tease about wanting April made his insides churn and his jaw clench. "Not for a minute, little brother," he enunciated each word clearly. "Not even in your dreams."

A knowing grin spread over Ford's handsome face as he lifted both hands to signify his surrender. "So it's like *that*, huh."

Decker nodded.

"Good. Now get your filthy ass out of my office before the dirt ruins my chair."

Decker rose slowly from the leather, placed his palms flat on the pristine desk in front of him, and glared down at his kid brother. "Watch it, boy," he growled. "While you sit here all suited up, looking pretty in your designer clothes and wearing fine cologne, I'm out there using my body and working my muscles." He blatantly flexed his biceps. "These are for more than just looking sexy, little guy."

Ford's nostrils flared just before he burst out laughing. "Dude, for real? You sounded like dad just now, and what I mean by that is… corny as hell. Seriously, man, do not use lines like that on the new chick, or she'll choose the douche over you."

A sense of happiness that he hadn't felt in far too long traveled through Decker's veins.

"Seriously, do you want me to send her that note?" Ford ribbed, reaching for a piece of BC stationary.

"I'll just call her myself." Decker chuckled as he reached for the office door. "But thanks."

CHAPTER FOUR

Gratuitous Winker

"I T'S BEEN THREE days, Rori, three flipping days!" April screeched into the phone, still watching from the window as her brother pulled out of her driveway with Elijah.

Their weekly guys' night was something August had started when Eli was just a baby. It was a way for her little boy to have quality time with an amazing male role model—August's words, not hers. Fact was, her brother was an incredible man, and both she and her son were lucky to have him in their lives. However, now that she had the house to herself, she could focus on the panic that was quickly taking over her rational thoughts.

"Are we talking about Super-Hot-Gym-Guy?" Her friend questioned, seeming distracted on the other end of the line.

"His name is Decker, and you know damn well that's who I'm talking about. So don't play that game with me, missy. He hasn't been to the gym in three days. He never misses three days. And he hasn't called." Pacing the first floor of her two-story house, April let her mind wander to the sexy man who had gone missing since their encounter only a few days earlier. "He basically told me he was going to call me. He even winked at me." April sighed.

Giggling, Rori asked, "He did? Was it cute? I feel like that gesture is only seen in text messages and reruns of *Seinfeld.* "

"Nope, he absolutely winked, and it was... sexy. His face got all soft and dreamy." April closed her eyes picturing Decker's long, thick lashes fanning as he quickly lowered his lid. "Anyway, after he winked and said he'd call—okay, he didn't actually promise—but when I told him I wouldn't call him, he said… wait, oh fuck!" April's head thumped directly into the window pane. The coolness of the glass felt nice in contrast to the flames licking up her neck and cheeks. "Do you think…?" She couldn't finish her sentence. Even thinking it made her sick.

"Do I think what, chica?" Whatever had been distracting Rori before was no longer an issue. "April, what's the problem? Wait, you actually told him that you weren't gonna call?" The musical sound that was Rori's laughter vibrated through the phone. "Oh, that's right! You told him about the phone call/orgasm connection. Do you know that you're a freak?" Her friend could barely form the question through her own hysterics.

"It's not funny, Aurora," April chided, unable to keep the smile from breaching her own lips. "Grrr, okay, it's a little funny," April conceded. "But it's also pathetic. I'm twenty-eight years old. Why is my mother still screwing with my sex life?"

"Why are you letting her?"

"I'm not *letting* her," April countered feebly.

"Good." A smile could be heard in Rori's voice. "Then call him."

"Aw, hell no," April snapped into the phone. "Have you lost your mind? What if Mom's been right all these years? I make the call and poof, no orgasms." April rubbed her fingers over her closed eyes in an attempt to relieve the tension headache that was building in her skull. "No way, I can't risk it."

A loud sigh came through the phone, followed by a pause. April knew her friend quite well. Rori was collecting her thoughts, measuring her words, and weighing the outcome of what she was about to say. "April, we've known each other a long time, so please know I say this with love, but the only times you've reached orgasm from something other than your own hand is when your phone is on vibrate and placed between your legs."

April's eyes popped open at the candid comment. "Rori, that is not true! You and I both know that the voice mail kicks in before any pleasure can be reached. Sheesh!"

Laughing, her friend continued. "Okay, fine. All I was trying to say was you haven't been with a man since Ben. That little bastard never worried about your satisfaction, and you followed all of your mother's rules with him."

It was true. April had fallen for Ben Spears in the tenth grade and followed every one of her mother's *make him love you* rules and look what they got her. Sure, she'd had her first climax with Ben—after all, he had been the first boy she'd ever fooled around with—but after a while, he stopped worrying about her release and only focused on his own. April had had orgasms in the years she was with her husband, but it was always her own doing that brought the release.

"Try something new," Rori nudged. "Call him."

"I'll think about it," April conceded as she climbed the stairs and made her way to the master bedroom.

"Sure, you will." Rori laughed.

The women said their good-byes, and April sat on her bed, replaying the conversation in her head. Rori wasn't wrong, but old habits were hard to break. April chose the option that fell straight in the middle.

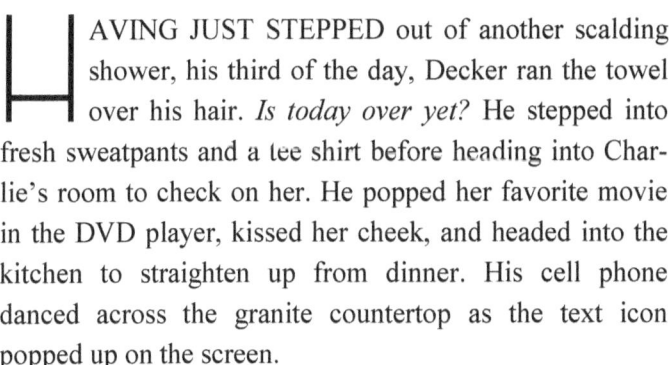

AVING JUST STEPPED out of another scalding shower, his third of the day, Decker ran the towel over his hair. *Is today over yet?* He stepped into fresh sweatpants and a tee shirt before heading into Charlie's room to check on her. He popped her favorite movie in the DVD player, kissed her cheek, and headed into the kitchen to straighten up from dinner. His cell phone danced across the granite countertop as the text icon popped up on the screen.

Like an athlete on a long distance run, he got a second wind when he swiped the screen of his phone and saw who the text was from.

Dimples: *It was my mom, wasn't it?*

He had no idea what she was talking about, but he was smiling for the first time in three days, and for that, he was grateful.

Decker: *Hello :)*
Dimples: *Oh, hi. So, was it what I said about my mom that scared you away? You can be honest.*
Decker: *LOL, do you mean about the orgasm thing?*
Dimples: *I knew it!! Shit*
Dimples: *I mean, sorry...*

She had him standing over the counter, reading her short notes and chuckling like a teenager with his first crush. He looked over his shoulder to make sure his laughter hadn't disturbed his daughter. While he loved his little girl to pieces, he was craving adult time, and April was the perfect prescription.

Decker: *Wait, why do you think I'm scared?*
Dimples: *Umm, you never miss 3 days at the gym*
Decker: *You noticed, huh ;)*
Dimples: *Ahh, so you're one of those...*
Decker: *One of what?*

His brows furrowed, but his lips quirked once again. The woman had him confused and delighted all at once.

Dimples: *A gratuitous winker.*
Decker: *Hahaha, I think it's just you, April, you make*

me… winky ;).

Decker laughed as he pressed send. He wasn't sure what had him more fascinated: April's immediate responses or her witty replies. Either way, he felt happy in way he hadn't known in a long damn time.

Dimples: *Anyway, you haven't been there… I noticed. The only thing that changed was me… so I assumed I scared you off*
Decker: *Wanna know what I noticed?*
Dimples: *?*
Decker: *You called me first ;)*

A minute passed then another, and there was no response. Decker stared at his screen, hoping he hadn't scared her that time. Just as he was about to tap out another text, his phone buzzed in his hands.

Dimples: *No, Decker, I TEXTED you. I've spent my life looking for loopholes to my mother's rules, and I figured out that texting was the technicality to the phone call clause. There were no texts when I was younger, therefore, I figure texts are safe for the Os :)*

Decker stared at her words. His cheeks ached from the smile that was plastered across his face. April Maddox was different from any woman he'd ever met before, and he needed to know more. He needed to know all.

That said, there were things he had to share with her

as well, the sooner the better. Over the years, he'd learned the hard way that plenty of women out there didn't want anything to do with a man who had a child. Not that he'd been looking for a relationship—hell, he hadn't been. Charlie was his baby, his heart, and his first priority. Much to his surprise and disgust, after dating one particular woman a few times before mentioning his daughter, he got the surprise of his life when she threw a toddler-sized tantrum during her *explanation* of how she hated children and refused to go anywhere near them. Laughing at the irony of her very public display of displeasure, Decker laid money on the table where they were dining and ended their date. From that point on, his parental status was disclosed up front, then he watched as the ladies either ran or swooned. Either way, he wasn't interested in a relationship, so their reactions didn't matter—but April's did.

Sucking in a deep breath, Decker touched the green button at the bottom of the screen instead of tapping out another text. He placed the phone to his ear and listened intently to the dull ring.

"Hello?"

Just one word from April's husky voice soothed his nerves and hardened his dick. The question in her tone had Decker grinning once again. She obviously knew who was calling. After all, she had contacted him first. Yet for some reason, she sounded surprised. Then again, there was a part of him that hadn't expected this call either, so he supposed the surprise was valid.

"Hello. May I please speak to April?"

"Umm…" There was a quick pause. "Decker, is this

you?"

He could hear confusion in her voice, which eased his nerves and caused a chuckle to escape from his chest.

"Yeah, April, it's me," he answered casually. "I wanted to show you that we all have parents who drilled rules into us when we were kids. For my brother, Ford, and me, it was phone etiquette. Our mother went berserk when we answered the phone like 'fools,' her words, not mine."

Her warm giggle covered him like a blanket fresh from the dryer. "Decker, phone etiquette is a normal thing for a parent to teach their children. Orgasm desertion is not. But thank you, thank you once again for reminding me that I told you that tidbit of information the first time we actually spoke."

He could tell by her light tone that while she may have been embarrassed, she was in no way upset with him for poking fun. A beautiful woman who could laugh at herself was a heady combination.

Padding from the kitchen to the living room, Decker sunk into the plush leather sofa and placed his bare feet on the coffee table—thank God his mother was more con- cerned with teaching them about respecting people and less about furniture, because he was a feet-on-the-coffee- table kind of man. Finally comfortable, Decker decided it was time to come clean. "You may find this crazy, but in a way, it was you telling me about the whole no-phone- calling thing that really sealed the deal for me."

"What?" Her inquisitive voice held humor.

"I'm not kidding, April. I told you from the start that I

thought you were beautiful, but when you shared that information, be it intentional or not, it brought you to a whole different level." He ran his fingers through his still-damp hair. "I knew then that I'd call."

"But… you didn't," she whispered.

Decker rested his head on the back of the couch. His eyelids lowered as he swallowed the lump in his throat. *If she doesn't want Charlie, then why would you want her?* The truth was he wouldn't want her even for a minute longer, but in that moment, they still had a chance, and in that moment, ignorance was bliss.

"You're right, I didn't call." He sighed loudly. "When I got home from the gym the other night, my mom was at my place, picking head lice out of my daughter's hair." The silence that filled his ear was so deafening that he checked to see if the connection had been severed. "April?"

"You have a child?"

Hearing the detached way she asked the question sent a chill up his spine. "Yes, I have a little girl," he confirmed softly. More dead air filled space and time before he heard what sounded like a humorless snort.

"Figures." Her snapped reply may have been short, but in that one word, all traces of the soft tenderness he'd adored were gone, replaced with a cold, hard front. "That's what I get for answering questions about my relationship status instead of asking them."

Decker shivered as he felt her iciness seep into his veins. How could someone who seemed so gentle be so callous? Even worse, how could he have misjudged her so completely? For over a month, he'd watched her, taken notice of the way she handled herself at the gym. While she didn't talk to people her own age, she offered kind smiles and soft words to the elderly men and women who approached her. She even went as far as to admit her interest in him.

"Wow, okay." He tried to keep the disappointment from his voice, but hiding the anger proved to be too damned difficult. "I didn't realize that men who had children were such a travesty, April—"

"Are you kidding me?" she interrupted, her laughter sounded forced and laced with pain. "I don't have a problem with kids! I have a problem with men who sneak around with women other than their wives. I have a problem with married men acting like they're single while their spouses are busy loving them exclusively with nothing less than their whole heart. That's where *my* problem lies."

Each of her words was an iron brander, and blue fire blistered his skin and seared his soul. They had him knifing up on the sofa and slamming his feet firmly on the hardwood floor. She thought he was an adulterer, a lying bastard. That alone would have sliced him in half had her agony not been evident in the shallow breaths he heard coming through the line. Were those quiet sounds sobs? *She was divorced. Had her husband cheated? Left her for someone else?* His anger defused faster than air leaving an unknotted balloon. "Oh my God, April, I'm not married. I would never, ever do that to any woman, especially not one that I pledged to honor."

Silence once again screamed through the phone until

he heard another shuddered breath.

"April, hear me out, okay?"

"Go on," she whispered.

"My wife, my daughter Charlie's mom, died more than five years ago." When he heard April's gasp, he knew the whole truth needed to come out before any more assumptions were made. "I would have never cheated on her, April, but I can also tell you that she and I wouldn't have stayed married. I'm sorry that she's gone, because no one should lose their life that young, and now Charlie doesn't have her mother, which breaks my heart. Does that make sense to you?"

ENSE? MY GOD, the last thing any of this made was sense. April's mind was a Tilt-A-Whirl, and her stomach was feeling the effects. Of course it was possible for the man to have a child and not be married—Jesus, hello, pot, meet kettle. She wanted to kick herself for being such a closed-minded little brat. Not every man was a low-life scum. Not every man was Ben. When he finished his explanation with the fact that his wife was deceased, April wanted to search for the nearest volcano and plunge headfirst into the darkened pit.

"Decker." She sighed as she held the phone between her shoulder and ear and hugged herself tight. "I am so unbelievably sorry."

"You don't need to apologize, April." While his

words rang true, his tone sounded defeated and exhausted.

She felt like such an asshole, treating a perfectly nice man like shit based solely on the mistakes of her ex. But Ben's betrayal cut deep, and even though years had passed, her wounds still ached. Sometimes they still bled.

Sitting back on the king-sized mattress, April pulled her knees up to her chest and wrapped her fluffy golden throw blanket over her chilled body. Decker had opened up to her. Now it was time to do a little sharing of her own.

"I do need to apologize, Decker. In fact, I owe you huge." He tried to interrupt again, but April hushed him. "It's my turn to talk, big guy, so simmer down." His deep chuckle made what felt like a tight fist around her lungs loosen just a bit, at least enough to allow some oxygen to flow and words to release. "So... I also have a child, a little boy named Elijah. And he is everything to me."

Unlike the ridiculous fish-out-of-water gasping shit that she pulled a few minutes prior when learning about Decker's daughter, Decker's response was appropriate. He asked Eli's age and if he had green eyes like his mother. His overall sense of interest seemed genuine, which both comforted and scared the hell out of her.

April circled her hand over her stomach in an attempt to calm the nausea that rolled around the coiled pit as a slight coating of sweat dotted the smooth skin between her breasts. It wasn't that she was ashamed of Eli. Hell, she thought her little boy was a superhero. It was just that she had a thing about not allowing people to get too close to her baby unless she knew they were going to stick around.

She didn't want her son to feel the sense of loss and rejection that had nearly broken her when Ben left and never looked back. Life was hard enough. Elijah didn't need people coming and going. It was her job to protect *him*... and she did.

In fact, since her divorce, April hadn't dated. At all. So the conversation was like opening a safe that had been sealed shut for years. If she wasn't so busy listening to the blood rush through her ears, she probably could have heard the squeak of unused vault hinges. While she had absolutely no immediate plans for Eli to meet Decker, the thought of discussing her son with a man she'd just met, a man she was insanely attracted to, a man she'd thought about while pleasuring herself made her uneasy. However, with said man waiting patiently on the other end of the line, she felt the indescribable need to explain her behavior. So she did.

While she didn't bore him with the play-by-play, she gave him the highlights or, as she referred to them, the lowlights. After four years of reflection, April was finally able to see some of the signs she'd missed along the way, and she shared those with Decker as well. Each time she felt as if she was divulging too much or going on too long, Decker would ask another question or express his disapproval over Ben's actions. April appreciated not just the fact that Decker listened, but the fact that he actively listened.

"I don't understand, April." Decker sounded perplexed.

"I threw a lot at you. What's got you stumped?"

"How the hell could any man lucky enough to have you be dumb enough to let you go?"

The heavy feeling that had sat like a brick in her belly mere moments before magically turned to fairy dust, all shimmery fine and satiny smooth. How did he do that? Still wrapped in the blanket and holed up in the corner of her bed, drained from sharing what was arguably the worst experience of her life, she was amazed to feel the small smile stretching over her lips. No, there would never be a day when what Ben did would be anything less than disgusting, wrong, and horrendous, but just the actuality that she wasn't crying buckets, hell, the reality was she was grinning? Decker Brand had to be some kind of magician.

His deep voice pulled her from her thoughts. "Seriously, April, no offense, but your ex sounds like a loser. As for the chick, she's his current wife, right? How the fuck could she be with a man who was not only married but expecting a child? Ech, that's a soulless woman right there."

Just the thought of Ben's wife, Becky, caused April to flinch. It was a knee-jerk reaction that occurred every time someone mentioned *that* woman. She sighed, "As much as I'd like to blame everything on the homewrecking whore, truth is, she wasn't the one who was married. That was Ben. She may have the morals of an alley cat, but she wasn't the one who was cheating." Ugh, thinking about it gave April a stomach ache, but actually admitting that Becky, while a nasty, skanky sleaze, was not the cause of her failed marriage… that made her want to vomit.

"We're home," August and Elijah chimed in unison

71

from the bottom of the stairs.

Wow. April glanced at the clock on her night table. Two hours had passed? Maybe the man did have super powers; he sure as hell made the time fly by.

"Hey, Decker, my brother, August, just brought Elijah home, so it's probably safe to assume that my kid is a sticky, exhausted mess in need of a bath and a bed." April smiled. Her son could be sugared up and shooting chocolate chips out of his nostrils, and she'd still be grateful for every minute August spent with him.

"Wait," Decker called, his soft chuckle sending tingles down April's spine. "Are you telling me that your parents had two children, and they thought it would be what... cute to name them both after calendar months?" His voice broke, sending ripples of laughter into April's ear.

Unable to control her own giggle, April replied, "No, I'm telling you that my parents had *three* children, and my mother, who we've already established is more than a bit crazy, decided to name us all after months. There's my brother, August, my sister, Ember, and me."

"Ember?"

"Yep, as in November." April held the cell close to her ear as she walked down the stairs. "Laugh it up, big guy," she teased, "but trust me, it's far from funny. My mother takes her names quite seriously. The woman is still holding a grudge over the fact that I was born a week late, making my birth month May instead of April."

Amusement evident in the contorted chuckle she heard in Decker's words, he asked the question so many had queried before. "A…April, why didn't she just name you *May* instead?"

The sound of the ridiculously handsome man's laugh felt like the sun warming her skin after a cold winter. So instead of answering his question with the bitterness that she usually felt toward the topic, she allowed herself to see it from an outsider's point of view. In all honesty, it sounded crazy, ridiculous, and funny as shit.

"My mother is a stubborn woman, Deck. She'd already had a mural painted on the nursery wall that said *April,* and she was angry that I, her third child, was overdue. According to my family, she demanded to be induced just so I could be born in April, but the doctors refused to do it." April rolled her eyes. "The woman has major control issues."

With his laughter under control, Decker replied, "Yeah, I'd say she may be a bit controlling. However, I'm kind of glad she stuck with the name April."

"You are? Why?" April couldn't imagine what his response would be.

"I don't know, May just seems so… pioneer-ish. Like the *Mayflower*." Decker's playful tone had April picturing the smirk that had been melting her panties for weeks on end. Decker continued to tease, "Or better yet, subservient. *May* I have my slippers and my pipe?"

"All right, funny man. I need to go get my boy ready for bed, and I'm sure you probably have another head inspection in your immediate future… but hopefully I'll see you soon."

"You just *may*." He chuckled and disconnected the

call, leaving April standing in the family room with a goofy smile plastered on her face.

⬥————————⬥————————⬥

APRIL SLID HER phone in her back pocket and moved toward her brother, whose arms were filled with sleepy little boy. "It looks like you guys had a ton of fun." She leaned in and placed a kiss on Eli's forehead, inhaling the sweet scent of ice cream and innocence.

"Hmm, someone else looks like they had quite a bit of fun tonight." August grinned, the question evident in his eyes.

April felt her cheeks warm. Her own built-in lie-detector had kept her honest her whole life.

"Tiny, did the guy from the gym call you?"

"Umm." Flames licked the soft surfaces of April's face, turning it from pale pink to blazing red. "Eventually."

August cocked his head to the right and smirked. "What does that mean? Wait, did you actually call him first? Holy shit, Tiny!" August's eyes rounded with pride. "I'm so proud of you! Don't worry, I'll never tell Mom."

"No!" April huffed. "I'd never call a boy first, jeez, August." She cupped her hand over her mouth and faked a cough. "I texted him." She used August's temporary state of shock to swipe Elijah from his strong but trembling arms. "Stop laughing at me, Aug. You're loud, and you're gonna scare my child. That will make me angry." She glared at her brother with the most evil stare she could summon. "You won't like me when I'm angry."

The Hulk quote lingering in the air managed to make August laugh even harder, as it always had in the past, but since August was the greatest uncle ever, August's laughter burst from his body, completely soundless, and his eyes watered, his face was red, and his hands ran through his dark blond hair.

April nearly lost her shit just watching her brother trying to contain his. "Stay down here," she whispered loudly through forced calmness. "I'll put him to bed real fast, and then tell you what happened. And since you are my favorite brother, I'll even let you laugh at me while I tell you." With Eli in her arms, April turned and headed up the stairs.

"Wait," August called quietly, "I'm your only brother."

She looked over her shoulder and smiled. "Good thing you aren't my second favorite." The sound of his chuckle followed her upstairs.

CHAPTER FIVE

You and the Floss Fairy

ECKER KNOCKED ONCE on his brother's office door and entered before Ford could instruct him otherwise.

"Deck, really, can't you even wait for me to invite you in? I could have been in the middle of a meeting." Ford's eyes held neither contempt nor any hint of chastisement.

Decker smirked, shook his head, and held up his smart phone. "But I knew you weren't. Our work schedules are synched now, remember? You went all crazy with your *knowledge is power* shit and forced your sweet little secretary to merge our phones. Christ, I know way too much about your damned itinerary. I'm shocked you don't have your daily jerk-off sessions tapped in." Decker tucked his phone back in his jacket pocket, sat in his favorite chair, and laughed when his brother flipped him the bird.

"You keep barging in, and you may just see something you can't unsee, big brother." Ford's words came through a smile, but the promise was no joke.

"Oh really, what does that mean?" Decker goaded in good humor. When Ford remained silent behind his desk, his face an impenetrable mask, Decker grew serious. Just because Ford was his best friend didn't mean they spilled their guts over cocoa on a weekly basis. "Seriously, what's up? I know it's not work-related because this place is booming." A sense of pride filled every pore in Decker's body. Their father would be proud of them. "Is it Mom? Is it you?"

Decker watched as Ford leaned back in his expensive Italian leather chair, his arms—muscular and inked with spectacular art hidden under designer suits—crossed lightly over his broad chest with his perfectly coiffed hair still in place even so close to the end of the work day. That kind of perfection used to drive Decker insane, but his brother appeared to thrive off of it.

"Relax, faux-pap," Ford smiled, using the nickname he'd given Decker after their father had died when Decker seemed to be so much more than just a big brother. "I'm fine, I swear. I just don't want your eyes to bleed if you ever barge in here and see more than just files spread out on my desk." Ford's brows lifted playfully. "You're not the only one who has a life outside of this place. You feel me?"

Laughter ratcheted through Decker's body. "Dude, just promise me I won't *feel* any part of you on my favorite chair here."

Ford leaned over and pressed a button on the phone

system. "Jovanna, can you please pick up some Clorox wipes before you come into the office tomorrow? Thank you."

"No problem, Mr. Brand."

Decker could almost hear the blush rising on the cheeks of the sweet young woman who sat at the front desk. "You're a dick, Ford." Decker shook his head but smiled at his business partner. "That poor girl has been lusting over you for months. And you have her running your errands?"

Ford loosened the knot in his tie and undid the first button of his shirt. "Don't you worry about Vanna." His eyes glittered with what Decker always clocked as a mischievous look. "She's doing just fine. Now what's your deal?"

My deal... Decker thought to himself, the reason he'd come to Ford's office in the first place. He ran his hands through his hair and stared at his brother before blurting, "I want to ask her out."

Ford's brows shot up to his hairline. "Jovanna?"

"No... April."

Ford nodded. "The hottie from the gym, gotcha."

For some reason, after the past two days of cute text messages during work and lengthy conversations late at night, hearing her described as nothing more than eye candy grated on Decker's nerves. "I told you, man, she's more than that, she's—"

"Stop," Ford interrupted his hands held up in defense. "Christ, I didn't mean disrespect, Deck, okay? We've spent the past couple of months referring to her as the gym hottie, and old habits die hard." Ford's eyes softened, and his lips ticked up on one side. "I'll be more careful."

"Sorry I jumped on you like that." Decker shoved his hand through his hair yet again. "She's different, this one... Christ, I don't know her that well, but I fucking want to." Decker glanced over at his brother and recognized the pensive look immediately.

Ford rubbed his hand across his jaw, over the shadow of hair growing where it had been freshly shaven and smooth just eight hours earlier. His brows were furrowed, and his lips pressed tightly together for a brief moment before he inhaled and began his assessment. "I don't see the problem, Deck."

"It's not a problem per say. We've being meeting up almost every day for nearly two weeks at the gym after work, and we're constantly texting or chatting, but it isn't enough. I want more."

"So take what you want." Ford shrugged as if the concept was as elementary as addition. "It's not like you've been celibate over the past few years. Women flock to you—they always have. She will too." Ford's face relaxed as he leaned forward in his chair, the sound of leather creaking in the otherwise quiet office. "I'm gonna give you a piece of advice you've been feeding me for years. Just be yourself. Whoever doesn't accept you can fuck off."

Decker snickered. "Nice. Sounds like brilliant guidance." The smile slowly left his face as realization hit. "But here's the deal. While you may choose to keep your acquaintances with women limited to them being bent over your chair or draped across this beast of a desk"—Decker motioned between the two men—"and you *know* there will never be an ounce of judgment from me, that's not what I want with April."

He knew he must have sounded insane. He was just getting to know the woman they spoke of, but all the same, he meant every single word that left his mouth. "I want to get to know this woman. I've seen her smile, and I wanna make that happen again. You should see her dimples, Ford, they're... fuck, they're sexy as shit." Decker felt his dick stir in his jeans as April's husky giggle echoed in his head. He had yet to hear her all-out laugh. It was a challenge he placed upon himself and one he couldn't wait to accomplish. "I wanna know what makes her tick, what makes her happy. Hell, I need to hear her laugh long before I hear her moan." With his mind and his body at odds, Decker stood from the chair, adjusted himself non-too-discreetly, and looked at his brother. "Thanks for the talk, Ford. I feel much better."

"Umm, okay." Perplexity passed over Ford's face as Decker turned to leave the office. "Hey, Deck?"

Decker looked back.

His brother wore a shit-eating grin. "Do yourself and the company a favor..."

Decker waited patiently for his partner to continue.

"Don't think of all of that sweet laughter and sexy dimples while you're working with the power tools." Ford shrugged. "You'll want all of your fingers when you finally get to the moaning part."

"Fuck you, little brother."

"I love you too."

Decker smiled as he closed the office door behind him and headed for the gym. It had been five days since he'd last worked out properly, the longest amount of time he'd gone in years. The physical demands of his job kept his body toned and his muscles cut, so it wasn't the actual gym he'd been missing as much as the smart, sexy blonde who made the extra time away from home more of a treat than a chore.

———————●———————●———————●———————

D ECKER RAN ON the treadmill, his incredible body fluid as each muscle moved in perfect form. April had been enjoying the inspiring view from behind while she rocked her own cardio routine. However, she did not enjoy the woman on the treadmill next to Decker, trying to garner his attention for more than thirty minutes. While jealousy was definitely good for April's workout, her elliptical practically begged for a rest. She was uncomfortable with the way jealousy made her feel inside. Instead of taking the time to dig into what the green monster was trying to tell her, she decided to intervene the way Decker had on the day they finally met.

"Hey, sweetie, you still want me to come with you to the doctor today? I'm thrilled you're finally getting that rash checked out." April looked up at Decker and grinned sweetly as she wiped the sweat from her neck before she continued to speak. "It's beginning to spread."

Decker's lips curled up as he nodded just once in April's direction without slowing his pace. The treadmill tramp to his left punched the big red "Emergency Stop" on her machine, bringing the belt to a halt. Wiping her hands onto her lycra-covered thighs, as if to rid herself of whatever ickyness may have jumped from Decker onto her during her thirty-minute eye-fuck, the jiggly-jogger stood slack-jawed. Her stare moved from Decker to April then back to Decker. Disappointment bloomed in her doe eyes before she quickly hopped off the treadmill and flounced in the direction of the ladies' locker room. April bit her lip in effort to contain the laughter that wanted to escape, but it was futile. Small snickers left her.

The whirling sound of the motor began to decline as Decker slowed his pace. His tank top, once pale gray, was drenched in sweat and nearly black as it molded to his broad chest. April's gaze roamed his body, his skin a natural shade of tan that covered divine muscle and sinew. The man was simply gorgeous, and while he was aware of his allure, he wasn't cocky or arrogant; he was just comfortable in his own skin.

"Okay, dimples, not that I'm complaining, because that girl was flat-out creepy, but what the hell?" Decker stepped down from the treadmill, his knuckles resting firmly on his hips. "A rash? For real? Couldn't you have come up and pinched my ass or kissed me? Why did you have to give me a rash?" He grimaced as he wiped the sweat from his face with the towel that had been draped over the hand bar.

April choked back a laugh, doing her best to keep a

straight face. "Look, you should both be thanking me. I saved you from her, and technically, I saved her life."

Decker looked perplexed by her claim. "What do you mean?"

"Oh come on, Deck, don't even try to pretend you weren't checking out her ass." April felt her cheeks flush. "Hell, I couldn't take my eyes off it. And while it was indeed a great ass, I need to know, who wears a thong bodysuit to the gym these days? Christ, I thought she was going to saw herself in half running in that thing." Unsuccessful in her attempts, a tiny snicker escaped. "I cut in the moment I smelled smoke."

Decker threw his head back as deep laughter poured from him, the sound so thick and rich it reminded April of melted dark chocolate. She wanted to revel in his mirth or, better yet, grab a spoon and eat it. Instead, she found herself laughing alongside him, deep hard laughter, the kind that had her eyes watering and her belly aching. It was the best kind of happy there was... the uncontrollable kind. After a minute or five, April wiped her eyes and realized that not only were several members staring at her as if she'd gone off the rails, but Decker seemed to be studying her too, no longer laughing, but his face happy none the less.

"Oh my God, I'm so embarrassed," April whispered through the hand that covered her mouth.

Decker reached for the hand she'd used to cover up her chagrin and engulfed it in his much larger one as he warned, "Don't you ever apologize for being happy, for laughing. Fuck, April." His voice was low and deep as he inched closer to her, making the space between them near-ly non-existent. "I swear to Christ, that was the sexiest sound I've ever heard." His free hand swept through his deep brown, sweat-slickened hair. His molten eyes re-minded April of the same sweet confection his laugh had just seconds before. The man was downright edible.

Tingles crept up her arm as she realized her hand was still nestled in his. It felt as though someone pressed the "pause" button on the remote control of life, leaving just the two of them in slow motion while the rest of the world kept still. April looked down to watch Decker's thick thumb rub circles across the top of her hand. While the motion seemed mindless, small even, he stood quietly sharing her space and her breaths. Each time his calloused thumb glided over her soft skin, waves of long abandoned desire burst through her already wanton body. "Un-pause"—her heart pounded behind her ribs in a frenzied rhythm that had nothing to do with the cardio she'd com-pleted more than ten minutes prior. Melting into a lust puddle by Decker's feet was certainly not on the top of her priority list. Then again, laughing like a clown hadn't been either. She needed to change the subject, fast.

April slowly withdrew her hand from Decker's and refastened the elastic on the ponytail that had fallen loose during her vigorous exercise. With some physical space between them, she was able to think with her head instead of her hormones. More stares and dropped jaws were aimed in their direction than before. A shiver of embar-rassment coursed through her heated body. She needed to get out of the fishbowl that was the workout center, because other than when she was teaching, she hated being the center of attention. She thought it best to lead them out to the lobby. At least the entrance was alive with people coming and going, not to mention the constant activity from the juice bar—the whirring sounds of the blenders that served up the protein shakes and energy drinks would be sure to steal the attention from her.

"Anyway," she said, attempting to steer the conversation back to its original content, "You should be happy I was in there to save you, Deck." April grinned. "Aside from the obvious, you know, the fact that she had a rockin' body, I can't imagine what you and Thong Barbie could've possibly had in common."

Decker tilted his head, questions blatant in his eyes.

"Oh, come on, she was one high maintenance chick. I don't know you well, but you certainly don't strike me as the type to go for a woman who works out with a face full of makeup."

Decker's brows furrowed as he cocked his head to the other side. *Shit, did I totally peg him wrong? Did I insult him? Why can't I shut up?* While April chastised herself silently, she noticed Decker's lips begin to lift. That smirk screamed "I gotcha."

"Hmm, well then, thank you, you kind and thoughtful woman." Decker's bright smile instantly put April at ease. "You truly are a selfless soul. I feel as though I owe you a great debt, you know... for saving me from the Thonged Villain." April giggled at Decker's mock horror. He shook his head, feigning torment. "I was going to ask her out for this weekend, but you opened my eyes and made me think better of it. Now what should I do?"

ELL, THIS COULDN'T have worked out better had Decker planned it himself. April's bright eyes sprung wide as he tossed out the question he'd been gearing up to ask. Her cheeks flushed an even deeper shade of pink than when she'd just finished her cardio. Was that bad or good?

"What do you say, April?" he teased. "The guys on the jobsite would say you cock-blocked me with the Thong Princess... so—"

April's eyes narrowed as her hands rested on her small waist. "Oh, big guy, I didn't realize I was interrupting such a love connection between you and the Floss Fairy."

Decker wanted nothing more than to kiss the woman who was dishing out silliness with the same ease she received it.

"You stay put, and I'll see if I can go find her. I'm sure she and all of her 90s hair could be ready for that date in about four hours." She winked and turned her back to him.

"April," Decker warned, his hand gently gripping her biceps to stop her retreat. He watched as her shoulders rose and fell and her blond ponytail swayed with each breath. Within two steps, he stood face to face with the smiling beauty and found himself at a loss for air. He could get lost in the dimples that hugged each side of April's lush lips. In fact, he wanted nothing more.

"What can I do for you, big guy?"

"Will you go out to dinner with me this weekend?" The timidity in his own voice threw him off guard for the first time in years. Shit, the only time in his entire life he'd lacked confidence were the years he was with Olivia, and even then it was conviction he was missing, not confidence. At the time, he'd been too frightened of making a mistake, of hurting the wrong people to follow his heart, and in the end, everybody lost. Now, as he looked at the woman who'd not only piqued his interest but sparked his passion, he knew that he needed her to accept his invitation.

"Umm, sure." April licked her lips then rubbed them together as if she were spreading gloss from bottom to top, even though the perfect skin was void of artificial color or shine. "Okay."

Decker's eyes dropped to her plump lips as he felt a stirring low in his groin. He shifted the towel he'd been holding to cover the front of his basketball shorts. "Wow, Dimples, I'm overwhelmed by your excitement. Seriously, try to tone it down a bit," he snarked, attempting to hide the disappointment her lack of enthusiasm caused.

April let out another sexy laugh. "No, I'd really like to go out with you, Deck. It's just... well, this whole thing is just strange." Decker wanted clarification. As if reading his mind, April continued to explain. "It's like something came over me when I saw that girl trying to get your attention." Again she moved her pink tongue across her bottom lip, and again he felt his cock twitch, but instead of pressing on, she looked away.

"April, truth, okay?"

She shifted her gaze back to his and nodded.

"That feeling, was it jealousy?"

"Completely." She sighed before muttering something unintelligible to herself.

"What was that?" He definitely liked how her cheeks flushed when she was embarrassed.

"Oh, it's nothing...just thinking about how that must sound, me admitting that to you. I promise I'm not the bunny-in-a-pot-of-boiling-water kind of girl."

The *Fatal Attraction* reference wasn't lost on him. Both he and his brother had come across more than one crazy stalker over the years, but thankfully, no pets had been harmed, unless of course one counted his pet rock, Rusty. Molly Martin, his third-grade girlfriend, had thrown Rusty out the window when Decker broke up with her for Samantha Park.

The same errant lock of hair had escaped her ponytail. Decker couldn't help but reach out and tuck it behind her ear. His heartbeat quickened when she leaned into the touch. "I get it, you know." Her arched brow told him she had no idea as to what he was referring. "Other than wanting to pummel that ass, Rocco, for trying to help himself to something that wasn't his and to someone who wasn't interested, I was jealous as hell that he was talking to you and I wasn't. Fuck, I've been jealous of every man who got you to smile, even if it was just your I'm-not-interested-now- go-away smile. So don't worry about feeling jealous, and don't worry about other women, April... there isn't anybody else."

As he waited for his words to sink in, he watched as what appeared to be concern, possibly even torment, drift across the planes of her beautiful face.

"I hear you, Decker, I do," she replied, nodding her head. "But I also believed my ex-husband when he promised to be faithful, and that got me nowhere. So while I truly look forward to going out with you this weekend, you're gonna need to give me a little time and a large learning curve with anything that comes after the check."

Honesty, she was giving him flat-out honesty. Shit, when was the last time anyone other than family had offered that?

Nodding, he smiled at the playful, genuine woman before him. "Dinner and drinks, April. Just two people who clearly like each other"—he winked—"getting to spend some time together. Sound good?"

The divots in her cheeks winked at him. "I look forward to it, Decker, but now I need to go and pick up Eli from day care... I'll chat with you later."

"I'll call you tonight," he promised, "after I put Charlie to bed."

When April flashed him another of her megawatt smiles, something inside him shifted. The satisfaction he felt from seeing her beam, from being the man who put it on her lips... fuck, it was incredible. Without thought, he leaned forward and pressed a kiss on April's forehead. When she didn't shy away from the embrace, he ran his finger along her jawline and under her chin, tilting her head back until her eyes met his. Her stare glazed over with questions and lust as her once smile shifted into a siren's grin—alluring, inviting, and intoxicating.

"I can't believe you just kissed me, Decker. I must have tasted gross, all salty and sweaty. Not my finest moment."

Decker chuckled. Her tone was sweet, and her words were adorable, innocent even, but it didn't match the sexy woman who was clearly begging to come out. He wondered if April even knew how many incredible sides she had. Something told him she had no idea.

"Mmm, I think you tasted perfect." He leaned down and kissed her cheek. "Yep, amazing. Dinner, April, Saturday night. I'm looking forward to it."

"Me too," April agreed once more before waving good-bye.

CHAPTER SIX

My Mother is Babysitting

"EEP!" RORI CLAPPED her hands together. "I can't believe my girl is going on a date tomorrow night. I feel like a proud parent."

"Oh my God, Ror, keep your voice down. The last thing I want is for my personal life to become fodder for the rumor mill here at school." April peered over her shoulder to see who else was in the staff lounge this early in the morning. "I swear, sometimes I think the teachers are worse than the students when it comes to gossip."

"Ooo, gossip. What gossip?" Janie floated into the lounge, her usual smile present and accounted for. "Seriously, girlies, what am I missing?"

"Oh, nothing," Rori said in a singsong voice. "Except that April here has a date tomorrow night with Super-Hot-Gym-Guy."

"Shut the fuck up!" Janie exclaimed, her eyes wide with interest. "I'm so excited for you that I'm not even gonna be hurt that you didn't call me as soon as it happened."

It wasn't that April was hiding the information from Janie; it was more like she hadn't been able to process it yet herself, let alone involve anyone else. Sure, she'd told Rori immediately, first because the woman was her best friend, and second because it was the first time she actually needed to find a babysitter for Eli. April had practically felt Rori's regret through the phone the previous evening when her friend explained why she was unable to help with the little guy, but that unease was nothing compared to what April felt when both of her siblings were also unavailable, leaving her mother as a last resort.

Sighing, April admitted, "It's true. I'm going on a date. It's the first date I've been on in more than ten years. And it's with the hottest, sweetest, funniest man I've ever met... I should cancel."

"Stop it," Janie and Rori said in unison as Janie pulled up a chair and joined the women at the table.

"I want details, all of them." Janie pointed from April to Rori. "And what she chooses to leave out, can you please fill in? We can't get her the help she needs if we don't have all of the details."

"I couldn't agree more," Rori said. "But from what I've heard about Mr. Six-Pack, he seems to manage our girl just fine. She's calm around him, not at all like the mess we've seen when she talks about him. The only thing I think she needs is a—"

"Umm, hello!" April interjected, waving her hands in front of her friends' faces. "You guys are talking about me as if I'm not sitting right here at the table."

"Oh, so you are here." Rori grinned, winking at a satisfied Janie. "Are you sure you're part of this conversation? Because the people at this table are getting ready for a date. They are not canceling or thinking about canceling on someone who makes them smile the way this man does you. So knock off your shit and dish the deets." Seemingly proud of her speech, Rori nodded her head as if to say she was finished speaking and took a large gulp of her coffee.

April looked at the two women who sat beside her. While Rori was her closest friend, Janie was much more than just a co-worker. The truth was, April was lucky to have these women in her life, and she could use some advice regarding her date so... "Okay, Decker made reservations at the new Italian place in Charistown, Amore, for seven o'clock."

"Ooh, Max, and I love it there. The food is amazing, and the service is great." Janie's eyes sparkled with the dreamy look she got every time she mentioned her boyfriend. "We intend to go back there as soon as the Grand Re-Opening for our bar is over and we have spare time. But anyway, back to you."

April bit her lip, unease filling her belly. "Well, here's the thing. I'm not sure I want him to come and pick me up. I think I'd rather meet him at the restaurant." Her comment was met with two pairs of narrowed eyes and pursed lips.

"Chica? It's a date. The guy is supposed to pick up the girl."

"Rori's right, April. What's the deal?"

April stared down at her hands, as if the state of her

un-manicured nails had all of a sudden become fascinating.

"Oh." Rori placed her hand over April's and squeezed. "I understand. You don't want Decker meeting Eli, right?"

Bingo. "Look," April answered quietly, "you know how I am with my son. The kid hasn't even met my hair dresser, and I've been going to her for three years. I refuse to have him meet people who are only going to hurt him when they up and leave." She could feel Rori watching her—hell, she could practically hear the thoughts whipping around in her friend's mind—but she refused to look up from her hands. "Anyhow, Elijah is only one of the reasons I can't have Decker come to my door." April looked up when complete silence met her comment. "Ladies, please, my mother is babysitting. Do you really think it's a good idea for him to meet her on our first date?"

"Nope," Janie answered.

"Hell no," Rori said at the same time.

"So I'll suggest just meeting at Amore?"

The three women nodded at once as the lounge began to fill.

CHAPTER SEVEN

Don't Test Me

"HERE YOU GO, sweet boy." April set a plate with triangular cuts of peanut butter and jelly sandwich and Doritos on the table in front of Elijah. "Let me get you a glass of milk."

"Thanks, Mommy." Eli plucked a triangle off the plate and took a four-year-old's equivalent of a huge bite.

April couldn't hold back her smile—she never could with him. Her son brought her so much joy, even in the beginning when there was nothing but sleepless nights and hormonal breakdowns, even now when she was completely exhausted and he wanted "just one more story" before bed. He was her sweet when life felt ridiculously sour.

She set the cup of milk next to his plate and planted a big, noisy kiss on the crown of his head. "Your head is so delicious, I think I'm gonna eat it like an apple. Nom nom nom."

"No, Mommy." Elijah's high-pitched voice giggled. "If you eat my head, I'll die." This was their game, and it made him laugh every single time. "Go get a real apple, Mommy. It keeps the doctor away."

"Okay." She stretched out the word, feigning disappointment, and went back to the refrigerator to grab the crunchy fruit.

"Mommy, can we watch *Cloudy With a Chance of Meatballs 2* again?"

Crunch. *Thank God I took a large bite,* April thought as she used the few seconds to chew and swallow the bit of fruit in her mouth. *Cloudy With a Chance of Meatballs 2* was Eli's favorite movie, one that they viewed almost daily, and April could recite the lines verbatim. That being said, she'd never say no to a movie with such a nice message behind it, and she did have quite the affection for the talking baby strawberry.

"You finish up, and I'll go get the movie started." Since the family room and the kitchen were attached, she could keep an eye on her little guy while cueing up the DVD.

Once he was settled on the sofa, she went back to the kitchen to collect her half-eaten apple and her cell phone. It was nearing three o'clock, and she still hadn't heard from Decker. In fact, she'd texted him the previous night, and he'd never responded. In the nearly two weeks since they'd been chatting, this was the longest they'd gone without any contact at all. Disappointment zipped through her. Was he getting bored already?

Crunch. The apple's crisp flavor pulled April's attention away from her thoughts just long enough to notice the text indicator blinking on her phone.

Decker: *Hey there, sorry I didn't get back to you last night. Got held up at work and then had dinner with my mom, Ford and Charlie.*

Hmm, she thought, taking another bite of the dense fruit. She scrolled to the next missed message.

Decker: *By the time I put her to bed and sat my ass on the sofa I fell asleep.*
Decker: *<<<OLD*

His self-deprecating comment had her grinning as she tapped out a response.

April: *No problem. I wanted to talk to you about tonight.*
Decker: *Actually, I need to talk to you as well.*
April: *?*
Decker: *Would you mind if we met at Amore tonight?*

April read the question. Twice. "Why would he want to meet me at the restaurant?"

"Mommy, did you say something?" Eli called to her from the sofa.

"Oh, no, baby, I'm just texting with Aunt Ember. I'll be in with you in a few minutes."

Eli didn't respond, already sucked back in to the animated talking food.

April: *Nope*

She knew her response was uncharacteristically short and would most likely grab Decker's attention, but that wasn't why she'd kept it brief. No, it was more because his request took her by surprise, and frankly, it upset her. The logical part of her brain chastised her for being ridiculous. After all, she had been going to make the same suggestion. However, her irrational side, the side that feared rejection, the side that questioned whether or not Decker had already begun to lose interest, that was the part of her that screamed the loudest.

Decker: *Are you sure it's okay?*
April: *Yep*

D ECKER STARED AT the screen on his phone. Two one-word replies? That was not like April at all. The woman texted like most people spoke—in full sentences. Even though he teased her about it, he found it endearing. There was something going on, and he had no idea what it could be. He only had about five more minutes left of the intermission, then he wouldn't be available for a while. But there wasn't any way he'd be able to stay focused when he was worried about April, so instead of texting, he called her number.

"Hey," she answered. Her aloof greeting confirmed the call was exactly the right move.

"Hey to you." He moved away from the crowded lobby so he could listen not only to her words but her tone. "I only have a couple of minutes, but I wanted to hear your voice. I can't wait to see you tonight." Thoughts of being close to her, getting to spend a little time with her without the chaos of the gym, call waiting, work, even their kids getting in the way had been absorbing all his extra brain space since the minute she accepted his invitation.

"Me too," she responded, her tone lacking all enthusiasm.

Decker's chest tightened. What the hell had happened to turn her from hot to cold so quickly? He'd done the whole bait-and-switch thing with his first wife, and there was no way he'd tolerate it again. "April"—he heard the edge in his voice but couldn't smooth it out—"did I do something to offend you? Because I'm lost here."

A beat of silence hit the air waves, then he heard her pull in a shaky breath.

"No, Deck, it's not you, it's me. Fuck, I mean, fudge … shit." The frustration he felt began to melt as he listened to her fumble with her words. "Okay, first, I can't believe I just used the 'it's not you, it's me' bullshit. I'm sorry about that."

He rolled his neck from side to side, relieving tension from his shoulders. "No prob, but what's the deal?"

He heard her let out a long sigh. "Umm, you don't want to pick me up for our date tonight and—"

"Wait, no, that's not it at all." *Shit*, he thought, slapping himself on the forehead. Of course that puzzled her. He'd dropped that on her without explanation. "I guess I forgot to tell you Charlie's dance recital is today. She takes two classes. One of the shows was this morning, and the other isn't until four o'clock. I usually take her for ice cream afterward, then I thought I'd have time to shower and pick you up—" April tried to interrupt, but Decker continued speaking. "However, as with all things *little girl,* the whole show is running behind. It's not a problem though. I'll take her for ice cream then come straight to you."

"Oh my God," April whined, "Deck, I'm a horrible person. No, absolutely not. Keep your plans as is, and I'll meet you at the restaurant. I'm so sorry for making you feel bad."

"Babe, it's fine." Hearing her embarrassment through the phone, Decker could practically see her cheeks flaring, and the image sent a burst of excitement through his body.

"No, Decker, it's not fine. I actually texted you last night to suggest we meet at the restaurant."

Her words drained his arousal like a cold bath in mid-January. Why wouldn't she want him to pick her up?

April continued, "And when you didn't respond, I began to wonder if maybe you were having second thoughts."

"Ah, so when I asked if we could meet at Amore—"

"Yep," April finished. "I thought you were trying to let me down easy."

"April, I told you, that's not gonna happen, but..." Decker needed to know why she was going to suggest meeting for their date. "Why didn't you want me to pick you up at your house, babe?" Silence hit his ear long enough that Decker had to look at the screen to make certain the call was still connected.

Finally, April spoke. "Well, there are two reasons, actually." Her voice dropped to a whisper. "The first is that I'm quite protective of Elijah. I don't let just anyone meet him. I told you I haven't dated since he was born, and I won't allow people in his life who aren't going to stick around. He doesn't need that kind of pain."

Decker understood all too well about not introducing random women to his daughter. He'd kept his dating, or should he say sex life, separate from Charlie. But he also knew the value of a passing stranger and a temporary friend, a person who entered one's life for a moment but impacted it for a lifetime. He kept those thoughts to himself. "So what's the second reason you didn't want me on your doorstep?"

"Umm, that one is easy—my mother is babysitting. There is no flipping way I'm letting you meet her unless…"

April didn't finish her thought, which had Decker practically dying to know what exactly was going to come out of her mouth. "Spill it, dimples. Unless what? If you don't tell me, I'll make certain Charlie's group gets moved up to an earlier spot, and I will be on your doorstep with a copy of the first text you ever sent me. You know, the one that started our communication. The *first* text."

April gasped. "You wouldn't."

"Don't test me." Decker's smile was so broad, his cheeks hurt from the effort.

"Fine," April conceded. "I was gonna say I wouldn't let you meet my mother unless you were completely in love with me. Because otherwise, there'd be no guarantee that you wouldn't run for the hills. Happy now?"

Yes, he was happy. The woman kept him on his toes but didn't make him question whether or not he was worthy. In fact, it was quite the opposite. "You have my word, April. I'm not running anywhere." An announcement was made over the intercom, requesting the audience to return to their seats. "I do, however, need to get back to the auditorium. But we're okay, right?"

"Yes, and I really am sorry, Deck."

"Don't be sorry, dimples. Just be at Amore by seven." He had the phone in his pocket and a smile on his face as he reclaimed the seat next to his mother.

Just as the lights dimmed and a hush fell over the audience, his mother whispered, "Don't think I haven't noticed all that grinning you've been doing lately, son. I look forward to hearing all about her... real soon."

Trying his best to squelch the smile, Decker shot a glance at his perceptive mother, whose eyes were locked on the empty stage. "Not sure what you're talking about, Mom."

Without saying another word, his mother patted his arm and nodded. As if on cue, the music started, and groups of little girls took the stage, making their parents and their tutus proud.

CHAPTER EIGHT

To Be That Spoon

"WOW." DECKER WHISTLED quietly as he appraised April from head to toe. "You look incredible."

He'd felt her presence from the moment she walked into the restaurant, as if there were a magnetic pull that drew her to him. The large swallow of vodka did nothing to moisten his throat that went desert-dry the second she'd slipped off her coat and revealed a black, V-neck fitted sweater over tight, dark rinse jeans. It took another swallow of the cool liquid to mask the groan that rose in his chest when his gaze drifted to the high-heeled leather boots that rested just under her knees, showcasing her long legs and firm thighs. Sure, he'd seen her countless times over the past couple of months, but each time had been at the gym. While he'd never deny finding her attractive as she pushed her body to new limits, dripping sweat and shaping her muscles, those instances didn't hold a candle to the image that currently stood before him.

With his heart pounding behind his ribs and cock pressed firmly against the zipper of his jeans, he rose from the bar stool he'd acquired ten minutes earlier, upon arriving at the restaurant. Decker's hands, as if acting on their own volition, reached out and caressed down the cashmere that covered April's arms, not stopping until they linked through her fingers. There was no hiding the anticipation that danced in her soulful green eyes, an invitation that Decker accepted by connecting with her skin to skin. Even though the move was middle-school-aged at best, when he pressed a kiss on her warm cheek, the world around them faded to black. Her fruity scent cloaked him like an embrace, much more intimate than what they were engaged in at the moment. Her silken gold hair grazed his cheek as he pulled back and watched how it cascaded down her shoulders, curling just over the swells of her breasts. *Fuck me, she's gorgeous.*

"You clean up pretty well yourself, big guy." She wagged her sculpted brows, acknowledging that he'd spoken and not thought about his previous comment.

While her words were playful, he could tell by her tone that she may be feeling a bit timid or apprehensive. After all, she had said this was her first date in years. Hopefully it would be the first of many for them.

T RYING TO MAINTAIN her composure after nearly turning to jelly from just the slightest brush of his lips against her skin, April inhaled deeply through her nose before releasing the breath from her mouth. Placing her purse on the bar, she noticed the half-empty glass he'd been holding upon her entry sat sweating on a cardboard coaster. She checked her watch then the clock behind the bar. The times were identical. Being a teacher, she was neurotic about punctuality, so how could he be halfway done with a cocktail if she was ten minutes early for the date he'd informed her that he'd arrive to at the exact time of the reservation?

"The clocks are correct," Decker acknowledged as if reading her thoughts. "I, however, got here about fifteen minutes ago, and that drink was exactly what I needed."

While the man looked ridiculously sexy in his gray button-down shirt and black jeans, the furrow between his dark brows said that the hours since their chat had been filled with more than just tap shoes and tights. He gestured for April to take a seat at the bar. When she did, he resettled in the one he'd been occupying when she arrived. With time to spare and nerves to settle before their table would be ready, April ordered a martini while Decker explained how the rest of his afternoon played out.

"Just like always, Charlie did want ice cream. However, she opted for a homemade milkshake... made by my mom... at her house." Decker ran his hand through his thick russet-brown hair, a grin so faint only a fellow parent would notice it lingering behind the curtain of chagrin. "So I changed *our* plans, which led to a misunderstanding between you and I, all so I could continue a tradition with my little girl, one that she'd been talking about for weeks, mind you, and in the end, she didn't even wanna hang out with dear old dad anyway." He lifted the glass, swirling the ice in the clear liquid. "I'll tell you, April, I love my daughter, I do." He snickered before swallowing a small sip of his beverage. "But tonight was one of those rare times when I wanted to sell her to the circus."

"Oh, believe me, I get it," April admitted. "Kids can be tough. I've often thought Elijah would make a perfect clown, but it just so happens that the Ringling Brothers and Barnum and Bailey Circus don't come around that often."

A comfortable silence fell over them as they savored their drinks.

"What are you thinking about, Deck? You're smiling." April placed her small hand on his thick forearm.

"I was thinking about something my mom used to say to me when I was younger. I never quite understood it back then, but with each year that passes, the damn statement rings clearer and clearer." April could have sworn she saw Decker's memory playing in his chocolate eyes. "Man plans, God laughs."

* * *

"AIN'T THAT THE truth?" she agreed.

Her sexy voice and soft giggles ignited tingles through his body, while the flash of her deep dimples gripped him like a firm stroke to his lengthening cock.

Then a gentle softness, an understanding only another parent could feel, settled on her beautiful face. "I'm sorry that you got stood up for your ice cream date with Charlie. Those little traditions probably mean more to us than to them." Her eyes lifted to the left before resting back on his. "And I'm sorry that I assumed the worst with you. It's just—"

Looking into her celadon gaze, Decker didn't need any more of an apology. This whole thing was new to both of them, and they were both bound to make mistakes. Her eyes told him everything he needed to know: she was sorry, she was happy to be there with him, and it was time to move on to a better part of their date.

"Dimples, the only thing you should be apologizing for is the condition of the lower part of my body." Watching her face transform from contrite to zealous did nothing to ease the condition he'd just mentioned. "Seriously, April, every time you move I smell apples." Decker leaned in, closed his eyes, and breathed in her sweet, fresh scent. "I've never smelled anything more intoxicating."

April threw her head back and laughed. "Um, you're sweet, big guy, but I'm thinking your nose is just extremely grateful for my apple-scented lotion. After all, I've smelled like a sweaty pile of laundry each time you've seen me in the past."

Before he could respond, the hostess arrived to lead them to their table.

"No, babe, that's not it," he murmured in her ear just

before they took their seats. "It just so happens that your brand of *sweaty laundry* has been one of my favorite smells over the last month or so."

Her rounded eyes and winking dimples made the strange look he received from the hostess well worth the effort.

Over a shared grilled calamari appetizer and separate meals, veal scallopini (Decker) and eggplant parmesan (April), the conversation flowed smoothly and the laughs came easily. Two people who'd never spent time alone together seemed as if they'd never been apart.

"So there we were, just the two of us, putting the finishing touches on the outside lighting at the neighbors' house. They were out of town, and I was packing up our supplies while my dad was fastening the sconces into the siding with the screw gun." This was one of Decker's favorite stories about his dad. Each time he told it, he relived the day, making his father feel not so far away.

Olivia had gagged the first time he shared this particular anecdote with her and rolled her eyes each time after. Judging by the way April listened to the things he'd said and engaged in their conversation thus far, he had a strong suspicion her reaction wouldn't be the same as his former wife's.

"It was my brother's birthday, and my mom, while loving that Dad and I spent quality time together when he wasn't working, requested we not take more than a couple of hours to do the job and return home. Delighting in our mutual love for all things construction, Dad and I got lost in the work and our time side by side, and before we knew it, the sun was setting and we were late. At first, I didn't hear him." Decker paused as much for a dramatic affect as it was to quench his parched lips. He rested his glass on the table eager to continue. "Between the clanking of the tools being tossed in the metal box as I cleaned up and the music blaring on the radio, nothing sounded off. But then I heard my name. It was a calm, lazy calling coming from my dad. 'Decker, can you come here for a minute, son?' April, I had no idea anything was wrong until I walked over and saw my father holding the power tool as steady as could be. When his jaw ticked, I followed his stare only to find he'd twisted the screw right through his index finger."

April's eyes flared as her jaw dropped. "Oh my God—"

Decker interrupted her before she could ask any questions. "My dad, in his calmest voice, said, 'Deck, would you mind throwing the gun in reverse, please? Gotta get this screw outta my goddamn finger.'"

"Holy shit, Decker!" Her eyes were still dinner-plate wide but filled with awe and not disgust. "What in the hell did you do?"

"Umm, first, I put that motherfucker in reverse and helped my dad get unattached from the house. Then once I realized the man was okay—and he was totally fine, like 'Oh shit, I got blood on my favorite flannel,' fine—I nearly peed myself laughing." Decker chuckled as he remembered that day. "I was fourteen, and we were a block away from home. My dad's hand was bleeding pretty badly, so he wrapped it up in his ruined shirt and let me steer the car while he managed the gas. It was the greatest day ever."

April's hand flew over her mouth. Judging by the tiny creases at the corners of her eyes, the fiery woman was no doubt trying to hide a full-fledged smile behind her partial hand-mask.

Decker shook his head. "You should have seen my mom when we got home. First she was pissed that we were late, but as soon as she saw my dad was bleeding, she morphed into nurse-mode. Mind you, the woman wasn't a nurse by trade, but when you're married to someone in our line of work, injuries come with the territory. Anyway, once she'd cleaned him up and he explained what had happened, my mom went from gentle and sympathetic to Nurse Ratched in the blink of an eye."

"Why," April asked from behind her hand.

"Why?" Decker questioned, laughter ripping from his gut. "April, my dad got into a truck, while bleeding profusely, with his vertically challenged fourteen-year-old son and drove home with said son doing the steering. It was not his finest decision-making moment. The guy was lucky my mother didn't screw his balls to the siding that night." Decker watched as April's dimples burrowed deeply into her cheeks. "Go on, beautiful, I can see the amusement just begging to come out."

She was fighting to hold it back, he could tell, and he didn't want that. No, he wanted her open and honest with real emotions from a real woman who wasn't afraid to just... be.

"Let it out, April, before you explode."

As if Decker's permission had been the only thing holding her back, April erupted in peals of laughter. The husky, rich sound was like fine scotch, running warm through his veins and fueling his soul. Every part of his body was live and stimulated like the electricity in the story he'd just told. Each of her jagged breaths sent more blood to his already hardened length, making him more than grateful for the long tablecloth that allowed him to adjust himself subtly without calling more attention to the table.

"Oh my God, Decker, seriously..." April gasped for air between fits of giggles. "Vertically challenged? Is that how you referred to yourself?"

He watched as a large tear drop rolled unchecked down her cheek until it hit her plump red lips. Decker sat frozen, enthralled as her small tongue glided to the corner of her mouth to catch the salty laughter. *Fuck me,* he thought as his cock pulsed behind the confines of his jeans. He felt a sense of disappointment when she swiped the remaining tears away with her palm.

He shrugged. "Look, I was a... late bloomer. At least that's what my mom used to call it. I didn't hit my growth spurt until I was almost seventeen."

April's gaze morphed from hilarity to heat in less than a blink as she covered his hand with her own. "I'd say you bloomed just right, Decker Brand." The words no sooner out of her mouth than the pink flush graced her cheeks.

"Why, Ms. Maddox, are you flirting with me?"

"Oh, hell, I hope so," she admitted. "Because I really suck at this shit."

"Mmm." Decker shook his head, wondering how the

hell he'd found her. "Beautiful woman, you have no idea how good at *this shit* you really are."

April rubbed her lips together before dropping her gaze to their joined hands. He wanted to taste those lips, wanted those hands on his skin.

"Can I interest the two of you in dessert?" the waitress asked when she appeared at their tableside with the pastry cart and a smile.

"Ooo, I'd love something sweet," April chirped, pointing at the chocolate mousse.

"And for you, sir?" the waitress asked Decker as she placed the dessert in front of April.

"I'll just have some of her... err, hers."

April grinned as the waitress left the table. Something sparkled in her eyes—desire, lust, intrigue. He wasn't certain yet, but he intended to find out.

"Hmm, I'm not usually one for sharing my dessert, but I loved the story you told me about your dad and you. In fact, I kind of liked all of the stories you told me tonight. Since you've been so sweet..." April pulled in a shuddered breath as if she was summoning courage. "I'll let you have a lick of me... err, my mousse." Her cheeks depressed as her lips turned up.

"I'd love to taste your mousse, April," Decker growled trying to figure out the logistics on how best to move from his side of the table to hers without the tent in the front of his pants becoming visible.

As if she could sense the desperation in his mind, April offered the perfect solution. "Would you like to move your chair a little closer to me so we can share?"

With his eyes practically glued to the silver spoon, Decker watched the utensil dip into the chocolate confection and move to the waiting channel of April's lush mouth.

"To be that spoon," Decker groaned as he took the silver from April's hand, loaded it with more whipped chocolate, and lifted it to her lips. *Fuck...* just before she opened for the spoon, he leaned forward and finally claimed her mouth.

He ran his tongue along her bottom lip, tasting the apple gloss that had enticed him the whole evening. When he breached her mouth, his tongue sliding against hers, the sweet chocolate flavor mixed with something uniquely April, his heart punched behind his ribs, and he knew there was nowhere else in the world he'd rather be—until he heard her quiet whimpers escape their joined mouths. Then he wished to God that they were anywhere else but at that table, no matter how tucked away it was.

The buzzing of a cell phone was like icy water on a campfire, making them quickly pull away from one another as the intensity of their kiss still crackled through the air. Scrubbing his hand over his roughened jaw, Decker watched smugly as April attempted to gather her wits when she answered her phone. The caveman in him was flexing his arms and pounding his club, proud to be the man to put that dreamy look in her eyes. Then it disappeared.

"Mom, what's wrong?" Her smile faltered then vanished, along with the color in her face. "Okay, I'm leaving now. I'll be home in about fifteen minutes... bye." April tucked the phone in her purse, slid her chair out from the table, and stood.

Decker felt a wave of nausea roll through his gut. There was nothing worse than getting a phone call from the person watching your child. "April, what's wrong? What did your mom say? Is Eli okay?"

"Umm." April rubbed her lips together, worry etched over her beautiful face. "She didn't give me any details. She just said I needed to come home." There was no doubting the complete despair bubbling in her small frame. "I've got to go, Decker."

Even though he wanted to follow her out to the parking lot, he hadn't yet received the check, so he couldn't just leave the restaurant. "April," he called, relieved when she stopped and looked at him over her shoulder. "Please call me tonight to let me know that you guys are okay?"

She nodded once and left him just as he'd started the evening—alone in Amore.

CHAPTER NINE

Everything Good Happens After Dinner

"MOM, I'M HOME." April announced around the lump in her throat as she bounded through the front door of her house. "Where's Elijah?" She did a quick scan of the family room, looking for her little boy, but found only her mother, Ellen, sitting comfortably on the sofa with a book in her lap. "Is he okay? You told me to come home." Panicked, April headed toward the staircase. The need to see her child had her pulse thrumming in her ears.

"April"—her mother's calm voice permeated April's hysteria—"Eli is fine. He's sleeping like the angel he is, so relax." Ellen sighed and closed her book.

Relax? April thought as she ascended the stairs. Her mother's phone call had shaved years off her life, and now the woman told her to relax? No, April needed to see her baby with her own two eyes before any relaxing could commence. Gingerly, so as to avoid the squeaky hinge, she opened her son's bedroom door and crept into the softly lit room. When her eyes landed on the small form snuggled tightly in the middle of the bed, April felt as if the boulder she'd been lugging around for more than fifteen minutes disappeared, leaving nothing but dust and unpleasant memories of its existence. Breathing deeply, she leaned down and rested her hand on his back, a habit she'd started when he was an infant. After a few respirations, she placed a light kiss on his head and backed silently out of the room. Clearly her son was fine, so why the phone call during her date? Why the cloaked message asking her to come home? As she descended the steps, all of the fear that had surged through her body rapidly turned to frustration or, better yet, anger.

"Elijah is fine, Mom," April shout-whispered as she closed the distance between herself and her mother.

"Yes, dear, I know. I told you as much when you got home." Ellen looked perplexed by her daughter's tone. "I'm not sure why you ran up there the way you did."

April pulled in a breath, held it, and counted to five before exhaling. When no relief came from her tried-and-true decompression technique, she repeated the process once again to no avail, causing her anger to spike even higher. "Mother, I was out... on a date. A *date*! With a really great guy, and you called me and told me to come home. How did you think I was going to react?"

Ellen leaned forward on the sofa, resting her forearms on her knees, "And *that* is why I phoned you," she answered confidently. "It was nearly ten o'clock, April, and you'd been out for several hours already. And if you want to get technical, it wasn't a *date* being that you met him at the restaurant." Ellen cleared her throat before delivering her final point. "And to be honest, nothing *good* happens after dinner."

April squinted as she tried to make sense of the craziness her mother was spewing. "What?" April shouted as she paced the room. Quickly remembering that Eli was asleep upstairs, she lowered her voice as she stalked closer to her mom. With her hands fisted tightly, her palms aching as her nails broke the skin beneath them, she hissed, "First of all, regardless if he came to my doorstep or not, it *was* a date. I didn't want him to pick me up because I'm not comfortable with getting Elijah involved, but more so, I didn't want him to meet *you*." Okay, so maybe that wasn't the whole truth, but at the time, April didn't care if she was leaving out details. She didn't give a damn if her words hurt—she was pissed. "Second of all, *everything* good happens after dinner! What's wrong with you?"

Shaking her head, Ellen rose from the sofa and walked silently to the coat closet to retrieve her jacket. She slipped her arms through the sleeves, cocked her head to the side, and stared thoughtfully at her daughter. "April, dear, why should any man buy the cow when he can get the milk for free? Think about it." She zipped her jacket and headed for the door.

"So, now I... I'm the cow in your story?" April shook with frustration as she spit out her question.

"Oh, honey—"

"No, don't 'honey' me. I've played by your stupid rules, and do you know what it got me? Do you? It got me Ben Spears. What a fucking prince he turned out to be."

She watched her mother's reaction to her words.

It wasn't the language that startled Ellen. The Maddox family had no issues with "bad" words, unless of course they were coming from a small child. No, it was the fact that April had stood up to her mother that made her frown with displeasure. Well, April thought, there's a first time for everything, and tonight her mother had gone too far.

"You know what? I'm tired, and I'm finished with this whole conversation. Good night, Mother."

"April—"

"Nope, all done listening. Thanks for watching Eli tonight. Talk to you later." April walked her mom to the door, closed it, and locked it behind her.

Nothing good happens after dinner—the woman had clearly never had mousse. April grinned at the thought. Memories of the heated looks and sexy things Decker said floated through her mind, but their panty-melting kiss... mmm. April rubbed her cool hand around her heated neck.

"All the good stuff came after dinner," she said out loud to the empty room as she walked to the kitchen, pulled out a pint of mint chocolate chip ice cream, and soothed her frayed nerves in minty delight. "It sure as hell isn't mousse, but it's damn good," she grumbled, popping the lid on the container and shoving it back into the freezer. She grabbed her cell phone from the table, turned out the lights, and headed for the stairs.

Thinking about the feel of Decker's tongue as it slid over her lips and into her mouth had April shivering with need. Oh, wait, that was her cell vibrating in her pocket.

She retrieved the phone and noticed she had two text messages waiting for her.

Decker: *Is everything okay?*
Decker: *Babe, I'm worried*

Staring at his words, April tried to articulate the answer to his question in her head. Another text buzzed through:

Decker: *April...*

Knowing his voice would provide comfort, a fact she was too scared to delve into, April's thumb pressed call instead of reply on the small flat screen of her smart phone.

———◆———◆———◆———

"THANK GOD," DECKER exhaled in relief. "Is everything all right?" Seeing her name light up his screen filled him with solace and concern all at once. Hearing her voice after more than an hour of apprehension released a flood of words he didn't have time to sensor. "I've been worried about you and Eli since you left the restaurant. I swear, April, it took strength I didn't know I possessed not to follow you home tonight, and then the tenacity I've refused to claim but clearly have not to hop in my car and pound on your door just to make sure you guys were safe and healthy."

She had given him her address earlier in the week when the plan was for him to pick her up for their date, so having that information and not going to her was even more difficult. He couldn't get her face out his mind. The haunted look that captured her eyes, the way the color drained from her cheeks, and how her lips quivered when she explained that she needed to leave.

He'd quickly paid the check and left the restaurant, only to pace in the parking lot while he processed what his next move should be. The grip on his cell phone tightened, as did his resolves not to call or text her while she was driving. Memories of his and Olivia's last conversation surfaced from the recesses of his mind, the outcome clawing at his heart as bile churned in his gut. It was then he finally decided to go home and wait to hear from April.

When the hour mark hit and he'd heard nothing, concern turned into panic. He'd tapped out a quick text to April, hoping by mistake she'd forgotten to call him, but when the message went unanswered, he texted the babysitter, who lived in the same building and just a few floors down. He asked if she'd come back if need be, then sent the next text to April, then the third. He was reaching for his car keys and waiting at the elevator for the sitter when his phone rang. He slipped the sitter a twenty, mouthed, "Thank you," and went back into the condo to talk to his woman. *His woman? Yep, feels right.*

"We're good, Deck." April's confirmation allowed him his first full breath since watching her leave Amore. "I'm so sorry to have worried you."

He could hear her exhaustion through her faked cheer, and every part of him ached to bring back the light that was in her tone while they were together. "Uh uh, no way, babe, tell me what happened with Eli or, better yet, the Queen of Orgasm Control." The melodic sound that sputtered out of April confirmed Decker hit the nail on the proverbial head.

"Deck, I can't even…" April sighed. "My son was fine, thank God. My mom on the other hand…" He heard her blow out another breath. "I just keep reminding myself that she loves me in her own very *unique* way. I swear I'm going to figure it out one day. Today just isn't it."

With the phone to his ear, Decker walked through his home, putting away Charlie's toys and turning off lights. They were typical things he'd been doing for more than six years, but tonight, he had April's voice in his ear, and for the first time, he had her scent on his clothes and her taste on his tongue. All of his senses had been affected by her, and he wanted more. He needed more. "So tell me, what was the reason for the call if it wasn't Eli?"

April snorted. "Oh, you'll love this—she was trying to save my virtue. Seriously, Decker. Does she forget that I was married? I have a four-year-old child, hence the reason she was at my house *babysitting*. I don't have any virtue!"

Decker could practically see the dimples forming in her cheeks as her giggle tickled him through the line. "Well…" He cleared his throat. "I hate to admit this, but your mother wasn't altogether wrong, babe. I had no intentions at stopping with just one kiss." Even though they'd been flirting and chatting for weeks, tonight was their first official date. While it was obvious that April was as attracted to him as he to her, he didn't want to scare her off, but he also wanted her to know he was no Boy Scout. The way she had his blood churning... mmm, one kiss would have been a mere appetizer.

"I'm glad to hear that, big guy," April cooed, her voice honey smooth but sinfully sexy, "because I would have been disappointed if one kiss was all you had to offer."

Decker pulled the phone from his ear and looked at the screen. Yeah, it was still lit and connected to April Maddox. No, he wasn't dreaming. The woman was sexy as sin. He closed his bedroom door, kicked off his shoes, and sauntered over to his bed. "April"—gravel and heat filled his tone—"will you let me kiss you now?"

Brief silence met his ear—no words, no breath—until she answered in a whisper, "Yes, Decker, I'd love for you to kiss me now. How do you plan to do that?"

The certainty in her answer, mixed with the innocence of her question, had Decker's cock hard as steel and begging to be released from its confines. "Do you trust me, April?"

A moment of time passed before she stammered, "I-I don't know."

Her honest response came as a bit of surprise. He'd never asked that question and received an answer other than "yes." The truth had him grinning; Ms. Maddox was a smart, sincere woman who told it like it was. He hadn't earned her trust yet, but he was going to.

"Deck, I didn't mean—"

"No, April, your answer was honest, and I respect that. So here's my honest answer—I like you, a lot. I'm not a liar, a cheater, or any of the things that fathers pray their daughters stay away from. I have no intentions of hurting you, and right now, in this moment, I just wanna make you feel good. Now, will you allow me to do that?"

"Yes," she murmured.

"Go to your bedroom, beautiful," he ordered.

"I'm already there, big guy."

While he couldn't picture the room, having never been to her house, the thought of her surrounded by a huge bed and her flawless skin draped on smooth sheets had him unbuttoning his jeans as he spoke his next demand. "Perfect. Now peel off that sexy top of yours. Just the hot little V-neck, honey. Leave the bra alone, and lie down. And April, keep those incredibly long fingers off your body until I say otherwise." The sharp intake of breath he heard followed by the soft hum gave him the incentive to continue their game. "Are you lying back?"

"Yes, Decker," her voice turned husky as she responded. "My shirt is rumpled on the floor, my head's resting on the pillow, and I'm laying here wearing just a lacy green bra and my jeans."

"Mmm," Decker rumbled while he removed his shirt and edged back on his mattress. Her breasts, so firm and round, had teased him all through dinner in that tight black top, and now imagining them in nothing but green lace… his hand grazed over his denim-clad dick. *First her, then you*, he thought, repeating his motto over in his head.

"Close your eyes, April."

"Decker—" His name wasn't a question but a plea.

He knew she was letting him in, and he wasn't going to let her down. "Shh, you said you'd let me kiss you. Now, trust me and close your eyes."

"Okay," she murmured, "they're closed."

His voice thick with desire, Decker closed his eyes as well and began to instruct April through the most erotic kiss of his life. "Good. Now imagine me beside you, our bodies so close, the heat of my skin warming yours as I lift your chin so I can look into your eyes.

"Imagine *my* breath, April, a hint of chocolate, sweet and close, caressing your skin with a promise of things yet to come." With each word Decker's heart skipped faster, but when he heard her shallow breath, his pulse began to race.

"Keep your eyes closed, beautiful, and lift your left hand to your face. Just before you touch your cheek, rotate your wrist so it's your knuckles that stroke your skin. Start by your ear, and slowly drag your hand down your jaw-line. That's *my* touch you feel on your soft skin, *my* knuckles that are making your breaths quicken."

"Now, move the index finger of that same hand across your silky-soft bottom lip. Do you remember how it felt when my mouth claimed yours? When my tongue breached your lips and slid into your warmth? Fuck." Decker groaned as the images he painted came alive in his head. "Let me feel your tongue, beautiful. Lick your finger for me."

"Oh, Decker," she whimpered, "Christ, how the hell

did you do that?"

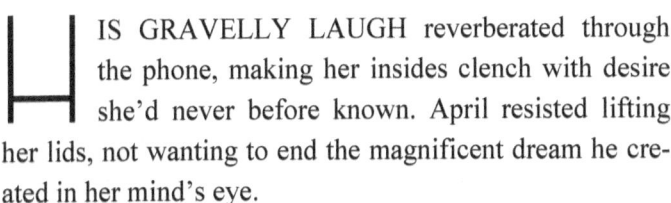

IS GRAVELLY LAUGH reverberated through the phone, making her insides clench with desire she'd never before known. April resisted lifting her lids, not wanting to end the magnificent dream he created in her mind's eye.

"I have no idea," he admitted, his voice sounding as rough with need as she felt.

Inhaling deeply, April forced her eyes open and looked down at her body. Her lace covered nipples stood in erect peaks, begging to be touched, while her stocking-covered feet rubbed together anxiously, like a cricket sending out a mating call. "Come on, Deck, I know you aren't a virgin any more than I am. It's okay. I just wanna know how you learned to have phone sex like that?"

Another deep chuckle infiltrated her ear. "Oh, sweet woman, that was not phone sex. That was… fuck." April could hear the exasperation in his tone. "Frankly, that was something I've never experienced in my life. To be honest, I wasn't certain how that was going to play out, but I just closed my eyes and pictured what you were doing and… it was like I could touch you, April. I could actually fucking taste your lips. That was phone-kissing and it was… mmm."

The timbre of his deep voice felt like his hands, thick and calloused. She'd only felt them a couple of times at the gym when he touched her shoulder or held her hand, but when he'd caressed her cheeks while kissing her at the restaurant, she nearly melted on contact. It was the thought of his rough on her soft that swept her away in his fantasy just moments earlier.

"It was absolutely 'mmm'," she teased. Having never experienced phone sex before, neither the full-fledged kind nor the type they'd just engaged in, April knew without a doubt if it was something that could make her feel that good, hell, she'd do it every damn day. "Deck?" She swallowed hard, summoning the courage to say what her mind was shouting.

"What do you need, beautiful?" There was a smile in his question, nothing cocky or crude, but it was as if he asked while fully knowing what she was going to say.

"Your kisses," she started slowly, "both in person and over the phone, made me feel things." She brought her hand over her breast and rolled her tightened nipple between her finger and her thumb, pinching the nub until small sparks lit in her core. "Things I haven't felt in a long, long time. I really liked it, Decker... I like you. And I need... more. I want more." She switched to her other breast, kneading the sensitive flesh, pulling at her nipple as she continued to talk to the man who'd lit her up more than once that evening.

"Are you touching yourself, April?"

"Yes." She heard the quiver in her voice, but she didn't have it in her to be ashamed.

"Good. Where are you touching, honey?" There was no hiding his desire. It was clear as day in each throaty question.

"Umm—" Shit, she had to answer him. She was a grown damn woman, and she could *perform* without a problem, but when it came to talking about sex in a *sexy way*... well, apparently she was missing that quality—at least according to her ex-husband.

"Do you trust me?" Decker asked for the second time that night.

"Okay…"

Chuckling, he repeated her answer. "'Okay' is better than *no*, so we're getting somewhere. April, feel free to stop me if I ever make you feel uncomfortable, okay?"

"That I can promise," she answered confidently.

"Perfect. Now, where are you touching yourself, babe?"

April sighed.

"April, are you touching your breasts? Christ, I hope you are. I've thought about your perfect tits for months, each time I watched you on the treadmill."

Oh my God, his words were like jolts of electricity zinging to the very center of her.

"Are you pinching your nipples, beautiful? Making them pebble beneath your long, delicate fingers? Are they begging for my mouth?"

April swallowed. Her breaths were shallow as liquid heat pooled between her thighs. "Mmm, yes, they're so sensitive, Decker."

She heard his muffled groan before he said, "Fuck, what I wouldn't do to sweep my tongue over those hardened points and suck until you screamed my name. But…"

His words stopped.

Confused, April pulled the phone from her ear to make sure the call hadn't dropped. "But what? But what, Decker?" The high pitch of her voice would have been amusing had it not sounded so pathetic to her own ears.

"But…" Decker sounded strained but more composed than her. "I asked you to kiss me tonight, and you agreed. But more importantly, I asked for your trust, and you gave it to me."

There was so much conviction in his words, so much intensity, April felt as if she could see him, touch him… trust him. She shook her head. *No, not yet.*

"I intend to keep that trust. So as much as it pains me to say this, this is where we need to get off."

"That's what I was trying to do before you so rudely interrupted me, Mr. Brand," April needled.

"Ms. Maddox," Decker mock-scolded, "are you trying to corrupt my morals? Because I will not allow it."

Unable to remember the last time her cheeks ached from smiling, April giggled into the phone. "I won't try to corrupt you, you sweet innocent man, but I will thank you for everything. I had a great time tonight, Deck."

"Me too, April. I know our schedules are crazy, but I look forward to seeing you again, outside of the gym," he qualified. "Sleep well, beautiful. I'll call you tomorrow."

Staring up at the ceiling, April replayed the evening in her head. Disregarding her mother's stunt, it was the best night she'd had in years. Decker's seductive voice massaged her memory—his sexy smile, kind disposition, dirty words… his coaxing ways—her body yearned for more. Then he'd given it when he kissed her. Oh God, that kiss. The way he ate at her mouth as though she was the richest chocolate and the finest wine. She'd never had a more amazing kiss until he managed to blow her mind yet again by recreating the embrace a second time, without even laying a finger on her hypersensitive skin.

Thousands of goose bumps blanketed her flesh as visions of Decker saturated her mind. For months she'd observed as he lifted weights. She watched as his biceps curled and his triceps flexed. She found herself practically drooling over the ripples in his abs, the muscles in his back, and the incredible form of his legs, but nothing had prepared her for what he would look like freshly showered and fully dressed. She'd locked on him immediately upon entering the bar and drunk him in, from his clean-shaven face that showcased his chiseled square jaw, to his strong bare neck, and the way his Adam's apple bobbed as he took a pull from his cocktail. Her gaze had continued its downward journey, reveling in the peek-a-boo patch of chest revealed where the top two buttons of his shirt remained open. The man was breathtaking, and after spending the evening in his company, tasting his erotic kiss and hearing his spicy words, April was aroused and wanton.

How had he affected her so profoundly with little more than a hot kiss and provocative words? How was it possible that he'd left her body coiled so tightly, there was no doubt with just a couple more touches, a few more thoughts … she'd shatter into tiny pieces of pleasure. Her middle finger swiped over her clit as her other hand went to her lips. After sucking on the finger she'd had in her mouth while on the phone with Decker, April moved her hand down to her breast. She pushed the lace cup down, exposing the firm mound, and traced the moist digit over her puckered nipple.

It had been a long time since someone spoken to her as he had, so fucking long since she heard hunger in a man's voice. Like a fog covering up her beautiful fantasy, reflections of her ex-husband rolled into her consciousness. Realizations of how, after all of the years she'd been with Ben and thought they were happy—thought she was happy—not once had he ever taken the time to see to her pleasure if his was not included as well. Never once had he taken the time to call her when he was out of town, especially in the last two years of their marriage; he certainly hadn't taken the time to make love to her over the phone. And never was their relationship built on trust—obviously, since the man cheated on her. Suddenly, the fire that had been raging in her body was extinguished, leaving nothing more of her arousal than smoke, soot, ash, and the longing for the release that wasn't going to happen. Goddamn, Ben—gone all these years, and he was still a selfish asshole.

CHAPTER TEN

You Talk, and I'll Listen

Dimples: *Eli is feeling much better. I was grateful that the pediatrician saw him today on a Sunday.*

EVEN THOUGH HE hadn't met April's little boy, Decker's blood had still boiled when she called him two days before to report that Elijah was bitten by another little boy in daycare. Not just a nibble either—the little cannibal had broken skin on April's son, requiring a trip to the emergency room. Had it been his daughter, he would have gone apeshit on the biter, then he would have demanded a pound of flesh from the brat's father. Not April. While he'd heard the worry in her voice when he listened to the message she'd left, she had calmly left work, picked her baby up from day care, and taken him for treatment. When Decker received the message during his lunch break, he immediately tried to contact her, only to get her voice mail. He left a message then worried for the couple of hours until she returned his call.

Decker: *The doctor doesn't think the redness is anything to worry about?*

Dimples: *No, Eli is on antibiotics so as long I keep the area around the wound clean, he should be fine.*

Decker: *I'm so sorry, babe. I hate that Eli got hurt and I hate that you had to deal with it alone. I wish you would have let me come by on Friday night or even yesterday to check on you guys.*

That was the part that was beginning to wear on Decker. It had been three weeks since their "first" date, and while they talked and texted multiple times a day, their schedules made it nearly impossible for them to see each other. Sure, they could get together if it was all four of them, but April refused to introduce him to her son, claiming she didn't want Elijah to get attached to people who may be *temporary*. There were so many things about that statement that bugged him, but the fact was, it had been only one date. He knew there were more dates to come, so he couldn't fault her.

Dimples: *Aww, Big Guy, thank you for worrying about me.*

Decker: *I worried about you both.*

He wondered if she could sense the intensity in his text. He didn't want to be the Sunday morning quarterback when it came to April and Elijah—he wanted to be part of their lives. As the seconds passed, he wondered if he'd come on too strong.

Dimples: **sigh* Thank you, Deck. But honestly, just like you, I've been going this journey alone for a long time.*

Decker: *But you don't have to be alone. I'm here.*

Her response shot back quickly.

Dimples: *Besides, August came by as soon as he got home from work and Ember and my parents brought pizza and ice cream over last night. Eli is good to go.*

Decker: *And you?*

Dimples: *I may need to color my hair I think I found 15 new grays this morning. Lol, but I'll be fine too.*

She was more than fine, Decker thought to himself. She was an incredibly strong, albeit stubborn woman, and he found himself falling for her more each day. He knew he wasn't falling alone, but the question was, would she open her world up to him and Charlie, or would she keep it on lock down indefinitely?

"Hey, Deck, you gonna stand out here all day, or are you coming in to eat dinner? We're fucking starving." Ford stood with his arms crossed over his chest and a scowl marring his face.

Anyone else in the world would have seen his glare and cowered in fear, but not Decker. No, Decker always searched his brother's eyes, and in those dark orbs, all he saw was laughter. "Starving my ass. Why don't you call your secretary and have her swing by with a sandwich? I'm sure she'd get right on you... err, it."

Ford flashed a devilish grin. "Vanna would happily bring me anything I wanted." His smooth, slow tone did nothing to hide his innuendo. He flipped Decker the finger and disappeared back into the house.

Decker: *I've gotta go. At my mom's for dinner. Call you tonight?*
Dimples: *Sounds good. Enjoy.*

❝**G**RAMMY, THE MEATBALLS are totes amazing," Charlie exclaimed with cheer only a six-year-old could conjure. She slurped up another strand of spaghetti, collecting even more sauce into the corners of her sweet little mouth.

"Thanks, sugar bug," Decker's mother, Robyn, replied. "I think you're totes adorbs."

Decker's jaw sagged as his glance shifted from his mother to his brother. Judging by Ford's arched brows and dropped jaw, Decker knew his brother's thoughts mirrored his own. "Dude, can you imagine Mom letting us speak in slang when we were Charlie's age?"

"Hell no," Ford answered, shaking his head in disbelief. "She would've grounded our asses for speaking like freaks." Ford chuckled.

"Excuse me, you two, but I will not have that kind of language used at this table and especially in front of my granddaughter. So knock it off." Robyn shot both Decker and Ford *the look*, and both grown men apologized to their mother and Charlie for their language.

Decker and his brother often joked about how a petite woman such as their mother was able to have a particular presence and influence over the Brand men. She wasn't pushy or evil-tongued. No, Robyn Brand just wanted the best for those she loved. She was honest and respectful. If someone didn't agree with her, she would back off, and in the end, when it came to be that she was, in fact, correct, she'd smile warmly and help said person fix what needed repaired. The two brothers could see why their father loved and worshipped his wife, because they too felt the same.

"Grammy, can I have dessert?"

"In a little while, sugar." Robyn patted Charlie's arm. "Now, please go wash your hands and your face. Pop in a movie, and let your dinner settle. I'll serve dessert shortly."

Decker bit the inside of his cheek as he watched his daughter's smile droop. His mother often claimed that he and Ford had been a challenge when they were young, but as he watched the color rise in his precocious little girl's cheeks, he knew she put them both to shame.

"No, Grammy." Charlie's head cocked to the side as her tone reached whiney levels. "I want dessert now."

When Ford kicked Decker under the table, the message was clear. Ford was excited to see how their mother would handle Charlie's little meltdown. Decker, on the other hand, had no doubt that Robyn would deal with Charlie with the same grace she'd shown since Olivia passed away, leaving Decker as a single father.

"Well, my sweet young girl, I've always dreamt of swimming underwater with tropical fish. I wanted to do it without scuba gear for miles and miles, without needing oxygen or rest."

The look of dreams not yet fulfilled in his mother's eyes was something Decker had never noticed before, and now it would haunt him. How long had it been there?

His mom continued, her tone gentle. "But we don't always get what we want the minute we want it."

Charlie sat on her chair, staring reverently at Decker's mother as Robyn tucked a strand of light brown hair behind his daughter's ear.

"The good thing is you *will* get your dessert if you are patient and wait until it's time." His mom lifted Charlie's chin so the little girl's eyes met her own. "If not, just like my dream of swimming for miles without air will never happen, neither will your cookies. Got it, sugar?"

"Got it, Grammy." Charlie slid off the dining room chair and planted a saucy kiss on his mother's cheek before repeating the gesture with him and his brother. She then headed into the bathroom, where he heard the water turn on and off before she went into the family room with a clean face and hands to watch her favorite Disney movie.

"Jesus, Mom," Ford muttered, "you're like the goddamn child-whisperer."

"We're still at the table, Ford," Robyn reminded.

"Fine," Ford gritted through his teeth, "then let's leave the table so we can talk like the crude adults we actually are. Because don't for one second think I'm deaf when it comes to your language down at the office."

Robyn's brow arched as her smile kicked up on one side. "Into the kitchen, boys. We'll talk where little ears can't hear."

Decker peered into the family room and saw his Charlie snuggled on the sofa, wrapped in a fleece burgundy throw, and belting out the lyrics of "I've Got A Dream," from Disney's *Tangled*. His daughter was so pretty, sweet, and smart, and he knew how blessed he was to have her in his life. Between her, his mother, and his brother, there was no doubting that he was a lucky man to be surrounded by so much unconditional love, but he also knew something was missing. Something he'd never had with Olivia and something he hadn't found in the years since… until recently.

Visions of shiny, thick blond hair and apple-green eyes clouded his mind. Deep dimples anchoring both ends of a brilliant smile captured his breath in his chest as his large hand swiped across his bottom lip, where her teeth had grazed just before she pulled away. *April*. Her name appeared in his head as his brother's voice yanked him from the fantasy.

"Deck, you gonna join us in here, or should I just go ahead and tell Mom all about the bangin' gym chick?"

Yeah, Decker thought to himself as he plotted revenge on his younger sibling. *Maybe I'd be fine as an only child.* Giving his brother the evil eye, Decker pulled three beers out of the refrigerator, grabbed the bottle opener from the drawer, and pulled up *his* stool at the breakfast bar.

"So are you gonna tell Mom about your new girl?"

Ford needled.

"Well, that depends, little brother." Decker smiled while glaring daggers at his brother. "Are you gonna tell Mom about the special services your secretary is providing?"

"And they wonder why I treat them like children at the table," Robyn said aloud to no one in particular. When both Decker and Ford stared silently at their mom, she continued. "Oh, now I have your attention? Super. Decker"—she gently placed her hand on his arm—"today is your day. I'm not blind, honey, I know that there's someone in your life. I can see it in your face every time I look at you. Now, I've given you plenty of space, but I can't take it any longer." Ford's snort drew Robyn's eyes away from Decker. "Ford Marcus Brand, don't you think for a second that you're off the hook. As I said, I am not blind, son, nor am I deaf. That Jovanna is a wonderful woman."

Ford dropped his gaze to the beer bottle in his hands.

"Look at me when I'm speaking to you, Ford." His mother's voice softened, "She's kind and sweet and loyal, but she isn't stupid."

Decker watched as Ford's brows snapped together. "What's that supposed to mean, Mom?"

Robyn let out a long sigh. "Oh, baby, women like Jovanna are special. She works hard and gives one hundred percent." Robyn pursed her lips and shook her head when both Decker and Ford went to make a sarcastic comment about the secretary. "But if you push her too far, treat her too carelessly, she may just close up, and you'll lose all of the things you like so much about her... as your secretary and more," Robyn narrowed her eyes. "You'd be smart to remember that."

Even though his mom directed her words to his brother, Decker felt like each of them applied to him. He didn't want to push April too fast, but he also didn't want to allow the opportunity between them to disappear because of her past and her fears. Decker took another pull from his beer, allowing the cool liquid to quench more than just his thirst.

Ford thumbed over to Decker and grunted, "I thought this was his day."

When his mother's deep blue gaze landed directly on him, she lifted the beer bottle to her upturned lips and said, "It is. So you talk, and I'll listen."

Decker sat at the counter and filled his mother in on everything April. He laughed when Ford offered his commentary about sappy smiles on Decker's face each time he received texts from April during the day.

"Seriously, Mom, he walks around sporting this ridiculous look, like... I don't know, like he's been clubbed over the head with Cupid's crossbow." Ford snorted then cocked his head to the side and seemed to study Decker quickly before adding, "That said, I wouldn't want him to look any other way. Happiness looks good on you, brother; it's been too damn long." The men tapped their long-necked bottles together in a silent toast.

His mother exhaled sharply. "Hmm, sounds like the girl's had a rough go of it."

"That's the thing, Mom, while there's no doubt that her ex is a piece of shit who deserves to have his ass kicked on a weekly basis for abandoning his wife and child"—Decker envisioned April, the way she held her head up high and rolled with whatever blows she was dealt—"the woman seems to handle her life with such dignity and grace…"

"I hear a *but*, Decker." The arch in his mother's brow asked the question her voice didn't need to.

His mom knew him better than he knew himself. It was amazing and it was annoying. "But…" He hesitated. "She keeps herself guarded when it comes to relationships, and I listened to what you just told Ford about Vanna. I don't want to push April too hard. Because I fear…" Decker looked up from the peeled and crumpled beer label in his hands to find two pairs of eyes waiting for him to finish his thought. "I fear that she may decide it's safer to stay behind her walls than to give what we have going a fair chance. I mean, shit, I *know* she's interested in me. We see each other several days a week at the gym, we speak multiple times a day on the phone, yet I can't pin her down for a formal date." Frustration bubbled in his gut as the depth of the situation unveiled itself.

"Sweetheart." Robyn placed her hand over his and squeezed. The small gesture had forever brought him comfort when he felt his most vulnerable, and that moment was no different. "Advice isn't one-size-fits-all, you know that. It's like construction. Just because a client comes to you because he loved the building you guys created for one client doesn't mean he wants the same exact structure for himself."

Both he and Ford sat quietly as they listened to their

mother speak. Decker gathered fond memories of their early childhood when they used to sit in practically the same fashion—albeit a less updated kitchen—as she dished out advice or punishment that swirled around their heads.

"If what you've told me about this young woman is true, then too much space and too much time may allow her to retreat further." Robyn looked thoughtful as she continued. "When a woman loses her spouse either through death or defection, it changes her on a fundamental level. Her life becomes based on providing for her children and showing not just the world but herself that she is not only capable but accomplished in doing just so. That said, the women who've had spouses leave of their own accord have even more to prove to themselves. The complete lack of confidence, self-assuredness, and understanding is an incredible cross to bear. A lot of times, those women find it easier to hide away instead of ever braving that kind of heartache again."

"Christ…" Decker's stare moved from his mom to his brother, who also looked taken back by the amount of information Robyn just laid on the counter. "Have you been watching *Dr. Phil* now that you're partially retired?"

Ford howled, but Robyn pressed her lips together, attempting and failing to scowl as a small grin kissed her mouth. She crossed her arms over her chest. "No, you sassy little shit, I pay attention to those around me. Not to mention I've attended a lot of support groups since your father passed away." His mother shrugged. "I'm more than just part owner of BC, your mother, and Charlie's grandmother, you know."

Decker did know that. The sad thing was he forgot that fact far too often.

"By the way, Deck, what did you say April's last name was?"

"Oh, it's Maddox." Decker supplied, "Her son bears her maiden name, and she herself reverted back to it as soon as her divorce was final." There was a spark of some unnamed emotion deep inside of Decker that delighted him in knowing that neither April nor her son carried the Spears surname.

"Maddox, huh?" Robyn murmured as a hint of mischief crossed her ocean blue eyes.

"What?"

"Nothing, honey." Robyn rose from her stool and disposed of the empty bottles. "Now please call your daughter in here. It's time for dessert. I think she's waited long enough."

CHAPTER ELEVEN

Yes, Decker

"**G**OOD MORNING, CHICKIES!"

"Ugh," Rori groaned, her head lodged in the staff refrigerator. "You are too happy for a Monday morning, Janie Silver."

April was thrilled to see Janie enter the teachers' lounge, because five minutes of listening to Rori complain about having to bring her least favorite flavor of Greek yogurt for lunch because strawberry was the only kind the yogurt thief didn't steal was five damn minutes too long, best friend or not.

"Hey, girl, how was the Grand Re-Opening of your bar this weekend?" April had been so happy for her friend's new business venture and a bit melancholy that she wasn't there to celebrate with her, but she hated leaving Elijah unnecessarily, and she'd just been out a few weeks before with Decker, so she hated to leave him again.

"I can't believe the band Your Toxic Sequel performed live." Rori cooed, "I kinda have a crush on Lucas Wolfe. I wish I could have been there."

"I wish you both could have been there also." Janie's face glowed with happiness as she threw her left hand out in front of her. "It *was* pretty awesome."

"Oh. My. God." April squealed as she grabbed her friend's hand and stared at the gorgeous engagement ring that adorned her finger. "Janie, oh, honey, I am so happy for you."

"Holy shit," Rori gasped. "That is some fucking rock. The man did well."

April embraced her friend then listened as she described how her boyfriend, now fiancé, Max, had given her the proposal every girl dreamed of. April was thrilled for her, truly… she was. If not for that small little piece of sadness that she kept tucked away, the part that reminded her that she wasn't good enough to hold on to her husband, she wasn't sexy enough to keep him from climbing into another woman's bed, that she wasn't smart enough to know he'd left their marriage long before he left their house.

She snapped out of her darkened thoughts when she felt a gentle squeeze on her knee. Placing her hand over the one on her leg, she turned her attention to Rori.

"Are you okay, chica?"

"Yeah, why?"

Rori shrugged, giving her the I-don't-buy-your-bullshit face. "You're gonna try that with me? For real?"

April glanced over at Janie, who was showing her ring to two teachers from the math department. The sun couldn't illuminate as much as Janie did, and it was a sight to behold.

"I'm fine, Ror. Or I will be." April whispered, "I really am extremely happy for her, you know that, right? Tell me you believe me." In that moment, Rori's confirmation meant everything. If her very best friend thought that she was as horrible as she was feeling on the inside, April wouldn't know what to do with herself.

Rori took April's hand in hers. "Honey, of course I believe you because you're an amazing person and a wonderful friend, April. It's okay to mourn what you've lost. It's not like you're trying to take what Janie's found."

Pulling in a shaky breath, Rori's words hit home, and calmness began to spread through April's body, relaxing her tightened muscles little by little.

"Sorry, chickies, but this whole engagement thing is so new, and to be honest, even though I've been living with Max for a while, wearing his ring just feels so… special."

"It *is* special," April agreed, pulling her friend into a hug as tears stung her eyes. "And you, my friend, will make a beautiful bride."

"Aww, April, no tears." Janie swiped the wet streak off of April's face. "You know what my best friend Lyla says about crying, don't you?"

April sniffed as she nodded her head. After all the years of them working together, she and Rori had heard a lot of Lyla-isms. While she'd never met Janie's friend, she felt as though she practically knew the woman.

"Crying is for pussies," Janie whispered so as to not

garner further attention from any of the other staff in the room. "So knock that shit off."

The three women snorted as they tried to keep their giggles caged in their bodies.

"Anyway, I'd really love it if you two would come celebrate with me and my friends, and Max of course, at Danny's on Main this Thursday night." Janie's eyes landed on April's. "I know it's short notice, but I also know you, and it wouldn't matter how much notice I gave you, you'd find a way to cancel. So I'm asking, can you please ask your brother or sister if they can watch Eli so you can come out? Please?"

There was so much hope in her friend's voice, so much optimism, April found herself accepting the invitation before she gave it any thought at all. It was both Rori's and Janie's delightful squeals that made her realize just what she'd done. Looked like she would be going out on Thursday night; how did that happen?

———————◆———————

WHEN ARE YOU going to let me take you out again, beautiful?" Decker racked his weights and turned to watch April complete another set of chest presses. *Fuck, what I wanna do with her on that bench has nothing to do with weight training.* "I'm a patient man, April, but you won't even commit to a date." *Christ, I sound like a naggy old woman.*

A feminine grunt escaped April's lungs as she finished her last rep, put down the weights, and sat up on the bench. "Geeze, Decker." Her playful tone lightened his serious mood. "I feel like conversations of this nature often happen in the opposite direction"—she wiped the sweat from her forehead—"and isn't there usually a wedding that's being avoided?" April's lips curled up, twin indentations appearing on either side of her lush mouth.

His mouth twitched as he tried to keep a straight face. "Are you insinuating that I'm acting like a girl, Ms. Maddox?" The mellifluous sound that flowed from her had Decker's dick hardening at an embarrassing rate.

"I'm saying if the garters fit, Mr. Brand…"

That, right there, was the reason he couldn't give up on April Maddox. Hell, it was the reason, no matter how hard he tried, he couldn't get her out of his fucking mind. She was the total package—beauty, intelligence, and a sense of humor to boot. But no matter how many attributes he mentally clicked off in his mind, the only one she seemed to care about was being Elijah's mom. While he certainly understood the bond between parent and child, especially the connection between a single parent and only child, he also knew how important it was to have a healthy adult relationship. They'd both done it wrong before. The difference was, he wasn't ready to give up. Not when he saw something worth fighting for right in front of him.

"Here's the deal." Decker picked up the dumbbells that lay by her feet and placed them on the weight rack. He gathered his words while his back remained to her, but when he lifted his eyes, his gaze met hers in the wall-length mirror. "I want more time with you, and you want the same thing. Let me take you out."

There was no question being asked, because he already knew that her heart and her head would give different answers. He wasn't a gambling man, so he wasn't going to take a chance. April opened her mouth to interject, but Decker pivoted took two steps toward the bench and kneeled down in front of her.

"You can avoid it, but you can't deny it." His heart thudded in his chest when she licked her lips before rubbing them together. "So save us both time, make us both happy, and just say, 'Yes, Decker.'"

The desire to run his tongue up the length of her throat as she swallowed was nearly as strong as his urge to moan when she licked her deep pink lips again. "Yes, Decker."

Knowing it would look amateur to fist pump, he quelled his excitement and settled on a silent nod.

———————◆———————◆———————

SHE COULD PRACTICALLY feel the enthusiasm brimming in his body, and no way did it match the slight inclination of his head when she accepted his offer. Although his smirk... that smirk screamed "gotcha" as his nostrils flared. Truth be told, she was just as excited to spend time with him, even if she had been stacking up reasons why dating wasn't a good idea. The thought of spending time with Decker alone made her body parts tingle. Sure, they'd kissed since their date. Each day as they left the gym, Decker would place his hands on either side of her face and pull her in for a leisurely kiss, one that warmed her skin and softened her insides. She savored those moments when his calloused hands met her soft cheeks. Each quiet whimper she released was a tiny crack in the wall she'd erected after her ex-husband shattered the very essence of her being. However, their kisses were rushed as they each had a child that needed their love and attention. As always, Elijah would come first. His needs were the most important, and his happiness was the only thing that counted.

However, having another date with Decker... mmm, even the thought was decadent. She'd ask her siblings if one of them could babysit, but she already knew her brother would gladly watch Eli without giving it a second thought. He'd repeatedly offered his nephew-watching services, especially since their Christmas chat on the porch swing outside their parents' house. *August will be thrilled.* April smiled. *He'd most likely cancel his own plans just so I can go out with...* the plans she'd made earlier with Janie and Rori popped into her head. "Shit."

"No way, beautiful." Decker's heated stare penetrated her. "I'm not letting you out of our date that easily."

Wow, was that unease she saw behind the dark eyes and firm jaw? *I really do suck,* she scolded herself, remembering Janie's words and Rori's agreement. *I guess I do cancel on everyone.*

"I'm not kidding, April." With her hands tucked firmly in his, Decker rose from his knees, leaving her no choice but to stand as well.

His six-foot stature, powerful and strong, towered over her five-foot-four-inch frame, yet she didn't feel daunted or afraid. In fact, her body snapped to full alert when, without further words, he lifted her hands to his mouth, touching his lips to her knuckles.

"Whatever excuse you're about to sell me, you can forget it, cause I'm not buying. This thing here, between us, is a relationship, babe. It may be undefined, but that doesn't make it any less real." He released her hands, only to obliterate what was left of the distance between them. "It's a give-and-take. You *gave* me a yes to a date, now I'm *taking* the reins and making sure it actually happens."

The combination of his commanding tone and soulful, tender eyes made it nearly impossible for April to breathe, let alone think straight, but she needed to keep her mind clear in order to figure out the best resolution for the situation she'd gotten herself into. As much as she wanted to spend time with Decker, and oh my God did she want that, she refused to be the stupid girl who dropped her friends for a guy—been there, done that, ended up with zero friends and Ben. Not a good trade-off and not a mistake she'd make a second time, but how the hell did she explain the scenario to Deck without making him feel like he isn't important?

"Um." She heaved a heavy sigh. "So here's the problem…"

"April, I can practically hear the cogs turning in your brain. Tell me what's bothering you, and I'll help you figure it out. But let's go out to the lobby." Decker's lips thinned as he looked around the weight room. "I wanna be able to concentrate on what you're saying, but if I see one more guy staring at your ass in those thin yoga pants while we're talking, I may lose my mind."

Gah, the man was a multitude of contradictions. Hard and soft, gentle and rough, sweet and crass, understanding and "no bullshit," caring and ... well, there was no opposite of that one. He was always caring, considerate, and kind. The problem was her; she couldn't let him in because she wasn't capable of that kind of trust. That said, she was perfectly capable of enjoying him and whatever time they had together before he moved on to the next woman who would enter his life. The thought stung, but she shook it off as they walked to the juice bar in the lobby.

Once they were settled on the plastic chairs with their bottled waters in hand, April explained the situation. Since almost all of their conversations were held over the phone, it was still novel—fuck, even sexy—the way Decker listened to her problem as if he truly cared and not just nodded blankly while he played on his cell phone.

"Okay, so let's see if I have it right." He brushed his large hand over the five o'clock shadow that spread across his squared jaw. "You already promised your friend Janie that you'd celebrate her engagement with her and a bunch of people over at Danny's on Main this Thursday, and you don't wanna leave Eli with a sitter two times in one week. Am I right?"

April looked at the sexy man addressing her and nodded. Why had she been putting off a second date with him for so long? She'd been a fool, and now she'd need to put it off even longer. She'd deserve it if he got bored waiting for her pathetic ass and walked away.

"April, I think it's really important for you to spend time with your friends—"

"You do?" she interrupted, incapable of hiding the astonishment in her question.

"Of course I do. After everything you've told me over the last month or so, it doesn't seem as though you've done nearly enough socializing since Eli's been born."

"Try since I was sixteen," April muttered quietly.

Decker's brows clinched together. "What do you mean by that?" When she didn't answer immediately, he asked the question a second time.

She studied the designer label on the plastic bottle. "I guess I never gave it any thought until recently, but Ben didn't necessarily like to share me." As the words left her mouth, realization entered her mind. "He claimed that he loved spending time with me, just the two of us. I had a lot of friends in high school, I was on a bunch of committees, and I had a lot of boys who were interested in dating me. Ben wasn't one of them... until he was. And once we got together, he preferred our alone time. Looking back, I should have known he was a classic asshole, but as a six-teen-year-old girl, I was in love with him, and I swore the feelings were mutual." April took a swig of water as Decker rolled his bottle between his hands. "Anyway, he used to tell me that when I chose my friends over him, it hurt him. Made him wonder if I loved him at all—"

"What an abusive son of a bitch," Decker growled.

"Yeah"—she shrugged—"but I didn't see it that way. I just wanted to make him happy. So I stopped going out with my friends and spent my time with him."

Decker leaned forward, placing his palm on her cotton-clad knee. The warm touch sent tingles up her thigh, directly to the juncture between her legs. "I know how it feels to be with someone who uses your love and kindness against you. That's how Olivia was, always putting her own needs first, believing that my loyalty to her and Charlie would stay steadfast even when her bitterness poisoned my love almost from the get-go." He reclined back in the chair, severing the connection of their bodies, a move that immediately had her eyes lifting to meet his. "I'm not looking to hold you hostage, April, nor do I need to be the only person who matters in your life, because let's face it, we're both coming into this *thing* with the most precious cargo." Her breath quickened as he leaned forward again, this time cupping her cheek in his warm hand. "I just want to know that I'm *one* of the reasons those sexy-as-sin dimples appear on your face each day."

Holy shit. April looked down at her body; yep, it was still there and not an ooey-gooey mess in a puddle on the floor. There was no doubt she needed to find a way to go out with Janie and still see Decker without taking any extra time away from Elijah, but how? "You want some dimple action?" There was no disguising the huskiness in her voice. "Then come up with a way for me to see you and celebrate with Janie and her friends without adding an additional night out this week."

She stared as Decker finished off his water. Transfixed, she followed his Adam's apple as it moved up and down the column of his neck with each swallow, wishing her lips were the rim of the plastic container.

E ALREADY HAD a solution in mind, but watching her drink him in, with wide eyes and plump lips parted slightly, left an insatiable thirst he doubted water would quench. Draining the remains of the liquid, Decker chastised his body, willing his erection to subside long enough for him to give his suggestion without sounding like an overprotective asshole or, even worse, her ex-husband.

"So," he asked casually, "Thursday night—the celebration at Danny's on Main, is it just a girls' thing?"

He watched carefully as she processed his words, waiting for the minute the meaning behind his question became clear. When her brows shot up to her hairline and her supple mouth formed a perfect O followed by a tiny smile, Decker allowed the trapped air to quietly leave his lungs.

"No, it won't be just girls," April professed. "Janie wants Rori and me to meet her fiancé, Max, as well as the rest of her friends, both the guys and the girls. They all co-own the bar and most of them work there, so it should be a pretty big group."

"Would it be okay if I joined? I figure it solves your double-booking problem, plus while you get to meet Janie's friends"—he shrugged with a grin—"I get to meet yours."

"Wow, big guy, you wanna meet my friends already? I don't know, it feels like a big step."

Even though her smile was bright and her tone teasing, there was no hiding the uncertainty he saw swimming in her bright green pools.

"Relax, beautiful," he implored as he stroked her knee, rubbing measured circles with the pad of his thumb over the black cotton pants. "It's not like you're taking me home to meet your family." Awareness struck him like a dart. He'd have no qualms about introducing her to Charlie and the rest of his family, because he knew even in a relatively short period of time that not only was he falling for her, but he saw her in his future. He did, however, understand that after everything she'd been through with the abandonment of her ex-husband, she was more than just a little gun-shy, and she felt strongly about protecting her son and herself from people who wouldn't be sticking around. Decker wasn't going anywhere, and he had no problem proving himself to her. "But I'd like to meet some of the important people in your life. So are you okay with me joining you on Thursday?"

The twin indentations in her cheeks answered before her words confirmed, "I'd love it, Deck." He couldn't contain his chuckle when she squealed, "Rori's gonna shit herself."

"You may want to tell her over the phone then, babe." April's quizzical look had him laughing. "Well, if you tell her at school, she'll walk around smelling all day and hating you. A teacher with a load in her pants is not something middle-school kids soon forget."

"You are an unbelievable man, Mr. Brand." April snorted as her smile grew even wider. "I'll be sure to give her the news on the phone." Glancing at her wrist, April let out a muffled curse. "It's getting late, and I have to go get my little guy from day care. Care to walk me to my car?"

Decker would have escorted her out to the parking lot regardless, but when she batted her long eyelashes in that flirty little way she did when she was trying to be cute, well… that would get her anything, anytime, anywhere. *I hope she never asks for a pony*, he thought, grinning to himself as he wrapped his arm around her waist and led her to her Acura RDX.

Those stolen moments were some of his favorites - the two of them alone together but out in the open where an audience could appear at any time, standing close, breathing the same air, near enough to touch yet no physical connection linked them together. It was erotic, and it was torture. He dropped his eyes to her parted lips, wanting nothing more than to taste their flavor and wondering what sweet surprise waited for him; sweet berry, tart apple, or maybe the youthful bubble gum that she seemed to favor.

There was no need for permission as her invitation was clear the instant she slid the tip of her tongue across her bottom lip. His patience turned to dust and his body to steel as Decker closed the remaining distance between them, cupping her face in his large hands and claiming her mouth. He loved how her warm body melted into his, their tongues caressing as an intimate dance began. Pulling her closer, he nipped at her sweet, flavored lips and inhaled her scent. The spicy sweetness sent a jolt through his body, causing his heart to pump a quick tattoo behind his ribs.

Decker heard the blood flow though his ears as April pressed herself closer to him, grinding her pelvis against his rigid cock. Her muffled whimper would have brought him to his knees if not for the voices coming from the gym exit.

"Fuuuck." Decker pressed his forehead to April's for a quick breath before placing some needed space between them.

With her eyes round like half dollars but shimmering with excitement, April grazed her lips with her fingertips. "I think we have a bit of a problem, Deck."

"What's that, dimples?"

"I really enjoy saying good-bye to you."

"Hmm, that is a problem." He leaned in and placed a quick peck on her forehead. "I guess I'm gonna have to start greeting you the same way."

"Sounds perfect to me." She grinned as her cheeks flushed.

"By the way, I couldn't tell." Decker ran his thumb across her bottom lip then placed the pad in his mouth just far enough to swipe the tip with his tongue. "What flavor did I just enjoy?"

"Passion Fruit." She winked before hopping in her car and blowing him a kiss.

CHAPTER TWELVE

Happy Face Pancakes

"HOW YA FEELING, Ror?" April spoke to her friend while driving home from the gym on Tuesday afternoon.

"I definitely feel better than I did last night and this morning." Rori still sounded weak, but at least she was able to speak, which was better than the partial conversation April had had with her that morning. Nothing said close friends like listening to someone vomiting on the phone. "Uhh, I'm so sorry about this morning, chica. I can't even imagine what that sounded like, but if it was even a quarter as bad as the real deal, then blech… I owe you big time."

"Stop it." April laughed. "You don't owe me anything. I called you out sick—it was no big deal. Clearly you weren't able to make that call on your own. My God, it sounded like there was an alien invasion going on inside you." Just the thought of the early morning call had April's stomach roiling. "Do you think it was a twenty-four-hour bug?"

The sound of Rori's snort made April laugh again. "Twenty-four-hour bug, my ass. I probably got food poisoning last night from the fool my mother set me up with. She thinks just because he's cute, he'll be a class act. She thinks if she gives me something nice, I'll forget about all she took from me when she uprooted me from my family in Los Angeles and brought me here."

The torment in her friend's voice was hard to miss, and it made April sad that in the years she and Rori were friends, Rori still hadn't let go of the resentment she held toward her mom.

"Umm, so why do you think"—April bit back a giggle—"the fool gave you food poisoning?"

Rori heaved a loud sigh. "Because God spent too much time on the guy's looks and forgot to fill his head with anything but air. Seriously, don't laugh, April."

The minute April heard the grin in her friend's voice, she started shaking her head. If there was anything she knew for a fact, it was that Aurora Velez could tell an entertaining story. Rori explained how in trying to impress her, Larry, the cute guy her mother had met while he was scooping dog poop at the park (which just so happened to be his full-time job), decided to *impress* her by taking her to a restaurant where she'd feel at *home*. While the small Cuban place only had a one-star rating, he claimed it would be perfect for her.

"Wait," April interrupted, "you're Mexican."

"Why, yes, I am, April. Thank you for pointing that out."

Uh oh, when sarcastic Rori comes out to play, no one is safe. April bit the insides of her cheeks so as not to interrupt her friend's story again.

"When I nicely explained that same thing to Larry, he said, 'Isn't it all essentially the same? Let's eat.'"

"Oh my fucking God! Rori, did you slap him? Kick him? What did you do?"

"What did I do?" Rori huffed. "I went against every instinct that my gut shouted, begging me to leave, but I stayed. I figured it wasn't right for me to judge the man based on his job any more than for him to assume all Latinos were the same. So I calmly gave a simple explanation on the huge difference between Cubans and Mexicans while we waited for our food."

"Okay," April asked, infusing as much hope as she could in the next question, "how was the conversation once you cleared that up?"

"Ha, the conversation turned to shit. Literally. I sat there and listened to him talk about his poop-scooping business for twenty minutes, April." Exacerbation ebbed from Rori's tone. "No joke, he got into detail about the different smells, textures, and colors of doodie. He even told me some story of how he saved a dog's life by telling its owner that the canine's poop smelled strange. Ended up the pooch had cancer, and now Larry thinks he's the high priest of poo." When April couldn't hold the laughter back another minute, Rori joined in. "You know I couldn't make this stuff up, right?"

"Oh my God," April gasped. Thankfully she'd just pulled into the parking lot of Elijah's day care center, because her eyes were filled with tears as the hilarity consumed her. "Okay, wait…" She pulled in a breath. "What did any of *that* have to do with your puking your guts up for ten hours?"

"Oh, please. Whoever gave that restaurant one star was being generous," Rori said flatly. "It didn't matter if I was Mexican, Cuban, or Martian, that food was disgusting. It tasted like shit… come to think of it, Larry loved it. Go figure. It looked the same coming up as it did going down, you know?"

April swallowed hard, doing her best not to picture what her friend was describing. "Oh, honey. I'm really sorry you had such a bad night. But I'm glad you aren't sick-sick, because I'd hate for you to miss Thursday."

"April Maddox, it wouldn't matter if I needed to come to Danny's on Main with a barf bucket and an intravenous line, I wouldn't miss meeting Super-Hot-Gym-Guy for the world."

April grinned at the memory of Rori's reaction when she'd informed her that Decker would be joining the celebration on Thursday night. Ecstatic didn't begin to cover it. "Aww," April teased, "you're the best friend a girl could ever want. That said, I gotta hang up with you and go get my boy. It's Tuesday, remember?"

"Ahh, IHOP night," Rori confirmed, having joined in a time or two on the weekly tradition April and Elijah had started when Eli was only a year old.

April nodded, and a kernel of warmth spread through her chest. She loved IHOP night; there weren't many things better than fluffy pancakes, sticky syrup, and her little boy. Well, maybe she could come up with a couple of things—Decker's sexy face flashed through her mind. He hadn't made it to the gym that day, but from their earlier texts, she'd known it was a possibility. Still, she missed him, and that was just as scary as it was exciting. But it had nothing to do with pancakes, and that was where her focus needed to be.

"All right, Ror. I'll try to call you later, but if not, I'll see you in the morning."

"Eat a pancake and give my boy a sticky kiss for me. Love you."

"You got it, and back atcha."

HEY, MOM, THANK you so much for picking Charlie up from the after-school program for me." Decker's phone was clutched between his shoulder and his ear as he scrubbed the day's grime from his hands. "This job is just one cluster-fuck after another." He swiped the horse-hair brush over his fingernails in an effort to remove the stubborn black gunk that refused to rinse off with soap and water alone. "It would help if the person writing the checks and the two guys showing up every damn day to 'oversee' the work being done were on the same fucking page. Or better yet, if the 'helpers' didn't come at all, being as though they do nothing but get in the way."

Every so often, Decker came across clients who were

fellow tradesmen. While he respected their opinions, it never failed that those clients were unable to step back and let Decker and his men do the job they were hired to do. Nearly one hundred percent of the time, that led to more harm than good. The person footing the bill was the one who had gone through the entire process with Ford and the architects. That same person had also met with Decker to discuss various options and issues. Often times, once the papers were signed, the "money man" stepped back and the job began, but there were occasions when the financer sent in his own person/people to "keep an eye" on the progress. The current job fell into that category, making the past three weeks not just a challenge but semi-unproductive. He'd already asked the men kindly to leave the property, but they'd returned. Now it was time to discuss with Ford about having the two men permanently banned from the site until the work was completed.

"Your father used to say the same thing, honey. But he usually found a way to handle things without alienating the clients, *if* he could avoid it. Be patient, you'll figure it out. In the meantime, you never need to thank me for playing with my granddaughter. It's my pleasure, you know that."

Even if the loving tone wasn't evident in her voice, Decker would, in fact, know that his mother loved spending time with his daughter. She'd always made it clear that she cherished every minute she spent with Charlie. Did it have something to do with the fact that her time had been quite limited when Olivia was alive? Maybe, yet even with finite time between them, Decker always saw the love that flowed between his mom and his little girl. More than not, her calming presence in his and Charlie's life is what kept him going, especially after Olivia's death.

"Thanks, Mom. Let me disconnect with you, finish cleaning up here, and I'll swing by and grab my girl." He peered at the clock that hung over the rinse basin in the trailer. "Shit, it's almost five thirty. I'll bet she's hungry." *I missed the gym*, he thought disappointedly to himself. *I'll text April after I get Charlie.*

"She is hungry, honey, but there's no need for you to stress. I've already promised her pancakes for dinner."

"Cool, you make the best pancakes." His stomach growled, as if agreeing with his statement.

"You always were a breakfast-for-dinner kind of boy," Robyn said, her voice warm with affection, "but I'm not making the pancakes, Decker. Your daughter informed me that she's never had IHOP's strawberry syrup before. Is that true?"

"Of course it's true, Mom. Why the hell would I ever bring her to IHOP when you make the best pancakes? Didn't we just discuss this?"

Robyn hummed. "Well, my sweet son, there are some things one just can't get in my house. One of those things is IHOP's strawberry syrup."

"And the other?" Decker asked, curiosity piqued.

"Meet us at the restaurant, and maybe you'll find out."

"I'll see you girls in fifteen minutes. Drive carefully, Mom."

"Will do, honey."

He disconnected the call and finished drying his hands. Taking a quick glimpse of himself in the battered old mirror that hung by the coat hook, Decker grimaced at his appearance: torn flannel shirt, mud-caked shit-kickers, ripped jeans, and a shadow of scruff covering his jaw. It wasn't great, but it was the best he had to offer. What did it matter? He was going for pancakes with his mom and his daughter, not like he was going on a date. Thoughts of April filled his mind as he reached for his cell and tapped out a text as he headed for his dirt caked Ford F-450.

Decker: *Sorry about today. Got held up on the site… again. Going for dinner with my mom and Charlie. Will call you later. XX*

He shoved the phone in the console and headed to the International House of Pancakes.

A PRIL PARKED THE car in front of the restaurant, but left the engine running while Elijah finished singing Pharrell's "Happy" song. It was a sin punishable by silent treatment to turn off the radio mid-favorite song. Thank goodness her son's cherished tune changed frequently.

"All right, sweetheart, you ready to go inside?"

"Yeppers," came the high-pitched voice from the backseat.

Smiling, she killed the ignition, hopped out of her car, and opened Elijah's door. "It looks like we may have a bit of a wait, sweetie. The parking lot is getting full."

Her son shrugged as if the news didn't bother him in the least. Hand-in-hand, they strolled from the car to the restaurant.

The normal Kids-Eat-Free Tuesday night crowd was already drifting in when April and Eli entered the restaurant. In another half hour, the place would be packed with families who had older children and later dinner times. After three years of trial and error, April had Tuesday night dinner down to a science.

"Hi, Sarah," April greeted the hostess. "We'd like our table for two, please."

"Sure, April, it's going to be about ten minutes." The hostess grimaced. "Sorry, we had a large party come in about an hour ago, and they're just getting ready to leave."

"It's okay. We'll wait."

"Hi, Eli! Hi! Eli... over here, Elijah!"

Stunned, April scanned the dining room for the body that belonged to the squeaky voice calling her son's name. Before she could ask Eli if he knew where the sound was coming from, he dropped her hand and took off like a shot down the aisle to a small table.

"Lee," Elijah squealed as he wrapped his tiny arms around the bright-eyed little girl.

Trying to squelch the panic she felt when Eli ran away from her, April breathed in deeply before slowly releasing the air. "Elijah, sweetheart, who is this?"

"Mommy, this is Lee," Elijah explained proudly.

The little girl covered her mouth and giggled. "My name is actually Charlie, but he calls me Lee, and I think it's cute."

Charlie. The name rippled through April's head before she shook it off. *No way, it couldn't be.* Crouching down, April looked at the two kids standing before her, smiling like the best of friends. "It's nice to meet you, Charlie." She looked between the two kids once again. Clearly there was an age difference between them, so they were not in the same class at preschool. In fact, the girl had to be in elementary school. "How do you two know each other?"

"Now that's an answer I'd love to hear as well."

The smooth voice that came from behind her sent shivers up her spine.

"Daddy, you're here."

April watched as Charlie edged around her and leaped into her father's arms, hugging him as if he'd hung the moon and polished each star just for her. Yep, she totally understood the feeling.

"Hi, son."

The greeting came from the table they were standing next to. Shit, she'd been so caught up with Charlie she hadn't even noticed the woman sitting at the table. *Responsible, April, real responsible.*

"Umm, hey, Mom." Decker placed his daughter down and kissed his mother on her cheek.

Judging by the way his brows drew together and the fact that he kept looking between Eli and April as if they were going to vanish, reality hit like a two-by-four directly to the back of her head. There, in the middle of the International House of Pancakes, her son was face-to-face with not only her boyfriend but his family. Bile churned in her stomach as the enormity of the situation revealed itself.

April assumed he played no role in the coincidental meet-and-greet. While that knowledge provided immeasurable comfort, her son was still meeting her boyfriend and already had a relationship with her boyfriend's daughter, not to mention having just met Decker's mother... April's heart slammed into her chest. It was way too close and way too fast.

"April, your table is ready." The hostess must have been doing double-time as an angel, because she'd just saved April's sanity.

April pivoted to face the hostess. "Thank you, Sarah. We'll be just a second." She hadn't even turned back before she heard two little voices requesting if they could have dinner together.

"Please, Mommy," Eli begged, "can we sit with Lee and her family, please?"

"Daddy, can they sit with us? We can pull up an extra chair."

Other than her bright blue eyes, Charlie looked just like her father, and the way she seemed to adore Elijah... well, that was just another reason for April to like the little girl. But it did absolutely nothing to settle the trapeze performers that had started spinning in her belly.

"There's no reason to pull up an extra chair, princess," Decker's mom announced. "I have a bridge game at the community center in less than a half hour, so I really must get going." The dark-haired, spit-fire of a woman then turned her attention to April. "By the way, I'm Robyn Brand, and it's a pleasure to meet you, April."

April nervously shook Robyn's outstretched hand. "It's nice to meet you as well, Mrs. Brand. Umm, I think my mom plays bridge at the community center on Tuesday evenings as well." April felt like an idiot trying to reach for something to say to Decker's mom, but it had been many years since she'd done the meet-the-parent thing. To have it thrown at her, and without preparation, was painful.

Robyn's lips turned up, a knowing look, kind but not a full-fledged smile, and patted April's hand. "Hmm, first, there's no need for formalities, so just call me Robyn, okay?"

April nodded.

"Second…" She looked at her watch. "Ooh, it really is getting late." She glanced at Decker and Charlie. "I'll chat with you both tomorrow." Robyn moved around the table and kissed Charlie before going up on tiptoe to kiss her son.

"I'll walk you out, Mom." Decker then leveled his sexy stare at her. "April, please, will you and Eli join Charlie and me for dinner? Apparently we are missing out on the great miracles of strawberry syrup." He lowered his mouth to her ear. "I promise you, honey, everything will be fine. Believe in me."

"No way," Elijah called out. "You've never had stwababbery syrwp? You're gonna love it, Lee."

Seeing the sublime happiness in her little boy's face

at the same time she got to see Decker's sexy smile made her inside warm like the sticky confection they were discussing. There was no way she could turn down that kind of invitation. "Okay. We'll join you guys."

"I'll tell the hostess you won't need your table." Decker leaned down and whispered in her ear, "Breathe, beautiful, everything is gonna be fine." He then wrapped his arm around his mom and led her to the door while April got the kids settled in their chairs with plenty of crayons and paper to keep them occupied.

"YOU SET THIS up, didn't you?"

"I have no idea what you're talking about," Robyn denied through pursed lips.

"Mom, I inherited my shit-eating grin from you." Decker stood just inches away from his mother in the tight lobby of the restaurant. "I know you're lying. I just want to know how you knew to do this." With work being such a disaster, Decker could barely remember what day of the week it was, let alone that April took her son to IHOP on Tuesdays.

"Okay, fine, I'll tell you. But not tonight. Go have fun with your girls and that adorable little boy. You deserve it. We'll chat tomorrow."

"Okay. Thanks, Mom." He wrapped his arms around his mother and tried to convey how much he appreciated her through his hug. He hoped she understood that she meant the world to him.

"You are so very welcome, my sweet boy."

He arrived back at the table to see April assisting the children with the menus. Despite the entire situation being sprung upon her, she seemed at ease while giving an animated description of the foods on the menu to two very interested kids.

"Daddy," Charlie beamed, "I'm gonna have a pancake that looks like a happy face. Eli says it's his favorite thing on the menu."

"Then you've gotta try it," Decker informed his daughter before sitting on the empty chair next to April.

Charlie and the adorable little boy who he now knew as Elijah immediately got lost in their own little world of crayons and chatter as soon as the orders were placed. They were so cute together, almost like brother and sister, doing the activities on the kids' placemats, such as tic-tac-toe and search-n-find.

"I didn't plan any of this," he stated quietly to April. "I mean, to be honest, I'm thrilled that we're all together and out in the open, but I would have never sprung it on you."

He followed April's eyes as they darted across the table to the distracted kids before they returned to his. Pressing her glossed lips together, her shoulders rose and fell with one respiration before she spoke. "I'm happy that you didn't set this up, because it would have upset me to know that you went behind my back. However…" She sipped from the glass of water that the waitress must have brought when he walked his mom to the lobby. "I'm scared, Decker." She nibbled on her bottom lip. "I've just wanted to protect his heart and... maybe my own." Her gaze shifted across the table to the children before reconnecting with his. "That said, I'm kind of relieved that it happened as well." The bridge of her nose crinkled the way it did when she knew she was wrong about something. "It was beyond time."

Relief washed over him as he savored her words. They could finally spend time together, all of them.

Charlie's peal of laughter grabbed his attention as the food was placed on the table, "Oh, you were right, Eli. If I move the banana slices on the pancake, the mouth goes from happy to sad."

"See, I told ya so, Lee." Elijah pointed at the unhappy-looking pancake. "He'll be sadder when you eat him up, right, Mommy?"

"No, he wants you to eat him, Charlie. He loves it," April explained while Decker nearly swallowed his own tongue. Did she realize what she was saying? "That's why he was created," she continued, "so both of you eat up."

Reaching under the table, Decker squeezed April's thigh. There was no holding back the chuckle when her eyes got as large as the pancakes and her cheeks as red at the strawberry syrup.

"You're right," he muttered under his breath, "*he* does want you to eat him, and it is why *he* was created."

April turned her head to him. A look of pure amusement glistened in her eyes as she whispered behind her hand, "I'm sure *he* does, but unless *he* is made of eggs and flour, *he*'s not getting eaten in an IHOP with the children around." She winked at him and turned her attention back to Eli and Charlie. "So, tell us, how do you guys know each other?"

By the time every sticky morsel of battery goodness was devoured, the kids had explained that they had met when Charlie's first-grade class made weekly visits to Elijah's preschool during the first semester to read to the four-year-olds. Apparently the two had bonded, and it appeared as though the four months apart hadn't affected their friendship at all.

While the children played with the fruit on their plates, Decker played with the sweetness sitting next to him. With his hand hidden under the table, he walked his fingers from April's knee to her inner thigh and watched from the corner of his eye as desire showed in the most subtle ways on April's composed face. If it were not for the gentle way her nostrils flared, the slight increase in her respirations, or how the tip of her tongue slid across plush lips each time his touch caressed the seam of her jeans at the apex of her thighs, it would have appeared she was just a woman enjoying a meal with her family. However, he knew better. He saw more, and he felt the chemistry that tethered them together. That she could keep collected yet stay warm and loving had him ready to combust. She was like no woman he'd ever been with, and her presence in his life was becoming more of a need than a want. Judging by the serene look on his daughter's face, both of the Maddoxes had found a special place in the Brands' hearts.

As the foursome left the restaurant and walked toward their cars, Eli stopped mid-stride. "Mommy, can Lee and

Mr. Decker have pancakes with us next week?"

"Aww, buddy," Decker cut in, trying to take the pressure off of April, "that's mighty nice of you to want to include us—"

"I think it sounds like a wonderful idea, sweetie," April replied, delight exuding from her features. "But only if they'd like to."

"We totally want to!" Charlie cheered as complete satisfaction took over Decker's body.

"Okay, E-man." Decker leaned down and extended his hand to his new friend. "We'll join you guys for IHOP nights, but you have to promise not to call me Mr. Decker. I'm too cool for that name."

Eli placed his tiny hand in Decker's and shook. "Can I call you D-man?" The little boy giggled at what he thought was hilarity.

"Absolutely." Decker winked. "It's a deal." While Decker would have thought the gleam in Elijah Maddox's eyes was heartwarming, it was nothing compared to the breathtaking one in his mother's.

As the children said their good-byes, Decker pulled April in for a quick hug. Her body felt incredible pressed up against his as he placed a chaste kiss on her forehead and released her from their embrace. Yes, he wanted April in a fierce way. Although they had been seeing each other, in some ways, for close to two months, their relationship was brand new for the kids. He wouldn't do anything to make anyone uncomfortable.

"Is it bad that I miss you even though you're standing right here?" April asked, her hand traveling up the arm of his dusty work shirt.

"Why do you think that is?" Shit, in all of the chaos, he'd forgotten that he'd come directly from work and looked disheveled and dirty. Although judging by the lust in her eyes, his messy appearance didn't seem to deter her one bit and knowing that made him want her even more.

She tucked her hair behind her ear and whispered, "It may be because you just spent close to two hours teasing me, and now you're standing here looking ridiculously sexy, and I can't kiss you or touch you." Her nipples had hardened beneath her long-sleeves cotton tee shirt—there was no way he could have missed it—and the sight had his blood rushing south. *Fuck*.

"I'm trying to be good here, beautiful. The kids would be scarred for life if they had any clue as to what was going on in my mind." Her lips curled up at his admission. "So let's wrap this up, and why don't you call me when Eli is asleep for the night? Maybe I can make you miss me a little less."

"Mmm." A low moan rumbled from her chest as April inched up on her tiptoes and placed a kiss on his scruffy cheek. "Now *that* sounds like a deal."

Yes, yes, it did.

CHAPTER THIRTEEN

Danny's on Main

ZZIP. THE HIGH-HEELED black leather boots that April purchased that afternoon from DSW were the perfect accessory to her outfit. Skirts weren't something she wore often, but she had a feeling that Decker would appreciate the look, especially paired with the V-neck red sweater. It felt as if it had taken weeks for Thursday to arrive when it had been only a couple of days. She regarded her reflection in the vanity-top mirror, happy with what she saw. Her golden hair lay in perfect soft waves over her shoulders, and the new eyeliner she'd bought enhanced the green tone of her irises.

"Hmm, I just need one last thing…" She'd always enjoyed her flavored lip balms and glosses but never as much as she had over the past couple of months. Decker seemed to savor her taste. He made a game of guessing her flavors, and in turn, she liked to play. "Ah, this one is perfect." She grinned, applying the fragrant gloss over her lip stain then dropping the tube into her purse. She'd definitely want to reapply later at the bar.

"Wow, Tiny, look at you." August whistled as April came down the stairs. Even though he was her brother, a compliment from him was worth its words, because, as she'd learned through a lifetime of gentle insults, the man didn't lie. "Seriously, sis"—her brother hugged her—"you look amazing."

"Thanks, Aug. I feel really good too," she admitted.

"I hate to say this," August whispered, "I mean, I *really* hate to say this, but I think Mom had the right idea when she got you that gym membership for Christmas. Look what's happened since you've started going there?"

He wasn't wrong. April had been thinking the exact same thing for weeks, but she hadn't been ready to admit it yet. "I know. I look and feel better than I have in years, and I met Decker… while things with him are new, he can still turn out to be no better than Ben—"

"That's not going to happen, April."

There was so much certainty in her brother's tone, she *almost* let the topic go. "You don't know that, August. You haven't even met him."

"I don't need to meet him to know that this guy isn't Ben." August crossed his arms over his broad chest. "Ben was an ass from the beginning. He was always out for himself, and your happiness was an afterthought. Judging by your perma-smile, this guy is clearly different."

Deep down, there was a tiny voice telling her that August was correct. However, she wasn't ready to let down all of her walls just yet. "You can't know that, Aug."

"Okay, you're right, but I can trust my nephew. Kids

innately know good people from bad, and my Eli is really fucking smart. The boy can't stop talking about this guy." August grinned. "I'd be jealous if I wasn't so goddamn happy." He winked.

Shit, Eli had been talking about Decker and Charlie a lot since Tuesday. That was exactly what she'd been trying to avoid. The last thing either of them needed was to get attached only to have two more people leave them when they realized there was something better out there. The last thing in the world April wanted was for her brother to feel less important; because when Decker did leave, it would be August picking up not just her pieces but Elijah's as well.

"Aug, maybe this is all a mistake—"

The doorbell chimes cut off her sentence.

"No, Tiny, this is all how it's supposed to be. Enjoy this, enjoy him... err, no details on the second part please. Now go open the door."

With one hand on the doorknob, April pulled in a deep breath to welcome Decker into her home. However, one look at the incredible man standing in front of her, and she was reduced to hand gestures and head nods.

The man looked like a dream in his olive-green button-down shirt with the cuffs rolled up, showing off his thick, corded forearms. Long muscular legs encased in well-worn, low-slung jeans begged for her attention, but they lost when her eyes roamed back up his body to his sexy face. Her mouth was desert-dry as she silently took in his freshly shaved jaw and perfectly messy hair. It took effort to keep herself from dissolving into a puddle when

Decker leaned down and kissed her cheek.

"You're gorgeous," he whispered in her ear as his scent permeated her senses, causing her heart to crash into her ribs at an alarming rate.

"Hey, I'm August, Chatty's older brother."

"Decker. Nice to meet you, man."

The handshake between her brother and her boyfriend snapped her out of what felt like a lust-induced trance. *How embarrassing.*

"Your sister here thinks the world of you, you know." Decker looped his arm around her waist before dropping a kiss on the top of her head.

While the gesture was new, other than the surprise meeting with his mom, there hadn't been other introductions, and the comfort his arms brought felt secure and warm.

"Ah." August chuckled. "I see all those years of brainwashing finally paid off."

"Nice, Aug, real nice." April poked her brother in the ribs. "Decker, would you like to come in?"

Before he could answer the question, Eli bounced off the sofa and ran over to Decker with energy only a four-year-old boy could possess. "Hi, D-man."

Out of the corner of her eye, April saw August's face soften, just as hers did, when Decker lowered to his knee and lifted his hand to high five her little boy. "Hey, E-man, how's it going, buddy?"

"It's good. You and Mommy are going on a date. It's okay if I still call you D-man, right?" Elijah asked enthusiastically.

April placed her hand over her mouth, her cheeks were already aching, and the night had just begun.

Being a dad himself, Decker took Elijah's subject change in stride and handled her son like a pro. "Of course you can call me D-man. You can call me anything you want, buddy."

"Oh, don't tell him that," August interrupted the sweet scene. "That boy has a mouth on him. Next thing you know, he'll be calling you D-bag."

"What's a D-bag, Uncle Aug?"

"August," April chided, "you're an asshole."

"I know what an asshole is," Eli giggled, covering his mouth.

A wave of laughter broke out in the room until April scooped Eli up in her arms and shot her brother a nasty look.

"Ooo, Uncle Aug, you're in trouble," Eli taunted. "Mommy just gave you the mean look."

Obviously finding humor in her family dynamics, Decker did his best to hide his laughter by pretending to cough. "My mom has a mean look too, E-man. And guess what?" Elijah, still wrapped in April's arms, waited patiently for Decker to finish his statement. "Even as a grown man, I know that when I see that look, it means I probably did something I shouldn't have done, and I need to apologize. No matter how old we get, we need to show our mothers respect. Got it?"

As Eli's little head bobbed with understanding, April, at first impressed with Decker's insight, thought about her own mom. She didn't have to always like the woman, but

Decker was correct. She did deserve respect. *Shit*.

"He hit a little too close to home, sis?" August cocked his head to the side, insight clear as glass in his familiar green eyes.

With a slight nod to her brother, she brought her attention back to the little boy in her arms. "All right, little man, you be good for Uncle Aug, okay?"

"Yes, Mommy," he confirmed, giving her a tight squeeze.

April then planted two loud kisses on each cheek and two on the top of his head. "Your kissy-bank is officially full. If you need any more, Uncle Aug will help you out."

Eli kissed her six times as well. "Your kissy-bank is full too, Mommy. If you run out..." She could almost see his little mind trying to problem solve. "Wake me when you get home."

The massive smile that etched its way on Decker's face, along with the quick wag of his brows, told her she wouldn't have any problems with kiss replenishment.

After a final good night, Decker weaved his fingers through hers and led her out of the house. Butterflies fluttered in her tummy as he opened the door to his Range Rover and helped her in. Hell, she couldn't remember the last time anyone, other than present company, had done that for her. Sure as hell had never been her ex-husband. When they were teenagers, she'd figured he was too young to know better, and when they were older, he dismissed the suggestion, claiming they'd been together too long for him to have to learn new rules.

Yet Decker opened doors and pulled out chairs each

time they were together. The man made her feel special. It was a feeling she'd long since forgotten.

April looked around the gleaming SUV. "Hey, not that I'm complaining, but where's the truck? I was kind of looking forward to taking a ride in that bad boy."

Decker stared at her, a flash of amusement crossing his face as he started the ignition. "That's my work car, babe. Even though the truck is safe for Charlie, this is what I drive on the weekends. However..." His gaze traveled from her eyes to her lips and back, feeling like a caress that sparked with electricity. "Now that I know how you feel about the truck, I'll be sure to get your sweet ass in there as soon as possible."

They pulled out of her driveway, and just down the street, Decker pulled the car over and parked.

"What are you doing?" April asked, clueless as to why he'd stopped the car.

"I wasn't sure if there would be little eyes watching out the window, so I figured it would be best to leave the driveway." While she still wasn't certain where the conversation was going, the steamy look in his eyes told her she was going to like the end result. "I know you said you enjoyed our *good-byes*, but I was hoping to take a minute to convince you *hellos* were just as good." Decker wagged his brows, leaned over the center console, and claimed her mouth in a bone-melting kiss. "Mmm." Decker ran his tongue over her top lip before sucking her bottom one between his teeth. "Is that lime lip gloss?"

"Uh ha," she admitted with a sheepish grin. "I figured, we're going to a bar and lime *is* very versatile... it goes with tequila."

He interrupted her by pecking her lips. "Corona." He gave her another kiss.

She smiled and said, "And margaritas."

Decker consumed her mouth as if it was the cocktails she'd described. Resting his forehead against hers, Decker agreed, his voice husky, "You're right, beautiful. Lime was the perfect choice."

With the butterflies still partying in her abdomen, April tried to voice her thought without tripping over her words. "I hate to tell you this, big guy, but *you* weren't right." She had to bite her inner cheek so as not to laugh at the perplexed look on Decker's usually confident face. "I know, you were wrong about something, can you imagine?" she needled, no longer hiding her amusement.

"Enlighten me, dimples."

"You said *hellos* were just as good as *good-byes,* but that's not the case." She loved having his rapt attention as she slowly shook her head. "Nope, *hellos* are so much better, because with them, I get to enjoy hours of your kisses and touches, where the other way, I only get the memories of how good you made me feel."

•————•————•

"CHRIST." DECKER EXHALED. Her words felt like silk across his naked skin. "Where the hell did you come from? And what did I do to deserve you?" Unable to form another sentence, he pulled her close and kissed her again. For a woman who'd been without a partner for years—according to her stories, hell, even when she was married she'd been alone—she possessed more passion than any person he'd ever encountered.

"I've been asking myself the same question about you," she answered breathlessly. "Now start driving or we may never make it to Danny's."

The new construction shined brightly, taking up the entire corner block of Main Street. Even from the driver's seat of the car, Decker marveled at the way the building blended in with the others around it, even though there was most likely fifty years separating the structures. "This place looks fantastic, and the way they managed to include several up-to-date features without losing the classic Charistown feel is impressive." Like a teenager finding his first *Playboy* magazine, Decker's insides felt electrified. After all, he had an awesome piece of constructive work in front of him and the sexiest woman he'd ever known to his right. Life couldn't get better than that.

"It is hard to believe that this place was in rubble just six months ago." April stared out the windshield. Her profile glowed from the dashboard lights, as well as the gleam from the parking-lot lanterns. Smooth skin, high cheekbones, and a straight nose with just a faint slope at the tip, the woman was stunning from all angles, yet the more he learned about her, the less the outer beauty seemed to matter. "Janie was devastated when Danny's was destroyed in a hurricane last year. She'd told me that her life had been unkind, and the only happiness she'd ever known started within the four walls of that bar."

Decker could tell April's words spoke of much more than just the building before them and the girlfriend he was about to meet. "And now look at her, she's marrying the love of her life." He ran his fingers through her silken hair, moving the strands behind her shoulder. "So much goodness can rise from the worst devastation, April. One just needs to believe in possibilities."

April released her bottom lip from the teeth that held it prisoner and looked him straight in the eyes. "I believe…"

She then proceeded to blow his mind by leaning over, running her smooth hands over his freshly shaved jaw, and kissing him. It was no chaste peck on the lips either. So when her velvety tongue brushed against the seam of his mouth, Decker felt both begrudged and thankful for the console between them. Lord only knew how embarrassed he'd be if she felt how hard he'd gotten, and just how quickly, from the taste of her sweet lips.

"Mmm." The groan left his chest as he pulled her closer, placed one hand on her cheek, and the other on the back of her scalp, gripping her hair at the roots as she deepened their embrace. Breathless, he broke the kiss. "Babe, you have no idea what you do to me. You look beyond sexy sitting here in my car, and the fact you initiated that kiss… I like the take-charge April. It's sexy as fuck. But we do need to stop if we intend to go in there and meet your friends."

"Oh, right"—her head bobbed—"we should definitely head in now." A pale blush crept up her neck and over her cheeks.

Part of him wanted to kick himself for stopping something that felt so good, especially when it led to the defeated look in her eyes. The other part knew stopping was the only right thing to do. However, pink cheeks he could handle, her embarrassment he could not.

"Woman, I've been wanting you for months, kissing you for weeks, and dying to touch you since the second you opened the door tonight." The way her chest rose and fell quicker with each breath indicated that his words were, in fact, being heard. "While you've initiated some pretty hot phone-play, not once have you brought that sweet little body over to me until now."

Deciding her reassurance was more important than his embarrassment, he reached for her hand and placed it between his thighs. Her eyes widened with desire as she gripped his hard cock through his jeans. *Fuck.* He watched as April pressed her lips together. Her grasp tightened as she stoked his length twice before releasing her hold.

Decker nearly growled at the loss of her touch but instead smirked when she said, "I told you, Deck, I believe. You make me want to believe." She shrugged. "I also wanted to make sure I was calling you big guy for the right reasons." He chuckled when she gave him a flirty wink.

"Kiss me, beautiful."

"You know if I do, it won't be *my* move, it'll be yours?" She eased her lithe body over to his, practically nestling herself on his lap.

"I don't give a shit whose move it is as long as your tongue is in my mouth... now." He smashed his face to hers in a hungry kiss, not caring if they ever left his car.

April's cell began to sing David Guetta's "Sexy Bitch." "Oh shit, that's Rori's ring tone. We're late."

Even though Rori was still a few minutes away, he and April took the call as a sign to stop fooling around. The last thing either of them wanted was to get caught in a compromising position in a public place. Once they stumbled out of Decker's car, and he adjusted himself, the two walked hand-in-hand into Danny's on Main.

***

IT'S ABOUT TIME you guys got here," Janie shouted from across the bar the minute she and Decker walked in the door. Her friend practically glowed as she waved them over to the corner she seemed to be occupying with her friends.

With Decker's fingers still twined around hers, they made their way through the thick crowd. Max was easily recognizable, being that Janie kept a picture of him on her desk. However, a picture did the man no justice. He was movie-star good-looking and ridiculously tall, especially in comparison to Janie's tiny frame.

"I can't believe I finally got you here," Janie bubbled, throwing her arms around April. "And it only took getting engaged to do it," she teased. "Speaking of which, April, this is my fiancé, Max DeLucca." April shook Max's extended hand before Janie continued, "Max, this is April."

"It's nice to finally meet you, April," Max said in a

deep, gravelly voice. "I was thinking maybe Janie had an imaginary friend at work."

When Max flashed his broad smile, April could see why Janie was captivated. However, its effect didn't hold a candle to the smile on the man who stood beside her.

"Hey, guys," Rori greeted in a singsong voice, "sorry, I'm late. There was stuff at home I needed to deal with before I left."

While both April and Janie nodded in understanding, only April truly knew the extent of Rori's home life issues.

"Well, you're here now, Rori, and your timing couldn't be better." The mischievous gleam in Janie's eyes combined with the "cat that ate the canary" grin warned April to brace herself. "Our girl was just about to introduce us to her man."

April felt Decker's body quake behind her, no doubt finding humor in the scene he was witnessing. He then squeezed her hand in a quiet show of support. Even though he was letting her take the lead, the gesture reminded her that she wasn't alone.

"Janie," Max playfully chastised, "you said this was the first time you've gotten her to come out in the five years since you two met. You think embarrassing the poor woman is gonna get her to come out again in the near future?"

"Max, thanks for trying to look out for me," April said genuinely before pointing at her two co-workers, "but working with these two for as long as I have... let's just say this doesn't even rank on the embarrassment scale." She laughed when both Janie and Rori had the gall to look surprised. "Anyway"—she stepped aside, loosening her grip from Decker's and sliding her arm around his waist— "this is Decker Brand."

She found herself swooning a little bit as she watched Decker introduce himself to both of her friends, as well as to Janie's fiancé. Just another side of him she'd yet to see—such ease and confidence with new people, but with none of the arrogance that someone as wealthy and good-looking as he was sometimes possessed. She stepped closer to his side, breathing in his cedar scent and finding happiness in his warm body, especially when he draped his large arm around her.

"I was telling April that the people you hired to re-build this place did an outstanding job," Decker stated, addressing both Max and Janie—who were two of the eight owners of the bar.

"Thanks, man. They were personal friends of the original owner," Max responded, "and they hired subcontractors that worked around the clock until the place was not only complete but perfect."

April wasn't sure if Decker realized he was doing it, but as he spoke to her friends, he casually stroked her—her back, her arm, and even her hair, almost as if he reveled in the connection as much as she did.

"Hey, baby, why don't you take Decker and grab a pool table at the back bar? Ryan's back there tonight, and Ashley said she'll switch places with Ando right now so she can hang with us," Janie suggested with a pleading look. "We're just gonna do one round of girlie shots out here, and then we'll join you."

"Whatever you ladies want. Just be careful—it's a school night," Max teased, tipping Janie's mouth up to kiss him.

"Seeing your cheeks flush and your eyes flash as you watch them kiss makes me wonder what you look like when you come," Decker whispered in April's ear. "I intend to learn the answer tonight." Decker took her mouth in a rough kiss before following Max to the back bar, leaving April breathless, horny, and wet.

"Holy shit, chica, whatever that sexy piece of man-meat just said to you must have been hot," Rori fanned herself, "because you look like you need to be extinguished."

April's skin burned as Janie announced, "No, what she needs is a lemon drop. Come on over to our corner of the bar, and I'll introduce you girls to my family."

Rori and April trailed behind Janie until they reached the far left side, where they were introduced to Lyla and Cate, who sat in front of the bar, and Ashley and Kyle, who worked behind it.

"Happy to meet you girls." Lyla lifted her glass. "I've heard only nice things, which don't surprise me, since this one"—she pointed at Janie—"likes to see the good in people. I'm not nearly as sweet—"

"Ly, don't scare off my friends." Janie poked her best friend in the arm. "Ash, let's do a round of lemon drop shots, then we can all go into the back bar."

The bartender smiled and started to whip together the shooters, while April focused in on Lyla. She could tell the woman wasn't trying to be mean or rude; there was just something about her that spoke of honesty, devotion, and kindness. Lyla reminded her of her own siblings, and there was nothing bad about that.

"Janie, Lyla isn't being scary, she's being... protective." She shifted her gaze to Janie's friend. "My own brother and sister would act the same way if they worried about me."

Lyla's mouth curved slightly as she lifted her glass once more. "To my ladies," Lyla toasted with a gleam in her eyes. April had heard from Janie that Lyla's toasts were always super funny, witty, and filled with sexual innuendo. "Let these shotties make mere men hotties, the liquid make us wicked, and the burn make us yearn. If one won't do, fuck it, we'll all have two."

Lyla's words mixed with the high-pitched chime of the shot glasses clinking together, had the women laughing riotously as they got to know each other.

"Hey, did I tell you that Larry texted me?" Rori informed the ladies as they made their way down the hall toward the back bar. "You remember him, the Priest of Poo?" She snickered. "Yeah, so he wanted to know..." Rori froze, and her sudden silence filled the crowded hall area, causing April to crash into her back.

"Rori, what's wrong?" April had never seen her friend's latte-colored skin look so pale.

"Ror, are you feeling okay?" Janie's concern had April even more worried.

Rori pivoted and stared mutely at the man in the staff shirt who'd just passed them on his way to the front bar. April thought she'd noticed him do a double-take when he saw Rori, but she hadn't wanted to interrupt her friend's story, so she'd kept quiet.

"Um, who… who was that?" Rori asked, her voice shaky.

"Oh, honey." Janie rubbed Rori's back. "That's just Ando Perez. He's a new bartender here, but we already love him, and so do the ladies." She winked. "Shall I introduce you?"

"No," she snapped, wringing her hands together. "I'm sorry, Janie. What I meant was, no thanks."

Janie shrugged. "It's okay, Ror, why don't you take a minute to breathe, and I'll meet you two over by the guys." She threw a concerned look at April and headed to the pool tables.

Once Janie was out of earshot, April took her friend's hand in her own. "Rori—"

"Not tonight, April. Please, for now, you just need to let it drop." Rori's tone was one that begged for time and understanding, and April had plenty of that to give to a person who'd shown her nothing but patience for years.

"Then let's put it aside and talk about how sexy my guy is," April teased as the women continued their way to the back.

"April, the man is hot, but so are all of Janie's friends. What the hell is going on in this place?" Rori sounded truly perplexed. "It's like every gorgeous guy in Charistown works in this bar. I think I may need to get a second job… here."

D ECKER TOOK A Swig of beer as Max took the reserved sign off the pool table and racked the balls. Decker was officially kicking himself for all the wasted years he and Ford could have been hanging out at such a cool place. Newly built or not, he had a feeling the vibe was probably the same regardless of the structure. *Son, it's the people that make success.* His father's often-used words rang in his ear each time Max introduced him to one of his partners. April was correct—this was a family-owned-and-operated establishment, regardless if it was blood bound or not.

"I've been looking forward to meeting you, Brand." Max's words were smooth like the shot he'd just made on the table.

Decker heard the clicking of the billiard balls and watched as several slid into the pockets.

"Stripes," Max declared.

"Yeah? To be honest, I didn't know much about you personally." Decker shrugged, eyeing up his first shot. "But April and I don't get much time together, and this was the only option I had." He took his shot, landing one solid ball in the side pocket, and stood up straight, looking a pleased Max DeLucca in the eyes. "I will say, however, that I'm happy as shit to be here, and I look forward to coming back."

Max rounded the pool table and stood in front of Decker. While the man had at least a couple inches on him and was clearly in fit shape, he didn't seem imposing. "I like your kind of honesty," he said with a smirk. "You're good people."

"Okay, so… are we gonna braid each other's hair now or something?" Decker asked, confused by Max's approval.

Gruff laughter boomed from Max's chest. "No, man. Here's the deal. Janie and I are getting married, and we'd like to move into a bigger place, but there isn't anything right here in Charistown that works for us."

Decker still wasn't following, but he wasn't going to interrupt either.

"I own a piece of land just minutes off the main stretch that would be perfect for new construction, and word has it that BC is one of the best companies around."

Sound stopped around Decker as he tried to process what the guy in front of him, a man he'd just met, but one who'd clearly checked out him and his business, just said. "You wanna hire Brand Construction to build your house?"

"Yeah." Max shrugged nonchalantly. "I looked into your company, and you do both commercial and residential, right?"

Decker tried to shake off the surprise and slip into business mode as his brother would have, but that was why he wasn't in the suit and tie, and Ford was. "Yeah, we do. And we have for three generations."

Max's face softened. "I know, man. When I mentioned building a house to my dad, he told me to look into you guys. Apparently our fathers knew each other a long time ago. And your dad left a lasting impression on mine."

Stunned, Decker ran his hands through his hair. "Well, that is a story I would love to hear."

"Perfect. How about if I call your office and set up an appointment?" Max suggested. "I know you guys are busy, but if we hire BC, I'd really like for you to be the one in charge. We aren't in a mad rush, so we'll wait for you if we need to."

Decker wondered if he looked as surprised as he felt.

"I've done a lot of research on you, Brand. No matter how nice of a guy you are, I wouldn't trust my woman or my life to just anyone. According to what I heard, you're the best."

Overwhelmed, Decker shook Max's hand. "Look, I think we have the best team working for us, but you have no idea how great it is to hear."

Max chuckled. "Gotta love the honesty."

"Hey, baby, did you talk to Decker about the house?" Janie asked, weaving her arms around her fiancé.

The puzzled look on April's beautiful face told Decker this was the first she'd heard on the subject.

Janie shrugged bashfully. "Sorry, girlies, I didn't want to say anything until Max talked to Decker. But we're looking to build our dream house, and we were hoping to hire Brand Construction, and for Decker to personally do it."

Happiness floated through April's eyes as a smile took over her face. "Gah, I'm not sure who to congratulate first: the two of you"—she looked pointedly at Janie and Max before returning her gaze to Decker—"or you."

"How 'bout we divide and conquer," Rori suggested, throwing herself at the couple.

The feel of April's soft body crashing against his as

she wound her arms around his neck made him feel fifty feet tall. "I'm so happy for you, big guy. I know how much you love doing custom homes." She nuzzled his ear. "You'll be able to get nice and creative during the design stage and then down and dirty during the build."

The tip of her tongue flicked his lobe. Fuck, he wanted her in a way that was so much more than carnal. The fact that in such a short time, she seemed to grasp that his work was a part of who he was, a part of his soul, that made her special. Hell, it made her invaluable.

"I'm a pretty creative man, dimples," he murmured as he pulled her tighter, lifting her chin so her eyes met his. "And it just so happens thoughts of getting you dirty turns me on." He ground his hardened length into her, whispering hoarsely, "You game?" Her sultry smile and pink cheeks had his dick pressed so tight against the fly of his jeans, that he swore there'd be zipper marks on the sensitive skin when he finally removed his pants.

* * *

THE NIGHT WENT quickly, too quickly in April's opinion. She had a wonderful time, not just being in the company of adults but surrounded by friends. While having an evening alone with Decker would have been incredible, being with him around others was amazing. She had spent most of her life watching couples interact with one another and wondered why her relationship with her ex never resembled what she saw. When Ben left, she assumed the problem was her—maybe she was un-friendly, cold, unlikable… unlovable. But each time she'd been in Decker's company, he made her feel special, wanted, and appreciated. While his words were flattering, romantic, and sexy, it was the small things that got her attention, like the way he was at IHOP. He knew how hard that situation had been for her, someone new meeting her son for the first time before they'd had a chance to discuss it, yet Decker was amazing with Elijah and even better with her. Subtle strokes on her back, a soft rub on her thigh, tiny gestures told her he was by her side but not in her face.

Here in the bar amongst friends, April had no ques-tions as to Decker's feelings toward her. No, he wasn't inappropriate, overly possessive, or nauseating, as she'd witnessed some couples be over the years. He was able to communicate his interest and desire with hungry glances, stolen kisses, naughty words, and sexy promises. Her body had been simmering for hours, and it was time to bring it to a boil.

"So, it's getting late, and it is a work night." She peered at Decker over the rim of her water glass. His eyes shifted to the clock on the wall, and she knew the very se-cond he understood where her thoughts had gone.

"You're right, babe. It's almost ten o'clock. We should definitely get you home." His voice dropped to barely above a whisper, only loud enough for her to hear. "Don't forget, I made you a promise earlier tonight, and I intend to collect."

"What are we waiting for?"

They quickly went around and said their goodnights to the crowd. April got squeals and thumbs-up from her friends while Decker and Max exchanged contact information. Before too long, they were back in the car and headed toward April's house.

The conversation flowed easily during the drive as they recapped the evening, marveling over the bar, discussing the relationships April had with both Janie and Rori, and the compliment Decker felt when Max approached him about building a house for him and Janie. Then the moment his Range Rover pulled into April's driveway and Decker switched off the headlights, leaving nothing more than the glow of her porch lanterns and the moonlight to illuminate their bodies, it was like a spell had been cast, changing the mood from energetic to erotic in an instant.

Clicks... swoosh... Decker's seatbelt released from its hold, breaking the silence in the cabin. "Do you have any idea how badly I want you?"

Was he kidding? Her body was vibrating with need for this man.

"Fuck, April," he groaned as he turned his whole frame to face her. "I'm going crazy with it." He slid his seat all the way back, placing space between him and the steering wheel. "Unfasten your seatbelt, baby, and come closer to me," he ordered, patting his lap.

Her fingers fumbled with nervous excitement as she followed his command. All she could think of was getting his tongue back in her mouth and his hands on her skin.

"Did you give much thought to your outfit, April?"

He didn't wait for her answer as he ran his hands up her bare thighs, pushing the fabric of her short skirt up around her waist. "Did you put this on knowing that I'd spend the entire evening imagining you riding me in the front seat of my car?"

"Maybe." She let out a shuttered breath as he grinded his pelvis into her wet, lace-covered core. Okay, no, she hadn't known he would spend his night fantasizing, but a woman could hope...right? He wrapped her long hair around his fist, gently tugging her head to the left as he dropped kisses from her earlobe down to the sweet spot where her neck and shoulder met. "Ahh, Deck, that feels... ahhh."

What he did to her body with small touches and spoken words completely astounded her, but there she was astride him, his denim-clad hardness pressed against her, and she was lost. With shameless abandon, she rocked against him, searching for release to the prison she'd been locked in for way too long. And while she saw an exit, there was no way she could reach it on her own. As if reading her mind, Decker released her hair and dragged his hand to her chest, sliding it into the V-neck of her sweater and palming her breast. His rough skin sent tingles rampant through her body as wetness seeped from her core.

"Mmm, I can smell your arousal, April." Decker groaned as his fingers breached the barrier of her panties, inching them aside. "Fuck, babe, you're drenched for me. Is this how you are during our phone calls?"

She could barely think, let alone formulate cohesive sentences, but when he stopped moving his fingers, she knew he awaited a reply. "No, Decker, no. I've never felt like this in my life. Please…"

"Please what, beautiful? Tell me what you want, and I'll give it to you."

———————◆———————

H E WANTED HER in a way he'd never wanted any woman before, with a hunger that one night would never satisfy. While he knew that the encounter would only lead to *her* sexual release, he couldn't wait to see the satisfied look in her eyes and know that he was the man to put it there. "Tell me, baby."

"I need more than just your voice. I want your touch." She grinded into his throbbing erection. "Your taste." She licked his lips. "I want you. Please."

The pressure of her sliding back and forth on his already stimulated cock nearly unmanned him before he could honor her request. Her brilliant green eyes focusing on him, begging him to bring her pleasure, brought him back from the edge just in time to help her over it.

Soft mewls and husky whimpers ripped from her throat as her body quaked beautifully over him, and she called out his name in release. It was magnificent. She was stunning, and he was a goner.

When her breathing leveled out, April lifted her head from his chest. "I know I should probably be embarrassed," she said timidly. "I mean, I haven't made out in a car since high school, and Deck—it was *nothing* like that."

Car groping is for teenagers and trash, Decker. Not for the upper class like us. His ex-wife's voice echoed in his head as his gut lurched. Christ, what the hell was he thinking mauling April in his car like an animal? "April, look, I'm—"

"I should be embarrassed, but I'm not." She pulled back the best she could in the limited space and looked him in the eyes. "That was incredible." She sighed. "I've never felt so… naughty and still so cherished at the same time."

What? Decker swallowed, trying to reconcile April's statement with what was going on in his mind. The smile that stretched over his face was unavoidable. The woman constantly blew him away. What she didn't understand was it was being with *her* that made the experience more than a casual hookup. She felt cherished because she was indeed cherished. He wanted her in his life, and he needed to stop comparing her to Olivia.

CHAPTER FOURTEEN

Hyundai and Ford

D AYS LAPSED INTO weeks as Decker and April, along with their children, formed a bit of a routine. Not only did they have pancakes on Tuesday evenings, but they spent a few hours together either on Saturdays or Sundays, depending on birthday party schedules and other obligations.

Decker treasured their time together, loving how his daughter and April seemed to connect in a most natural way. He also found himself turning to mush every time Elijah wrapped his little arms around him in a tight embrace. He knew there were still pieces of April that were locked behind the battered wall, hiding from the hurt she feared would one day return. Decker knew in his heart that he would never betray her, but it was April who needed to believe it, not him. So Decker held back on declaring words of love, but he no longer abstained from showing the affections. It was clear that both Eli and Charlie knew their parents were dating, and they didn't seem bothered by the fondness that was forming between them. In fact, often the children piled in for group hugs and sweet gestures.

"I love when the sun is out and we can spend time at the park." April pushed her sunglasses down the bridge of her nose. "Let's set up over there under the tree. That way the kids can have some shade when they get tired." Sliding the shades back in place, she grabbed the picnic blanket and the Thermos, leaving the cooler to Decker's capable hands.

"Come sit with me, beautiful. The kids are fine. We can see them from here," Decker said, relaxing on the soft blanket. "Besides, I'd like to taste what kind of fruit you brought me today." When April sauntered over, kneeled next to him, and placed her soft lips on his, his heart began to thunder in his chest. "Mmm, strawberries. I love strawberries," he growled, leaning in for another kiss.

"Umm, you kids do know that this is a public park. Jeeze, there are impressionable young minds running around." Ford chuckled his hello before reaching into the cooler for a soda.

* * *

"NICE TO FINALLY meet you, Ford." April was grateful for her large sunglasses. Hopefully they hid most of the embarrassment that no doubt showed on her face. She'd spoken to Decker's younger brother on the phone before, when he intercepted a call. The man seemed funny and sweet, and seeing him in the flesh, she knew that good looks ran in the family. While he didn't exactly light the fire inside her the way Decker did, she could see how other women would get in line to gain his attention, just as Decker described.

"Rein it in, little brother," Decker teased as he stood to give his sibling a side-hug-back-slap.

April could see the easy camaraderie between the two men and loved that Decker seemed to have a close family unit, just as she did with her siblings.

"So this is April Maddox," Decker introduced.

"It's a pleasure to finally meet you." Ford stretched his arm out to shake her hand and pulled her up to a standing position, wrapping her in a hug instead.

Charming characters, these Brand men are.

"I've heard a lot of great things about you, but the most memorable fact is that you and your siblings are all named after calendar months."

April saw, out of the corner of her eyes, that Decker glared at his brother.

"What?" Ford questioned animatedly. "Come on, that's awesome!"

Decker stepped beside her and wrapped his muscled arm around her torso. "Babe, it really is unusual." He pressed a kiss into the top of her head. "I happen to love it."

"Yeah, it's great," she grunted sarcastically. "Can you imagine if *your* parents were into theme-naming their kids?" She looked from Decker to Ford. "You could have been Decker and Painter or, better yet, Hyundai and Ford."

Both pairs of brown eyes widened at her statement. "Not so awesome now, is it?"

She felt Decker's body pulse with controlled amusement, but there was not an ounce of control in Ford's uninhibited cackling. Turned out his charm was in fact contagious, because the three of them were howling like lunatics and gasping for breath by the time Eli and Charlie joined them for lunch. Once the meal was over, the kids hopped on the swings while April, Decker, and Ford chatted and joked for a bit longer.

"I like her," Ford declared as he crumbled up his lunch trash and wiped the grass from his jeans. His gaze met hers when he added, "Keep her around, big brother. We both know that gorgeous, smart, *and* funny is a rare find."

"Trust me, I know"—Decker laced his fingers through April's—"and I plan to keep her by my side."

Decker's words sent shivers down April's spine and curled her toes. The man was a shot of whisky—potent and warming to the insides—that left her tingling in all the right places. She squeezed his hand, hoping he understood that by his side was exactly where she wanted to be.

Once Ford had left the park and the picnic was packed up, April and Decker quickly collected the children and strolled to their cars. It was Saturday night, and they were finally going out on a date, just the two of them.

"I'll see you tonight, big guy." Excitement oozed from each of her pores as she stood outside of her idling Acura with Eli strapped into the air-conditioned car, listening to music.

Flames licked Decker's chocolate-brown eyes. "I can't fucking wait to have you all to myself, April. I need to feel you come apart in my hands."

Seeing his big body tremble made her insides turn to mush. "I'd like to finally get my hands on you." Her brows bobbed suggestively. "Or better yet, my mouth."

"Fuuuck."

Quickly calculating the best plan for the evening, April suggested they once again meet at the restaurant. "We both have babysitters, Deck, so if for some reason an emergency occurs, I'd like to have my car, and you should have yours."

He reluctantly agreed. They shared a quick kiss and went their separate ways.

CHAPTER FIFTEEN

(For real…this is all of Chapter Fifteen)

Super Heroes and Mime Sex

HER GREEN EYES shimmered, revealing mutual desire as she lifted the glass of merlot to her full lips, parting them to take another small sip. Christ, those lips, so soft and sweet… Decker could practically taste them as he tried to convince himself to look away from what shouldn't have been such an ethereal sight. It seemed as though everything April Maddox did was sexy as hell and erotic as sin. He couldn't fool himself into thinking otherwise therefore, why bother missing any part of her beautiful show? With his gaze focused squarely on the delectable vision next to him, he inhaled—there was no ignoring the erection pulsing behind the zipper in his slacks. Everything the woman said or did affected him, and he'd venture to guess she was not clueless to her role in his torture. No, he could see the hunger in her eyes, the mutual ache of sexual desire. She was wanton. As the glass touched her mouth and the deep burgundy liquid ran up the tapered bowl of the wineglass, caressing her glossy painted lips, Decker's mind automatically fixated on apples. When he claimed her lips after dinner, would they still taste like the apple gloss he enjoyed earlier that evening; or would the sweet grapes of the wine touch his tongue and flavor their kiss? Not that it mattered, as long as he got to own her mouth for a few minutes. Got to taste the essence of the woman who was quickly changing the very foundation on which he'd built his life. She could taste like wood filler and he'd relish it. A man could easily become addicted to those lips, as well as those mind-bending kisses—lord knows he had, and it'd only been two real dates. Well, this being their third...

"Decker?" Just the sound of his name in her honey-smooth voice had his heart beating faster and his length hardening to an aching throb. "Deck, is everything okay?" April lowered her glass to the table, shifting her lithe body smoothly in the U-shaped booth.

As they turned toward each other his knee gently brushed her leg, and he watched her questioning gaze descend slowly from his eyes to where his hands gripped his upper thighs. His thumbs all but digging into the cotton of his perfectly pressed pants. April's perusal paused briefly, the minute she noticed what was practically impossible for him to hide. The audible catch of her breath as it held for a beat, and the slight flush that kissed her cheeks a fraction of a second before she licked her lips and brought her steamy green gaze back to his face, nearly set him ablaze. Yeah, everything would be just fine once he finally got her alone and beneath him. His body vibrated with need for the incredible woman beside him. It had been far too long... too long since he'd felt this way. Had he ever truly felt like this before?

"You look... stiff, Deck." Her shy smile now charged with a vixen-like confidence he'd never seen on her before.

That look that made him want to sweep the dishes from their table—and to hell with the mess or the prying eyes of the other diners. He wanted to spread her out before him like a main course, and finally see if her whole body tasted as sweet as her damn lips. When she placed her small hand over his and began tracing small circles with her index finger over his sensitized flesh, Decker was pulled from a lustful haze. April Maddox knew exactly what she was saying, knew just how her tiny touches were affecting him.

"I've heard massage can help with *that* sort of problem." Her gaze flitted to his lap then back to his eyes before a smirk curled the ends of her upturned mouth. The innuendo played openly on her beautiful face.

Lifting both of their hands from his thigh, he twisted his wrist to bring her palm to his lips. Decker breathed in her warm, fruity smell then placed a kiss on the soft skin. "You're a funny lady, you know that?"

He could barely contain the laughter in his voice, and truth was, he didn't want to. He liked April as a person, her humor, intellect, and warmth set her apart from so many of the other women he'd dated. When his libido wasn't sucking the blood from his brain and depositing it directly into his balls, he could tell the feeling was mutual.

"Yes, I'm freaking hilarious." Her brow arched. "In fact, I may be one of the funniest people I know," she confirmed, a smile stretching across her face as the deep dimples in both cheeks winked, practically begging him to touch them, taunting him to kiss them.

Extending his arm, he cupped her face, stroking the divot in her right cheek. Silk... her skin felt silken beneath his touch and as the backs of his fingers traveled down her neck, reveling in the supple skin, electricity jolted through his body.

"April Maddox, *you* definitely are amusing, but you're so much more. You're smart, sweet, and... well..." His gaze traveled from her face to the scooped neckline where the swells of her breasts subtly formed the perfect amount of cleavage. "Let's face it, you're fucking gorgeous."

Watching her chest rise and fall with her shallow breaths as his words resonated sparked a fire in his gut. As her cheeks flushed, his blood heated. Her scent flooded his nostrils as he breathed in slowly while recomposing himself in the leather booth. The moment her pink tongue slid over her plump bottom lip, Decker knew all attempts at being suave were lost. He was lost. *Take her home*, he told himself. *Charlie will never find out*, he promised his troubled conscience, then took the leap he'd wanted to take for months.

Slipping his thumb under her chin and tilting it back, Decker stared into her hooded eyes. "I can't stop thinking about your mouth, the way it tastes, the things you say—I want you, April. I need you in ways that makes no sense." Desire clawed its way up his chest demanding its release. "But right now, I don't give a shit about making sense…"

"Decker." April sighed, her voice low and husky as her chartreuse eyes practically glowed with anticipation. She leaned forward and pressed her lips to his.

Her moaned agreement had his heart pounding double time as he did his best to keep his cool exterior from melting onto the leather booth. She pulled her plush bottom lip between her teeth, and for a brief second, the world faded away. He heard nothing, saw nothing but those lips.

As if she sensed his momentary loss of time and space, April gently stroked his jaw until his eyes once again made contact with hers. "And I've wanted you since the first second I saw you at the gym." Her lips curved. "Any man who can bench-press that much weight and not make those silly grunting noises is someone I pay attention to." Her dimples sunk deeper. "It didn't hurt that you were easy on the eyes and compassionate to boot. When that older woman tripped and fell getting off of the treadmill, you helped her up and got her ice for her ankle. You were so kind and gentle with her. Kind of like a superhero that day, Decker Brand."

"Are you saying I'm not a superhero every day, Ms. Maddox?" Dimples, again… it was like playing Skee-Ball and scoring in the coveted top ring. No matter how many times you win, you always feel like a champ. Seeing April's dimples and knowing they were aimed at him… yeah, totally fucking winning.

With one hand placing whisper soft touches on his

throbbing cock, April lifted the cloth napkin from her lap and laid it gently on the table. "Do you wanna get out of here?" Her wide eyes showed she was just as surprised by her brazen actions as he was.

After three dates, hours spent at the gym, and countless dirty chats and texts, maybe April Maddox was dying to get her hands all over him like he was her. Maybe she, too, wanted to feel the length of him pressing into her as they came together for the first time. *Fuck, I want her.*

Decker lifted his hand and signaled for the check.

WITH THE CHECK paid at lightning speed, Decker placed his large hand on the small of April's back and led her to the restaurant door. The heat from his palm sent tingles up her spine and moisture between her thighs.

Oh my God. Is this really happening? Holy shit, this is finally happening! Like one of her preteen students instead of a grown woman, her thoughts flipped-flopped from excited to nervous, from giddy to curious. Had she made the right moves? Brazen had never been her way, but the years she'd spent tucked away inside herself hadn't brought her happiness either. So at the advice of her friends and siblings, she decided to leap outside of her comfort zone and reach for what she wanted, and she wanted Decker Brand. Due to circumstances beyond their control, their timing seemed to veer on the opposite end of opportune.

There was no questioning the desire they shared—Christ, she felt as though she could drown in its depth—but her past had taught her a bitch of a lesson, and it wasn't one she'd ever care to repeat. Therefore, she'd taken the tortoise's route instead of the hare's. Slow and steady kept her safe but left her horny as all hell. Although that would be remedied shortly because she intended to hop her ass to the finish line no matter what, and she couldn't wait to collect her reward.

Walking through the small parking lot with his arm draped protectively around her waist sent small jolts of anticipation zipping through her already hyper-aware body. Everything about the man to her left was imprinted into her memory—the way his tall, hard frame gave balance to her knees that just barely kept her upright, his scent, a spicy blend of cedar, pine, and Decker, hung ever so lightly in the spring, just enough to make her mouth water and her heart race. The man was a sensory feast, and she suffered from insatiable hunger.

They stopped in front of her car. They'd agreed to meet at the restaurant because she still felt more comfortable having her own transportation.

"I'll drive slowly so you can follow me back to my place," April's skin bloomed with goose bumps as Decker's thumb glided up and down her arm as he spoke. "But just in case, please enter my address into your GPS." Decker shifted closer, his mouth mere inches from her ear. "I don't wanna lose you tonight, April." Yep, those seven words had her blood pulsing through her veins while eagerness clenched at her core as she tapped in his address.

"Are you sure you want to take this back to your place, Deck? I mean, I've never been there before and… what if Charlie finds out?" She saw a quick flash of something pass over his face. If it was guilt or the thrill of getting caught, April had no idea; but as quickly as the look had come, it was gone.

Decker opened her car door and waited until she was tucked and buckled safely into her seat before speaking. His brow arched as his chocolate eyes glittered. "It's late, April. Charlie's been sleeping for a while." His lips curled up in the half grin that April had named his *gotcha* smirk as his voice dropped to a gravelly pitch. "As much as I look forward to hearing how you sound when you're screaming my name as you come"—he winked—"tonight, we're gonna have to go on touch instead."

"Ahh, so kind of like mime sex," April teased, squeezing her thighs together. Everything the man said sparked her libido, and she was one flare away from detonation.

Her heart revved up, pounding wildly into her ribs as Decker's brown eyes blackened at her comment. Their relationship flourished due to their easy banter, snarky remarks, and similar sense of humor, but as he licked his lips and leaned into her car, the only thing that occupied her mind was getting his mouth closer to her own. She didn't have long to wait. Decker tipped her chin up and crushed his lips to hers. His tongue breached the seam of her lips and demanded entrance into her mouth. Her breathless whimper seemed to rev up the fire between them as their bodies fused as one. He nipped her bottom lip before ending their scorching kiss, his forehead pressed gently to hers as she breathed in his warm sweet breaths.

"Fuck, April. Let's get out of here before I strip you down and take you in the backseat of your car like a horny teenager."

Lust struck and aroused, April grazed her fingers over Decker's stubbled jaw. She loved the way his brown eyes were practically black with desire—desire for her... her and no one else. "Deck, I'm not opposed to a backseat romp." She sniggered. Hell it had been so damn long since she'd had sex, she wouldn't be opposed to any kind of romp.

Breaking their physical connection, Decker slowly shook his head once as he backed away from her vehicle. It appeared as if the common sense that she felt returning to her brain was quickly creeping into his as well. "No, beautiful. Not our first time together. Let me take you back to my condo so I can lay you out and savor every part of your delectable body the way you deserve—hell, the way I've been fantasizing about for months."

The kiss he blew her would have been cheesy had it come from anyone else, but from him—ahh... she wanted to grab it and tuck it away for later. Of course, she'd never do such an embarrassing thing. Even the thought was something she'd keep to herself. Instead, she closed her car door and rolled down the window.

"I'll see you in a few," he called over his shoulder as he walked to his black Range Rover.

Mmm, the view from behind is as delicious as from

straight ahead, April thought as she spent an extra second admiring his tight ass. She shook her head to clear the mental haze she so frequently slipped into whenever Decker Brand ghosted into her thoughts which, frankly, happened more often these days. Still uncertain as to if she was ready to give more than just her body, a decision not made lightly, to another man, April decided to listen to some recently dispensed advice and, for the first time in a long time, *just enjoy the damn moment.* Excitement filled her Acura RDX as she twisted the keys into the ignition and brought the car to life.

Just before pulling out of the parking lot, April checked her text messages. Only one new message awaited her attention. Tension immediately gripped her shoulders when she saw who the sender was. She practically never left her house other than for work or the gym. She never allowed herself time to be a woman, and now that she had, guilt threatened to consume her. Would Eli be jealous? Upset? She opened the message.

Everything is fine here. Doesn't even know you're gone. Enjoy ~ A

Exhaling, her shoulders slumped as the tension expelled. It was hard enough trying to make a relationship work when only two people were involved, but there were complications in their relationship that couldn't be ignored, people they were trying to protect, others they were trying to forget. She'd left her *comfort zone* tonight, and this was her reward—Decker. And oh, what a delicious reward it would be.

After about a minute on the road, Real McCoy's version of "Come and Get Your Love" filled the otherwise quiet cabin of April's car. She giggled at the nineties song she and Rori had selected as a ring tone to represent *Smokin'-Hot-Gym-Guy.* Well, he was, in fact, smokin' hot, and she felt her smile widen.

"You missing me already?" April teased.

"You have me on your *hands-free* device, right?" Decker asked by way of greeting. His familiar seriousness about this particular subject was present.

"Yes, dear." April smiled at the stern voice coming through the speaker. The man was an intoxicating blend of sexy and sweet, compassionate and considerate, domineering and delicious, and those were just the few layers she had seen so far. "So…why the call, Deck? Not that I'm complaining, but according to my GPS, it looks like we're gonna be arriving at your place in just a few minutes."

"Yeah, we are," he admitted. "And I can't wait another minute to finally touch you—"

"Well, big guy, it seems as though you'll have to be-cause—"

April's attempt at interruption was cut off when Decker continued to speak, his voice dipped low and smooth, like warm dark chocolate coating her cool, needy skin. "When we get up to my place, April, every hot kiss, every touch, every look we've shared up 'til this point will be like a spark compared to the inferno I intend to unleash the moment I get my hands on you. Do you understand what I'm saying, beautiful? We are going to burn together, and I can't fucking wait."

Her breath hitched as his seductive words caressed her. April removed one hand from the steering wheel and placed it on her bare thigh. Slowly, she inched her fingers up and down, allowing her thumb to tease but not breach the satiny edge of her panties. Goose bumps broke the surface of her skin. Her nipples tightened into sharp points, already sensitive as they rubbed against the lacy bra that cupped them. Her body was reacting to mere words spoken by a man too far away to touch her but close enough to unravel what had been tightly spun for too damn long. *Holy shit, this is really gonna happen.*

"April, did you say something?" Decker's voice came through the speaker, a smile evident in his tone.

"Umm." April pinched her upper leg, bringing a sting to where pleasure had been only seconds before. The man was a constant witness of her incessant silliness. "No, Deck, I was just, umm…" *Think, April, the guy just told you he wants to fuck your brains out, and now you're acting like an escaped patient from a psychiatric ward.*

Decker chuckled. The sound was sensual like the man himself. "Ah, are you having one of your little self-chats, as you like to call them?"

April stayed silent. Had she not been driving, she'd have been pounding her head into the hardest surface she could find.

"I told you, I think the concept is great. I've been doing a bit of it myself lately, and you're right, it's great to talk and not have anyone interrupt."

April took deep breaths. It amazed her how easy it

was for Decker to calm her down. After only a couple short months of friendship, and okay, she could admit, some pretty serious lusting, he'd grown to have an important role in her life. He seemed so confident about her…them, but they had more to think about than just each other. Shaking her head, she forced herself to stay in the present. Looking to the future had gotten her nothing but trouble in the past.

"We're here." His voice sounded different as it came through the speaker. His confidence from only moments before seemed a bit shaky. Was he nervous? "This is our place. Pull in the spot next to mine. I own them both."

The call ended, leaving April's car completely silent. Exiting her vehicle, she craned her neck back to look at the tall (well, tall by suburban standards) apartment building before her. It was a newer place, probably only about five years old. She remembered when it was built. God, her life had been so different back then. *Here and now, April, here and now,* she reminded herself as strong fingers laced through her own, kicking her libido back into overdrive, where it seemed to stay whenever Decker Brand was near.

✦━━━━✦━━━━✦

"CHRIST, APRIL, YOU Smell incredible." Decker ran his nose up the column of April's long, slender neck, inhaling the sweet scent of apples and cinnamon. The never-ending elevator ride to the top floor of the apartment building would be the death of him.

"You've got the whole 'apple for the teacher' thing going. When I'm near you, I can't decide if I want you to teach me a thing or two..." He sucked gently on her earlobe, taking pleasure in the way her breath hitched briefly. "Or if I wanna just take a bite out of you." He nipped her lobe with his teeth, relishing the hiss that escaped her lips as he laved where he bit once more.

"I think a little of both can be arranged," April purred. "Don't you think?" A blush crept up her cheeks. "Deck, I'm getting better at the sexy talk, right?" She giggled. "I never could have pulled off that cat noise when we first met."

Laughing, he pulled her close to his chest and placed a kiss on the top of her head. "Oh, babe, you never needed any practice being sexy." He guided her hand down the front of his pants, over his hardened length. "You do that to me just by being close. Hell, I get hard practically every time we talk on the phone. However, the naughty texts and that sweet little purr... yeah babe, there is no doubt it's time I get you underneath me." Just as he leaned in to take her lips, the elevator door slid open, spitting them out on the sixteenth floor.

"To be continued." April winked over her shoulder as she exited the car, and the simple gesture caused his heart to pump faster.

Fueled by urgency and determination, he took one long stride and stood before her in the lavish hallway. The need to claim her lips overpowered his desire to get her into his apartment. He cupped her beautiful face in his hands and stroked her satiny cheeks with the roughened pads of his thumbs.

"Have I told you lately how much I love the way your hands feel against my skin?"

Her words caused a searing pain to lance through his gut, an icy splash of water quelling the fire that had been burning within him. Dropping his arms to his sides, Decker closed his eyes to keep the shame at bay and inhaled slowly. *Fuck, my goddamn hands. 'My skin is too fine for hands that rough,'* the memory screamed inside him. When he lifted his lids, there she stood—her brows furrowed, confusion clear in her eyes. But instead of allowing him to keep his distance, April stepped closer to him, her heat seeping from her body to his, her scent captivating his thoughts. She lifted his hands in her own and pressed them back against her soft cheeks.

"Decker, your hands are strong." She turned her lips to his left hand and placed a gentle kiss on his roughened palm. "They're sturdy." She kissed his right palm. "And they are the sign of a man who creates amazing things." He stared into her bright green depths. "I can't wait to finally have these hands all over my body."

Where has this woman been my whole life? "Ms. Maddox, you really have gotten damn good at the sweet talk, now haven't you?" Without waiting for a response, he leaned down and captured her lips. When a soft moan escaped her, Decker knew it was past time to get them both in his place and in his bed. "Fuck," he murmured while trying to casually adjust himself. "I can't go in there looking like this." He pointed at his tented pants. "She'll know, and the poor girl will never sit for me again."

April giggled. "Sure, she will, Deck. She's sixteen, and you're hot. You know she brags to her friends when you call her to babysit. God, she probably sneaks into your bedroom and sniffs your cologne."

"Now that's just creepy, April. Jeez, and people think teenage boys are bad." Shaking his head, he laughed because April wasn't wrong. He'd overheard a thing or two about how the girls in his building thought he was *super-cute*—their words, not his.

———•———•———

"THANK YOU, MR. BRAND." The babysitter, Jessi, smiled sweetly, and slipped on her shoes as she gave him an account of the evening. "Charlie was a princess as usual. But she did complain of a tummyache around bedtime. I read her an extra story and rubbed her belly. That seemed to work, because she fell asleep before the second story was over."

"Hmm, okay."

April watched silently as Decker's brows knitted together. She recognized that look. He was concerned but trying not to overreact. Charlie wasn't necessarily a drama queen, but she was a six-year-old, so only time would tell if she was actually sick.

"Well, you never know with that little one," Decker continued. "She was fine earlier today at the park, so hopefully it was just a passing bellyache, and she'll wake up perfect tomorrow."

"I sure hope so, Mr. Brand," the babysitter cooed, smiling brightly as Decker pulled some bills out of his side pocket to pay her for her time.

April pulled her bottom lip between her teeth, biting hard to keep from laughing. Could it be more obvious that this poor girl was crushing on Decker? She was proud that the teen was stringing together full sentences. At sixteen, April would have never been so collected in the face of all that beauty. The bitter taste of regret formed in the back of her throat as she remembered how she was at sixteen. Yeah, this girl was much better off.

"Well, thank you for babysitting tonight, Jessi. As always, I really appreciate it." Decker walked her out the door and into the hallway.

April looked around the large open floor plan. The space was magnificent, clean, and perfect. Not pristine, not at all. It felt lived in by a man and his little girl, but it was still beautiful.

"Oh, you're *so* funny, Mr. Brand."

She heard Jessi giggle from the hallway. April felt her lips twitch. Decker was probably waiting for the elevator to come, and the teen loved the extra attention. *So cute*, she thought. *I'm so gonna have to bust on him about that later.*

Even though the front door quietly clicked closed, the sound reverberated through April's body. They were finally together, in his home, alone. Leaning up against the door, his eyes met hers from across the room. She felt his stare stroking her, touching her, wanting her, yet she was rooted where she stood. The ease that had been floating around the room only seconds before was replaced with a tension so hot, so sexual, and so electric, April felt the charges moving through her bones. She would combust if she didn't turn down the heat.

"Umm, Deck, your home, it's beautiful." April licked her bottom lip, unable to break their eye contact, therefore unable to cool the fever burning her flesh. "It's so clean and well decorated." She knew her voice sounded shaky, maybe even husky. The question was did he notice the change?

"What did you expect, babe, a frat house?" His smile widened slowly, showing off his bright white teeth. "April, I wear a tool belt, not a toga." April's heart pounded in her chest as Decker pushed off the door and began to move toward her. Like a predator, he stalked slowly, and his eyes glittered with intent. "I'm a thirty-three-year-old father of a little girl who means the world to me. The reason I chose to live in this building instead of a single-family home is for companionship for Charlie. Several of her school friends live here, so while it may not be permanent, it's been a great home for the two of us."

With those words, softness appeared in his eyes that April only ever saw when Charlie's name was mentioned. That look was one of the things that had her falling hard and fast for the sexy Decker Brand, even though everything in her head kept questioning if she could really trust her heart.

Standing face to face, he dragged his knuckles from her ear down her jawline. The gesture sent tingles spreading through her body, multiplying at an alarming rate.

Once her chin was cupped between his thumb and index finger, he tilted her head back and looked directly into her eyes. "I'm a man, April, who wants you more than any woman I've ever known before. So are you done avoiding this now? Can I have my sexy kitty-cat back?"

Exhaling the breath she'd been holding for too long, April began to laugh quietly. "You're so funny, Mr. Brand," she mimicked the babysitter before wrapping her arms around Decker's neck and pulling him close. "Purr, Decker, purr."

"Oh my God, April." Decker chuckled. "What am I gonna do with you?"

"You can kiss me."

She'd barely finished her sentence before he pulled her against his hard chest and smashed his lips against hers. Cedar and spice filled her nostrils as she rolled up on her toes and wrapped her arms around his neck. His tongue traced the seam of her lips, demanding entry as his hands caressed her scalp. His fingers twirled in her long, blond hair, tugging at the tresses and sparking desire just on the cusp between pleasure and pain. His large hands traveled quickly down her back as he grabbed her ass cheeks and pulled her flush against his hardness.

"Mmm, Deck," she moaned, feeling him lengthen even through the thin fabric of her dress and his slacks. Fuck, her thong was already damp with arousal, and he'd barely touched her. As his mouth left her lips and trailed wet kisses from her jaw to her ear, she let out another breathy sigh.

"Fuck, April," Decker growled in her ear. "I've been

dying to have you close again, in front of me, where I can smell your arousal and know that your pussy's begging to be touched…"

His dirty words were potent as hell, but when combined with his tongue running up the shell of her ear, it was almost a miracle she was still standing upright.

"Come on, beautiful. I seem to have worked up quite an appetite since dinner." His gaze stayed locked with hers as he lowered his hand and reached under her dress.

Was it possible for one's heart to pound hard enough to fracture one's ribs? If so, April feared she may require an ER visit by the evening's end. Calloused fingertips glided up her inner thigh, the coarse sensation stimulating her soft skin. As his thick fingers slid beneath the satiny barrier, April saw his gaze go from sexy to smoldering.

He dipped one finger into her opening and stroked her inner wall. "You're so wet for me, babe, so fucking drenched."

Her eyes closed as his touch, and his words lapped waves of pleasure over her heated skin, a sensation that was gone too quickly. Slightly embarrassed by the whimper she was unable to contain at the loss of his touch, she forced her lids open. There he stood so close, so sexy, and so smug. His crooked *gotcha* smirk spread across his plump lips.

Decker lifted his middle finger, still glistening with April's wetness, and placed the digit in his mouth. "Mmm, April, you're exactly what I had in mind as an after-dinner snack. I need more of you now."

Breathless, April laced her fingers with his and followed him through his penthouse. She was finally ready, finally able to move on from the past, and she couldn't have found a more perfect man. Her body was thrumming with anticipation as he looked over his shoulder and gave her a look that nearly melted her into a puddle. He wanted her as much as she wanted him. He'd made it clear. No more games, no more bullshit. Just him and her and some mind-blowing sex.

"Daddy! Daddy!"

Decker halted mid-stride.

"Daddy, I'm gonna be sick." The little voice sounded frantic and scared as she called out for her father.

He dropped April's hand and ran in the opposite direction toward what April assumed was Charlie's bedroom.

CHAPTER SIXTEEN

Did You Get Some?

S TANDING OUTSIDE OF the little girl's room, April listened, the mother in her wanting to rush in and help, especially since she'd come to love Charlie as she did. But the single parent in her didn't want to interfere in the interaction between father and child.

"Come on, sugar, let's get you to the bathroom...oh ...oh..."

(Retching noises followed by crying)

"It's okay, honey. Shhh, it's okay. Daddy can get a different shirt." His voice became distant and echoed. There must have been a bathroom attached to the little girl's bedroom. "Let me sit you down on the fluffy mat, sugar. I'll give you a bath and get you fresh pjs, okay?"

April could feel her throat tighten as tears began to sting the backs of her eyes. He was an amazing man straight to the core. Why couldn't she have found him sooner?

"Hey, babe?" Decker poked his head out of Charlie's

room. Worry had replaced desire on his beautiful face. "I can't believe this is happening tonight of all nights, but she's obviously sick"—he lifted his vomit-covered shirt—"so can I ask for a rain check?"

April's gaze had left his face and traveled down his naked chest. While she'd seen his upper torso before at the gym, there was something intimate about seeing him shirtless and wearing dress pants instead of basketball shorts.

"April?" Decker called her name, his voice gentle but hasty.

"Oh God, of course, Deck." April had been so focused on his biceps that she'd almost missed his question. "Never apologize about taking care of your child first. You *know* that out of anyone, I get it. You go bathe Charlie, and I'll change the sheets on her bed. Then I'll sneak out to give you guys some privacy."

Decker tipped his head to the side, gratitude evident in the soft set of his mouth and the slow exhale of his breath. "Babe, you don't have to."

"I know, big guy." April placed her hand on his warm shoulder. Just touching him brought her comfort that she couldn't explain. "But it's nice having help when they're sick, isn't it?"

"I meant, you don't have to leave." The request was plain in his gaze, but it was one she refused to see.

"Daddy!"

Understanding replaced hope as Decker kissed April's lips quickly before pointing her in the direction of the spare sheets and running back to his daughter. "It's okay, Charlie. Let it out, baby girl."

April replaced the soiled pink sheets with powder blue ones and left the little girl's room. She washed her hands in the kitchen sink and allowed herself one last look around the beautiful home before letting herself out the front door.

Once she was in her car, she made a call. "Hey, August, how's my boy?"

"He's good, sis. I told you, he didn't even notice you were gone. He loves being with his uncle A. Now, why are you calling me? It's still early, and while I don't necessarily want or need details, I'm wondering."

April heard the hesitation in his voice. She could have made it easy on him by giving him details, but where was the fun in that? She giggled. "Wondering what, Aug?"

"Fuck, come on, sis. You know what I'm asking. Did you guys finally… did you… err… did you get some? You pain in the ass."

August was the best big brother a girl could have. Honestly, April knew she'd won the lotto with him. He'd spent her entire life protecting her from danger or helping her recover from harm.

"No, I didn't get some, Aug." April sighed. "Charlie woke up vomiting."

"Cock-blocked by the kids again." August chuckled. "Remind me not to have children, like ever."

"Shut your trap, Aug. You love Elijah like he's your own son."

"Yeah, baby sis, I do," August admitted. "However, when I wanna get laid, my nephew is with his mom."

"Bite me, big brother." April giggled before disconnecting the call, effectively cutting the sound of August's laughter off mid-chuckle. She wondered how long it would take for him to realize he was laughing to himself. Her cheeks ached from smiling as she replayed the evening in her head. While she'd have never guessed it would end with sickness instead of sex, she'd still had an incredible time with Decker, even if the aching need between her thighs told her otherwise.

A FTER THREE ROUNDS of violent vomiting and two baths, Charlie was asleep in her bed and hopefully out for the night. After taking a long shower to rid his body and his nostrils of the revolting stench, Decker locked up his apartment, grabbed his cell phone, and got into bed. The two missed texts from April, inquiring about Charlie, helped to ease some of the tension in his shoulders, but it did nothing for the sexual relief he'd been waiting for since first meeting her.

Decker: *Are you awake?*

It had been more than an hour since her last text, but he knew she stayed up late reading her romance novels, and it was Saturday night.

Dimples: *Hey, How's Charlie?*
Decker: *She finally crashed.*

Dimples: *And you're still up?*
Decker: *You have no idea.*

He groaned as his cock ached, begging for relief. His phone trilled in his hand as the screen lit up with April's picture.

"Hey, beautiful." His voice sounded rough to his own ears as exhaustion settled in. Nothing was more draining than a sick child.

"Aw, Deck, you sound like you need sleep. Can I do anything to relax you?" The coyness in April's question told Decker that she wanted to play, and it was his pleasure that would be the focal point.

"Mmm, sounds like the second-best option," he teased. "But first, I wanted to ask you something at dinner, but you were so damn distracting that I forgot. So let me ask you now before you distract me again."

"Um, okay."

"Every year on Memorial weekend, I take Charlie up to Great Wolf Lodge in the Pocono Mountains. Have you and Eli ever been there?"

"N… no."

He had anticipated her hesitation with the whole topic. Christ, what he was going to suggest was a big fucking deal, but it felt right, and if she thought about it, she'd know it too.

"We haven't been there, but I hear it's amazing."

"Oh, April, it's fantastic. We've been going for the last four years. Charlie and I head up first thing on Friday morning for some family time, and then my college friends—Michael and Janine, Bobby, his wife Shawna, and Marc and his wife, Tammy—meet up with us on Saturday with their kids, and we make a weekend of it. No cell phones, no computers, no outside world. Just family and close friends for a few days. And I'd, well… we'd, because I did ask Charlie, love it if you and Eli joined us."

Silence.

"April." His voice lowered and fear of her rejection began to take root as he tried to sell her on the idea. "Separate bedrooms so there isn't any confusion for the kids. I just want to spend the time with you and Elijah."

The sound of her breathing was the only indicator that she was still on the line until she finally broke her silence. "Okay." She hesitated. "We'd love to join you guys."

"Are you serious?" he asked unable to believe that she'd agreed so quickly.

"Yeah, Deck, I think it sounds awesome." Genuine excitement bubbled in her voice. "Just please don't say anything to Eli just yet. It's still weeks away, and he will ask me every day if it's time to go."

"My lips are sealed, beautiful. And April, thank you. You have no idea how happy you just made me."

A sweet little purr came through the line. "It's late, big guy. Let me make you a little happier, and then we can both get some sleep. Okay?"

She'd gotten so damn good at phone sex over the past couple of months that by the time their call ended, Decker drifted off into a deep, sated sleep.

CHAPTER SEVENTEEN

Have a Nice Weekend

"**I**T FEELS LIKE I haven't talked to you in ages, chica." Rori frowned as she sat in the seat next to April's and unwrapped her brown-bag lunch.

"I know, Ror. It's like I see you every day, but I haven't really seen you, you know?" Guilt weighed on April as she tried to figure out where the days had gone and how she had let her friend fall through the cracks of her life.

"Oh, April, I'm totally not placing blame. I know you're busy with Eli and Decker, and I've had my hands full at home. I just miss you, that's all." Her poor friend had the weight of the world on her shoulders, and April wanted to offer support the way Rori had so often done for her.

"Honey, are you busy tonight? Eli would love to see you. Why don't you come over for dinner?"

Rori heaved a heavy sigh. "I can't tonight. How about Wednesday?"

"Sounds great." April grinned. "Oh, do you think

you'd want to help me pick out an outfit for my date on Saturday night?"

Rori's eyes widened as her hands went to her hips. "Dates on back-to-back weekends? I'm so happy for you, April."

"Well, August isn't." April shook her head. "Ember was supposed to babysit and canceled because she got a better offer. Can you imagine?" she deadpanned. "You know my brother. He's a saint, so he rescheduled his own plans so I didn't have to cancel my date with Decker."

Rori swooned. "Your brother is the best, you know that?"

"Ha, I do. However, some of his motivation is selfish." The confused look on Rori's face made April giggle. "Aug keeps telling me that his babysitting services are only available until I finally end my 'dry spell,' and let me tell you, Ror, his face scrunches up like he ate bad sushi every time he discusses sex and me in the same sentence. He says that my getting laid would be doing his nephew, and the world at large, a favor, and he's willing to sacrifice his social life if it means helping mankind. His words, not mine."

"Oh my god." Rori snorted. "The man is loco."

The women laughed until tears rolled down their cheeks. By the time lunch was over, April felt refreshed and excited for the rest of the week.

ECKER KNOCKED ONCE then entered his brother's office without waiting for an invitation. "Ford, we gotta talk." His eyes traveled to Jovanna, who was perched on the arm of Decker's favorite chair with a notepad and pen in hand. "Sorry, Vanna, but this can't wait. Please excuse us... now." The anger that surged through Decker's veins made it nearly impossible for him to speak in anything more that grunts and commands.

"Of course, not a problem." Jovanna quickly stood up, smoothed down her skirt, and exited Ford's office, closing the door behind her.

"Deck, what's goin' on?" Ford pointed at the closed door. "That's not like you."

Decker exhaled, frustration and agitation twisting in his gut. "I thought we discussed weeks ago about having those two *punks* tossed off my job site." Decker didn't need to use proper names for Ford to know exactly who Decker was referring to. "I went about it... nicely," Decker seethed. "I told them to leave, I had them escorted from the property, and I asked you to contact Marvin Randall, the goddamn guy who's funding the whole fucking project, and inform him that his *helpers* were a liability."

The color drained from Ford's face. "I did. I followed protocol." Ford attempted a smile. "What happened that got your shorts all twisted?"

"It's not funny, man." Decker ran his muddy fingers through his hair, not giving a shit if the dirt transferred. "Those fuckers came back today and started directing my men, giving orders and declaring that Randall wanted specific things changed. Of course, my guys didn't make any change without coming to me, but that was the point. They wore a goddamn path coming back and forth to me. The chaos was out of control."

Even through his anger, Decker could see the gears in Ford's business mind churning. Ford's fingers flew over the keyboard of his computer just before he pressed the intercom button on the phone and asked his secretary to get Marvin Randall on the line immediately.

"What are you doing?" Decker asked as the knot in his gut began to loosen.

Ford shot him a look of disbelief. "Taking care of things."

That was one of the reasons Decker loved working with his brother. The guy was incredible under pressure.

"Mr. Brand," Jovanna's voice came through the intercom. "I have Heather from Mr. Randall's office on line three."

"Thank you, Vanna."

"Hmm, judging by the way she said Heather's name, it doesn't seem like there's a secretarial sisterhood between those two," Decker pointed out.

Ford mindlessly waved his hand as if dismissing the entire topic. "I went out with Heather once... maybe twice." Ford snickered. "Well, we went out once and stayed in the second time. Heather complained to Vanna that I never called her again and... you know women. V got all bitchy about it. Whatever, let's handle *this* situation and move on."

Decker shook his head and gestured to the phone. "Put it on speaker so I can hear what his goddamn excuse is."

Heather's voice filled the room, and her tone was aloof, if not cool, as she explained that her boss had already left the office for the weekend.

"I just emailed a letter restating the fact Tommy and Vincent Allen were banned from our work site," Ford stated. "I also attached the original email which Marvin Randall, your boss, signed and dated nearly a month ago when the topic was initially raised." When Heather tried to interrupt with a flirtatious comment, Ford cut her off and continued his spiel. "Please make certain your boss sees the email immediately, Heather, because the next time Tommy and/or Vincent trespasses on our property, we will press charges. Have a nice weekend." He ended the call before the woman could fit in another word.

With relief finally settling into his system, Decker sank into his favorite chair. "Thanks, I wanted to tie up the little fuckers with cable and duct tape their mouths closed, but I thought my actions may be frowned upon."

Ford sat back in his chair. "That's why we have each other, Deck. Because I'd rather handle this part. If I had to look filthy like you every day"—his nose scrunched up as if he'd smelled a skunk—"I'd kill myself."

The men quickly discussed their weekend plans before Decker left work to meet April at the gym for their daily workout.

CHAPTER EIGHTEEN

A Proper Date

"MORNING, BEAUTIFUL."

Hearing Decker's sexy voice first thing was the best way to start the weekend. Eli was sitting at the bottom of her bed, watching cartoons, and barely noticed that she was even awake.

"Morning, handsome. I can't wait for tonight," she purred as butterflies took flight in her belly. It didn't seem to matter how often she saw him, the fluttering never lessened. In fact, it seemed as if the beautiful winged creatures multiplied.

"Actually, I wanted to talk to you about tonight."

Dread took over the fluttery feeling as April sat up in her bed. "Decker Brand, if you're canceling..."

His husky laugh was an instant balm to her irritation. "No, babe, I'm not canceling. I am, however, making a demand."

"A demand?"

"Yeah, I want all of you, from start to finish. None of

this meeting at the restaurant bullshit. So tonight, I'm picking your sweet ass up at your house, wining and dining you, and then I'm taking you home. I want the goodnight kisses, the opportunity to run the bases with you," his voice dropped to a gravelly tone, "and if I'm lucky enough to score a run, I want to drive home with a goofy grin on my face. A full-fledged date, April."

His words left her breathless and wanton, a mere tease that would keep her on the edge for the entire day. Christ, the man was sex and lust and romance all wrapped in the most magnificent package. "Okay, Deck. You can pick me up here… and big guy, I see a goofy grin in your near future."

The catch in his breath told her she'd made him a very happy man. "I'll see you tonight, babe."

Just as he'd promised, Decker arrived at her house at seven with gifts for everyone: lavender tulips for April, the latest Disney DVD for Eli, and a six-pack of root beer and a bottle of aspirin for August. After good nights were given and kissy-banks were filled, they left the house for their first *proper* date.

"I've wanted to come here for ages," April said as they pulled into the parking lot of a Mexican restaurant in the center of Charistown. "Janie is always talking about how much she and her friends love The Sombrero. She says the food is great and the margaritas are even better."

"It's true, the food is awesome, and while I'm not a margarita kind of man, the Coronas are ice cold." His eyes dropped to her lips. "And seeing as you're wearing the lime lip stuff, I think this visit will be my favorite yet." He reached around, cupped the back of her head, and pulled her close, taking her lips in a fiery kiss that could rival any hot sauce the restaurant could offer.

She threaded her fingers through his hair, deepening their embrace. "Mmm, I don't want to leave this car."

"Uh uh." He shook his head, puffing out a shaky breath. "A proper date, beautiful." With that, he got out of the SUV and walked around to her side to open the door and help her out.

The restaurant was packed with every table occupied, but they had a reservation and were seated immediately. Both Decker and Janie were right—the food was incredible. As usual, she and Decker filled the hours with easy conversation, arousing flirtation, and witty banter. It wasn't until the restaurant started to clear out and the tables started to empty that April saw the couple sitting just across the small dining room.

Each delectable morsel of dinner turned to boulders in her stomach, and her airway began to constrict as a huge lump formed in the back of her throat. Praying to whoever would listen that she could keep her composure, April stared at the duo and concentrated on her breathing.

ECKER WATCHED AS the easy smile hardened on April's face and the ever-present blush quickly drain from her cheeks. "Hey"—he reached for her hand—"what's wrong, babe?"

Without a verbal response from her, he followed her line of vision and began to piece together the puzzle on his own. It was clear by the smug smiles, loud giggles, and indiscreet whispers from the couple who garnered April's direct attention, they could be none other than her ex-husband and his current wife. It was also apparent that those two found more than a little pleasure in displaying a nauseating if not embarrassing amount of affection toward each other while making sure their eyes were trained on April. Their behavior was an act, of that Decker was certain. He'd lived that life before, pretending everything was perfect when inside, things were at a boiling point. But he wasn't going to express his thoughts to April, because in the moment, his opinion didn't matter. All that mattered was April and how her breathing hitched when Ben and his wife stood up from their table and he rubbed his hand affectionately over her clearly pregnant belly before leaning down to press a kiss on the baby bump.

"Unbelievable," April murmured.

Decker wondered if she realized she'd said it out loud. "I'm here with you, April," Decker whispered, kissing her temple. "You're not alone."

"Hello, April," her ex-husband drawled in an oily tone as he and his wife approached the table. "Glad to see you've moved on… finally."

Decker kept his hands under the table, resisting the urge to choke the weasel in front of him.

Pride bloomed in his chest as April sat back casually in her chair, lifted a brow in her don't- give-a-damn way, and painted a cool smile on her beautiful face. "I've never been happier."

She didn't cling to Decker or use him as a tool to get back at her ex, which was quite sexy, but she also didn't look to him to have her back, and that was not okay. His desire to claim her was as strong as his need for air. So when the smarmy fuck-twit leered at April, allowing his eyes to roam from her face to the plunging neckline of her sexy black sweater, Decker wanted to toss away the table that separated them and pummel the loser. Instead, he took great pleasure in squeezing April's hand and slowly rising from his chair to introduce himself to the much shorter guy.

"I'm Decker Brand, her man. And you're...?" He knew it was a childish move, but between April's smile and the outraged look on Ben's face, it was worth it.

"I'm her ex-husband," the guy seethed. "I'm the father of her son, you... ignorant ass. You do know she has a little boy, don't you?"

"Oh, that's right." Decker tossed a quick glance over his shoulder at April before returning his attention to Ben. "She did tell me Eli's father lived close by but chose to have no responsibility for his own child." Decker sat back down next to April and draped his arm around her shoulders, pulling her chair closer to his. "For some reason, I always think of the guy as dead."

Ben's eyes widened at Decker's statement.

"No, he isn't dead." April shook her head as sadness filled her eyes. "Just said he wasn't cut out to be a father." April turned her focus to Becky. "So you're looking... well."

Becky gleamed, rubbing her hands over her extended belly. "We're pregnant!" When her announcement fell flat, she continued to babble. "We are so excited our little guy is due in less than two months."

Decker felt April's body stiffen with each of Becky's words. His gut churned as he watched the column of her throat work with each swallow.

"That's great." April's false cheer left her mouth in little more than puffs of air. "I hope he's a better father the second time around."

Decker glared at Ben, who at least had the decency to look ashamed.

"Well, that's the thing," Becky chattered confidently , a bright smile plastered across her horse-like mouth as she grabbed Ben's hand and placed it across her belly. "Everyone makes mistakes, April, and Ben made his. He can't be forced to spend the rest of his life dwelling on the past." She leveled her eyes to April's and shrugged. "Therefore, we're thinking of this as *his* first baby as well."

Decker heard April's breath hitch as her spine went rod straight. He firmly gripped her knee to both offer comfort and to keep her seated. He knew in hindsight, she'd hate it if she made a public scene.

"Oh, really? Well, guess what, Becky? I don't give a shit how the two of you think of it, but DNA says he's been a father for close to five years." Her voice lowered to slightly above a whisper as she continued. "And if either of you ever refer to *my* son as a mistake again, you will live to regret it." April turned her fury on her ex. "I will never forget when you came to serve me the divorce papers five days after I'd delivered our baby. You held your son, stared into his eyes, and then placed him and the papers in my lap before leaving." April's voice was quiet, but her tone was strong. "You didn't just sever our marriage. No, you signed away the rights to your firstborn child like he was nothing more than a used car."

Decker's stomach clenched at the new information. How the hell could any man do such a thing? He'd walk through fire for his daughter; in fact, he'd lived through hell for her. April's ex appeared to shrink with each stone cast in his direction.

"So I guess you're right." She pointed at Becky's belly. "That is your first fucking child. Because my son has been and will always be better off without you. Now walk the hell away from our table before I decide to make a scene." April twisted in her seat so her back was to the unwanted couple as they stood with shock etched on their faces.

"Would you like some dessert, beautiful?" Decker tenderly kissed April's knuckles. The pain on her face tore at his insides, but there was no way he was going to let the two assholes who still lingered at the table see anything less than the strength he saw each day.

"Sure." April breathed in deep, clearly trying to firm up the walls that had been damaged through the confrontation. "What did you have in mind?"

The flirty tone in which she asked the question had Decker forgetting about their unwanted audience. "How about the strawberries in chocolate sauce? I know how much you love warm chocolate." He wagged his brows, earning a genuine smile. "What do ya say, dimples?"

"Ick." The disapproving sound came from Becky, who stood table side with her hand tucked tightly in her husband's. "Come on, Benny. Clearly there's nothing more to say, and my feet hurt."

Ben's response came in the form of silence.

"Will you rub them when we get home, baby?"

The high-pitched question, which Decker was certain was supposed to come off sounding sexy, grated on what little nerves he had left and seemed to fall on deaf ears when it came to her husband as well.

"Ben," Becky pouted, "you love rubbing my feet. You know it always leads to—"

"Let's go, Bec."

Without another word, the couple headed toward the exit. It was when Ben helped his wife into her coat just before opening the door and ushering her through that Decker saw tears well in April's green eyes.

◆————————◆————————◆

EACH SHAKY BREATH was an effort as April tried not only to pull in oxygen but to keep the tears that blurred her vision at bay. It wasn't seeing Ben that devastated her—quite the contrary, in fact. On the rare occasion she'd seen him over the years, she'd actively avoided him; his entire being made her cringe. No, it was seeing him happy—his pregnant wife by his side, the way he catered to her needs and looked forward to their future—that crushed her.

"The whole time, it was me." April didn't realize she'd spoken her thought out loud until Decker responded.

"What was you, sweetheart?"

She saw his thumb stroking her thigh but was too numb to feel the comfort it was meant to provide.

"April, let's get out of here so we can talk."

She wasn't sure if she nodded, but Decker saw what he needed to see, paid the check, and led her from the restaurant.

The cardboard boxes that held years of pain and rejection split open as the tears finally escaped her eyes. She swallowed down the lump of shame that had formed the moment she witnessed Ben and Becky head in her direction with upturned mouths and laughter on their lips. "All these years, I forced myself to believe that my husband left me because *he* was an ass. Because *he* couldn't handle commitment. Because *he* didn't want children." Warm sadness trickled down her cheeks as the reality she'd kept hidden in the dark thrust itself directly into the light. "It wasn't that he didn't want those things. It's that he didn't want them with me."

She wasn't sure how or when she'd gotten into Decker's car, only that she was seated and buckled in the passenger side with him in the driver's seat. The engine idled as the heat warmed her chilled skin. She was always cold, no matter how many layers she wore. Even though the spring air was warm, she shivered as her nerves wreaked havoc on her body temperature.

Decker raised the heat and shifted in his seat. His

touch was soft as he wiped moisture from her face, but his gaze was guarded. "Do you still love him, April?"

"What?" Her throat was scratchy from sobbing and her head a mess from the whole encounter, but she couldn't have heard the question correctly.

Decker closed his eyes and exhaled slowly, as if speaking the words caused physical pain. "Do you still love your ex-husband?" His lids lifted, "Do you want him back?"

Was he insane? "Are you insane?" Anger and humiliation mixed together with anguish, creating a bitter cocktail she had no desire to imbibe. "Do I still love him? I loathe him. The sight of him makes me ill." She heard the shrill tone seep into her voice but couldn't pull herself back from the proverbial ledge. "Do I want him back? He didn't just leave me—he abandoned my son, Decker. My Elijah. I couldn't care less if he fell off the face of the earth."

"What? Do you think I've waited over four years for *him*?" April's heart slammed into her chest as the years of loneliness replayed in her mind. During all of that time, she'd never wanted for the Ben she grew to know. She only wished for the dream she'd started with. When Decker opened his mouth to speak, April cut him off. "Just take me home, Decker."

The car was silent on the way back to her house, but her mind was filled with static. The way Ben and Becky smiled, and how he rubbed her stomach and opened the door for her... *we're thinking of this as his first baby,* she said as she looked proud to be the one who carried that honor. *Do you want him back?* Decker had asked, the look in his eyes like a hot poker. Did he not want her after all?

Before she knew it, the lights of her driveway surrounded his car, and her house stood proudly before them. Her home, the place she'd bought for her and Elijah after the divorce was final. She'd made a life for the two of them, a good life, and regardless of how much she cared for the man sitting beside her, she'd never let another guy tear her apart.

"Look, I can't—"

"April," he interrupted, "it's my turn to talk." He unfastened his seatbelt and turned his body to face her. "I'm sorry if my question upset you. It wasn't my intention, but…" He paused. "We've been seeing each other for close to three months, and I just watched you fall apart over a man you once shared your life with. The father of your son." His head tipped to the side. "I had to ask."

April sighed. "Deck…"

"Let's go inside like we planned. Charlie is sleeping at my mom's tonight, so we'll relieve August of his babysitting duties and spend quality time together, just the two of us."

The conversation they'd had earlier in the day felt like a lifetime ago. She'd craved him, his touch, and his taste. The thought of having him, all of him, finally, had made her mouth water and her body ache, but the confrontation with Ben and everything that had happened since left her feeling exposed and raw.

"You actually still want to fuck me?" she hissed, the question crude to even her own ears. "What is it, Decker, some kind of a pity fuck?"

She watched as his clenched jaw ticked and his brown eyes blazed with an emotion she'd never before seen. His silence was deafening as he switched off the ignition, opened his car door, and closed it behind him. Frustration, anger, and sadness warred through her, each battling for top billing as she watched his solid form cross the front of the Rover to her door. When the passenger side opened, she couldn't help but stare at the captivating man who suddenly seemed larger than life.

"Look at me, April," he growled, nostrils flaring as he took measured breaths. "I'm not kidding. You take a long, hard look and tell me if you see—hell, if you've ever seen—pity in my eyes."

The interior light of the car illuminated him, showing fierce emotions as they played across the lines of his face. While she was used to seeing sentiment in his chocolate gaze, he was correct—pity had never entered it. She'd never attached names to what she saw and felt coming from him each time he looked at her, touched her, and smiled at her. In that moment, words continued to fail her completely.

Without thought, she ran her hand over the coarse planes of his cheek. "I see something. I…"

He placed his one large hand on the dashboard and the other on the headrest behind her and leaned forward, bringing their faces just inches apart. "Yeah, you do. You want to know what you see?"

She just nodded quickly.

"You see sadness, because the woman I love is hurting, and it's fucking killing me."

She swallowed. He loved her?

"I needed to ask you those questions earlier, April, because I'm in this"—he gestured between the two of them—"eyes open, parachute off, no safety net. And I wanna make sure I'm not jumping alone."

I'm in this. His words floated in the air as her world stopped spinning. She wanted to reach out, pluck each one, and place them safely in a box where she could cherish them forever. Keep them guarded where no one, not even he, could take them away. Then, as if someone pushed "play," all that he said sunk in.

"You love me?" she croaked as the blood whooshed through her ears.

"Actually, no, I misspoke." Decker's calloused fingers grazed April's chin as he tilted her head back and looked into her eyes. "I'm *in* love with you, April. I have been for a while. I don't need to claim your body for you to have claimed my heart. It's been yours since the beginning."

"Deck, I..." She stopped herself, swallowing a bitter pill of truth that she refused to give voice to. "I can't..." Her feelings ran miles deep, but she had to keep them protected, even just a little longer—not just for her but for Elijah. If she didn't let Decker fully into her heart, maybe she'd survive if he left.

"April," Decker spoke, anguish suddenly replaced by assurance before he kissed her gently on the lips. "I love you, and whether or not you're ready to admit it to yourself, I know you feel the same way about me. I can see it in your eyes, feel it in your touch, and taste it in your kiss. You show me your love in ways you can't even begin to know but ways that mean the world to me." Decker ran his hand through his messy hair. "Earlier, at the restaurant, when everything went down with Ben, I was proud to be by your side. You were amazing and strong, everything you always are... but the things you said afterward, the blame you shouldered..." He scrubbed his hands over his face and turned away from her.

Understanding crashed over her like waves. Slipping down from the SUV, she grabbed his thick arm and urged him to face her, allowing the light from the car to shine on her face. "I understand, Deck. I get why your mind went there, and I'm sorry." When his shoulders sagged, she found relief as well. "I got... I don't know, angry or sad when I saw the life he was making with someone else, a life he claimed he never wanted with me." The memory of Ben smiling as he stroked his unborn child sent a shiver through April. "The thought of him excited for a baby when he threw ours away made me sick, Deck. Can you understand that? Everything about them was the opposite of how he'd been with me. So while I don't and I wouldn't ever want him back, it just stung knowing that he'd found happily ever after even though he was a villain of the worst kind."

Decker sighed, pulling her tightly into his chest. His familiar scent embraced her just as lovingly as his arms. "Sweetheart, I know what you think you saw tonight, but trust me, I was a man living in a marriage of lies. What you think was between them and what was actually going on"—he tsked—"it was two different things, babe."

She smiled to herself as she tightened her grip around him. He was trying to be kind, inserting his own messed up former marriage in place of what she'd seen with her own eyes. She also knew she'd given her ex-husband too much head space on a night when the only man she wanted was standing right before her. While she wasn't ready to return Decker's words of love, she was ready to *show* him exactly how she felt. "Hey, big guy, I'm feeling kinda done with the whole topic. We've wasted enough time."

———————◆———————

D ECKER HELD HER hand as she opened the front door and entered her house. August promptly ended a phone call, grabbed his keys from the coffee table, and stood up from the couch. April looked pleased at the full report August gave of the evening: what he and Eli had done, eaten for dinner, and what time he'd gone to bed. As a fellow parent, Decker knew exactly how much better he felt when he knew his daughter did well with the sitter, no matter who it was.

When August asked how their night had gone, Decker stayed quiet as April described their run-in with Ben and Becky. August's face grew fierce as he listened to each detail, but instead of questioning his sister's responses, he kept his jaw locked and his arms crossed.

"I'm just gonna run up real quick and check on Eli," April announced. "I'll be right down."

The moment she was out of earshot, August gritted out, "Is she okay? That motherfucker did a number on her."

"She was great with him, Aug, but after we left the restaurant, she kind of lost it." Decker squirmed. "And I may have asked her if she still had feelings for him."

August shook his head. "I'm sure she took that well." Sarcasm was evident in both his voice and his expression. "No, seriously, man, I can understand why you'd wonder, especially if she reacted the way you say she did. But I can tell you, that piece of shit disgusts her. Knowing my sister, the whole scene probably wounded her pride more than her heart."

Why hadn't he thought of that himself? *Because you were too busy looking out for your own heart, you moron.*

As if seeing his internal struggle, August clapped him on the arm. "Don't let Ben Spears take up any more time between you and my sister. You're a good guy, Decker, and you make her happier than I've ever seen her. But being left by the *first* man she ever loved, well, that changed her. So when she tries to run, and knowing my baby sis, she will try"—August leveled a sympathetic stare on Decker—"give her space, but don't give up on her, okay?"

"I'm not leaving her, Aug."

"Is August being the protective older brother again?" April bounced down the stairs.

Gone was her sexy black top and tight-fitting pants, and in their place was an old Bon Jovi concert tank top and sweat shorts, yet still his mouth watered at the sight of her.

"Umm…" A familiar blush kissed her cheeks as she

looked from him to her brother and back. "I just figured I'd get ready for bed while I was up there." As soon as the words left her mouth, her cheeks turned a deeper shade of crimson. "Not that he's staying for bed," she denied adamantly to her brother.

"Chill, Tiny." August laughed. "I hope he does stay for bed. Just remember, if he's not gonna cover his head"—he glared between the two of them—"make sure she's covered instead."

"Oh. My. God!" April gasped. "You didn't just say that." She swatted at her brother. "You're just as bad as Mom!"

Decker chuckled as he watched them banter back and forth before hugging goodnight.

"I like him," Decker confirmed as he stood behind April while she locked the front door. He swept her long blond hair over to one shoulder and pressed feather-light kisses over the other. "But I like you more." He nibbled the sensitive flesh between her shoulder and her neck, a spot that had proven to heat her up on more than one occasion.

"Mmm, that feels so good."

"So, beautiful, I know tonight didn't go the way we planned." He moved his hand to her front, sliding one finger slightly under the hem of her tank top, just enough to graze the soft skin of her taut belly. "But am I really not invited to stay for bed?" An accomplished smile graced his face as her breath halted in her chest. The smile turned hungry when she turned to face him with pure desire burning in her eyes.

"Decker…" She swallowed. "I want you, I want you so badly. I've been fantasizing about it for months, touching myself to the sound of your voice and to the image of your face." She pressed her cool hand to her stained cheeks, no doubt trying to rid some of the color. "No pressure, big guy, but I can't imagine how incredible sex with you is gonna be. But I believe the invitation was for a baseball game. No?" Her wink had them both laughing quietly, so as to not awaken the sleeping child in the room at the top of the stairs.

His dick jumped in his pants at the mere thought of sliding into her tight body. As he glided the tip of his tongue up the column of her neck, shivers wracked her body and goose bumps covered her flesh the moment his teeth grazed her ear.

"There will be no sex tonight, beautiful." Placing his index finger over her mouth to stop the protest, he continued. "No, baby, sex is for clumsy teenagers and those looking for a quick release." He walked her backward until she was pressed against the wall, trapping her with his body, his hardness pressing against the soft curves of her abdomen. "That's not us, not now, not ever. First, I'm going to lay you down, strip away your clothes, and taste, touch, and cherish every inch of your sexy body while I slowly make love to you." The feel of her breasts pressed firmly against his chest as her heart pounded had him aching with pent-up need. "Then only after we've both found a small slice of ecstasy"—he dropped his hand to the frayed edge of her shorts and slowly lifted the fabric as his fingers inched up her inner thigh and moved aside her damp lace panties—"I intend to ravish you like the starved man I've become. Goddamn, April, the pleasure of having your sweetness convulse around me while my name tears from your throat, that's been *my* fantasy."

"Yes."

"Yes what, April?" His fingertips traced the skin at the scoop-neckline of her tank.

She licked her lips and pressed them together. "Yes, I want to be your fantasy."

Desire and heat flushed through him as April stood there, glassy-eyed and wanton. They'd waited so long for this moment, had so many almost and close calls, he practically felt like a teenage boy just before his first time. The difference was he was an experienced man who knew exactly what he was doing, and there was no way she'd have the what-the-fuck-was-that look on her face when they were done.

"Does E really sleep deep?" He'd really grown to adore the little guy over the past month or so. He didn't want the poor kid to walk in on anything... life-scarring, nor did he desire *another* interruption. They seemed to be perpetually blocked when it came to carnal matters.

"That little boy sleeps like the dead," April said, running her hands from his broad shoulders down to his rippled abs. "So will you be coming upstairs? Or will it be another entertaining round of phone play for us tonight?"

Decker covered her hand in his and slid it from his torso to his arousal. "I'll be *coming* upstairs... a couple of times, I hope." He winked. "Now lead the way, beautiful."

A bright smile flashed in his direction before April

turned and led him up the steps. The firm globes of her ass peeked out of her sweat shorts, teasing him, taunting him, arousing him further.

"Nice view, babe," he whispered in the hallway, careful not to speak too loudly.

She looked over her shoulder with a grin as she crossed the threshold to her bedroom. "So glad you like what you see."

The door was barely closed before his hands molded against her supple ass. "*They* say seeing is believing. I say, ya gotta touch it to trust it."

The way she laughed at his ridiculous joke just before her eyes widened and filled with heat made his body burn with need, but her verbal response had his heart thrumming with tenderness. "Then touch away, Decker. Touch *away*."

⎯⎯⎯⎯⎯⎯⎯⎯◆⎯⎯⎯⎯⎯⎯⎯⎯

"DON'T EVEN THINK about moving," Decker uttered, his voice gravelly from exhaustion, as he gripped April's naked body to keep her in place astride him.

The feel of his calloused hands gliding on her bare skin made every part of her tingle with arousal. They always had. Although nothing could compare to the explosion the man caused when he finally slid into her body. Christ, there weren't words to describe that kind of pandemonium. As she lay on top of all his masculine beauty, both of them sweaty and breathing each other's air, she couldn't stop herself from leaning down and swirling her tongue over his flat brown nipple.

"Mmm, babe," he groaned as she felt him harden between her thighs once again.

"Impressive," she muttered. She reached between them and swiped the bead of moisture, breaching the head of his shaft. The way his nostrils flared and his eyes bore into her when she lifted her thumb to her lips to lick off his juices made her feel like a goddess. "You taste so good, Deck. I can't wait to get you back in my mouth, but"—she grinded herself on his erection—"right now, I just need you inside me again."

"Fuck," Decker growled as he looped his arms around her waist and flattened her to the mattress. "You have no fucking clue what you do to me, April." He stared into her eyes. "No clue."

Stroking his hardness, April quipped, "I may have some idea."

Decker shook his head, grabbed both of her wrists in one of his large hands, and held them still above her head. "Now, my stunning sassy woman, I'm going to rock your world."

Believing he'd already accomplished that mission, April couldn't wait to see what he still had to offer. So quickly he'd mastered her body, the places that made her squirm and those that made her melt. She'd nearly cried when he found that place inside of her, the special spot she'd read about in romance novels and magazines but never experienced for herself. With his teeth grazing her hardened nipple and his fingers and thumb bringing her indescribable pleasure, April found herself awash in a searing climax that claimed every part of her soul.

"Goddamn." She may have heard wonder in his voice, but her head still spun in orgasmic bliss. "I need you, April."

"Take me, Deck."

As his hardness pushed into her heat, a muffled trill sounded in the room.

"What the…?"

She felt Decker tense, his body still embedded in her own. The trill sounded again.

"That's my phone." Coldness blanketed her hot skin as Decker disengaged and sprang from the bed, reaching into the pocket of his discarded pants.

The red digital numbers on April's clock by the bed told her it was after eleven. Her stomach twisted. No calls at that time were good news.

"Griff, slow down," Decker huffed into the phone, the color slowly draining from his face as he listened to the person on the other end of the line.

"Is it Charlie?" April whispered across the bed, the sheets the only barrier between her nails and the palms of her hands. Nearly tangible relief flooded her system when he shook his head, indicating his little girl was fine.

Decker yanked on his clothing with the phone pressed to his ear. "Motherfucker," he spat into the line. "So where are they?" He listened for a moment before speaking again. "Okay, okay… I'm heading over there now." He listened for a beat while he tucked his feet in his shoes.

"No, I'll call him. Thanks, Griff. I'll talk to you in a few." He disconnected the call and headed for the bedroom door.

"Decker?" April called out. Obviously something horrible had happened—she wasn't an idiot—but was he just going to leave without telling her anything? Was it is Robyn? Ford?

"April," he snapped, "I've gotta go. Now. Sorry." His face was stone, his posture rigid. Nowhere was the man who'd taken her body and claimed her soul.

She followed him down the stairs to the door, wrapped in nothing but a sheet. "Is there anything I can do?"

"No." Though he was still in her home, he was already miles away. "I'll talk to you soon."

April saw him bring his cell up to his ear as he pulled her front door closed behind him.

———•———•———•———

D ECKER PEELED OUT of April's driveway and headed to his job site. "Goddamn it, Ford. I told you those bastards were trouble."

"I know you did, Deck. I'm sorry, I should have called Randall on his cell phone personally instead of leaving the message with that twit of a secretary. Goddamn it!" The strain in his brother's voice echoed through the speakers in Decker's Range Rover.

"Well, Marvin Randall is a clueless asshole, and we could be looking at a very large lawsuit. Fuck!" Decker slammed his hand on the steering wheel.

"I'll call our lawyers, and I'll meet you and the police at the site. You said Griff is already there, right?"

"Yes, Ford. Listen when I talk, man. Dave Griffin is the police chief who's on duty tonight. He's the one who called to tell me those punks cut through our gates, broke the windows, and tried to do some construction of their own." Decker used one hand to rub the cramp that was forming in the back of his neck. "Fucking morons trespassed on our property, screwed with our materials, and when the scaffolding fell on them... we're screwed. Unfucking-believable." Anger ebbed through his body as he recalled the endless weeks of frustration the two men had caused.

"Deck," Ford's voice went from apologetic to authoritative, finally gaining his brother's attention. "Decker, calm down and drive carefully... please."

The call disconnected, leaving Decker alone in his car to process the shit storm that was about to hit BC.

CHAPTER NINETEEN

I'm Supposed to be the Village, Asshole

O
NE HUNDRED TIMES…one thousand… April had no idea how often she checked her phone on Sunday, but it was to the point of insanity. She'd gone as far as to have her sister call and text her to make sure her cell phone was working. It worked just fine.

After waiting up most of the night, hoping to hear from Decker, she'd fallen into a fitful sleep around the time both the birds and her son were waking for the day. Thankfully, Elijah was easily entertained and quite mellow in the early morning hours, so when he entered her room with his blanket and stuffed penguin, all April had to do was pop on a movie, check her phone, snuggle her boy, and go back to sleep. Unfortunately, her mind refused to quiet, and the sleep refused to return.

While Decker denied the problem had anything to do with Charlie, worry about his mother and brother sat in her gut all day, festering like an infected wound. Several times during the day she tapped out a text to inquire if he was okay, but then the harsh sound of his voice and the distant look in his eyes before he'd left the night before haunted her. He'd been buried deep in her body, claiming love, desire, and need, then... he was gone. The physical emptiness jarred her, but the way he shut down was unnerving. Sure, there was obviously something wrong, something very wrong, but he didn't bother to fill her in. He just left her... standing in her house... alone. The familiarity of the situation was uncanny, the anger just as hot, the pain... worse.

She did her best to keep busy that afternoon, taking Eli for new sneakers then to the market for their weekly food-shopping trip, but her concentration was split, her stomach in knots and her head aching.

"Mommy, can I have ice cream?" Elijah asked while sitting in the shopping cart.

"Sure, sweetie."

"Really?" Eli's surprise gave April her first real smile of the day. "You never say 'yes' *before* dinner," her son whispered, as if saying it louder would cause her to change her mind.

April kissed the top of his head, sniffing in the sweet scent of shampoo. "Sometimes, my sweet boy, you just have to say, 'what the fu...fudge.'" She pinched the bridge of her nose, grateful that she stopped the cuss before months of hard work was undone.

"Hmm, no," Eli said thoughtfully. "I want vanilla ice cream, not fudge."

That time, April laughed as she strolled the cart to the dairy counter.

A couple of hours later, April's already frazzled patience was tested further while she and Eli were at her parents' house for dinner, a bi-weekly event that was enjoyable as long as her mother kept her opinions to herself.

"April," Ellen sighed. "I see you checking your phone under the table every five minutes and, like drying paint, watching it won't make whatever you're waiting for happen sooner. Put the phone away, dear, and enjoy the family time."

Had April been in a better frame of mind, a calmer place, she'd have noticed that there was no bite in her mother's voice, no pinched expression on her face. However, the whole day had passed, and still Decker never reached out to her. He'd left her without explanation and clearly without concern. As far as her mother's advice, she could shove it up her judgmental ass.

"I'm going outside for a minute... or ten," April huffed quietly, trying her best not to worry her son, who stared amazed at his grandfather's hands, trying to figure out just where the coin had disappeared to.

Thank God for Dad and his ageless magic tricks. She looked down at the cell phone gripped tightly in her fist, where it had been since the previous night. It suddenly felt too cumbersome, too pathetic. She placed the device on the table and headed out of the house before she said or did anything that couldn't be retracted or explained to Eli.

The squeaking of the porch swing brought instant comfort to her battered heart, allowing slices of reason to filter into her conscious thoughts. Maybe her mother wasn't completely wrong *this time*. Decker had made his choice when, after he voiced his deep devotion and soul-searing love, he left her practically naked with his cum still warm inside her body and a glacial look on his face. She'd have understood if he'd explained what was going on, but obviously she warranted nothing. His love meant nothing. Once again...her heart meant nothing.

"Tiny..."

"Honey..."

Both August and Ember startled her when they joined her on the porch.

"Move over, girl." Ember said wedging herself on the left side and August on the right. "Hopefully this old swing can still handle the three of us."

The comment was more like a prayer as the old swing winced under the additional weight.

"April, it doesn't take a rocket scientist to see that you're hurting. Christ, even Mom was being sympathetic," Ember mused. "Tell us what the hell happened so August can kick this guy's ass and I can ruin his social life forever."

"That was Mom's sympathetic side?" April shook her head in disbelief. "No way, how does the woman have any friends?"

"Tiny, you and she have been battling for so long that you see and hear everything she does as a jab or an insult." Understanding filled August's eyes. "I don't blame you, I really don't, and she's treated you differently than the rest of us for, well, always." He and Ember shared a look that April didn't care to decipher. "Ember and I have never understood it, and trust me, we've tried to figure it out. But

I can tell you this, tonight, Mom really was trying to be helpful, kind even."

"Aug, I'm thrilled you're all pro-Mom and shit, but she's created the relationship we have. I'm trying my fucking best to be considerate toward her especially in her own home …" *No matter how old we get, we need to show our mothers respect.* Those had been Decker's words to Eli. She'd not only listened to them but taken them to heart, hence why she'd bit her tongue just moments before and left the house. What a shame his advice didn't include respecting one's girlfriend. Her throat tightened and a pit grew in her belly as she breathed in through her nose and out through her mouth, doing her best to avoid tears. Shaking off the melancholy, April resurrected the wall of indifference she'd lived so many years behind and pulled out her armor suit.

"It was strange to see her so… what's the word I'm looking for?" Ember stared blankly into the twilight sky. "Nice. Yeah, let's call it nice, for lack of better words."

Even stifling their chuckles, both Ember and August sounded like nasally lunatics.

Her siblings always made her feel better. They didn't even need to try—just their presence provided April with a sense of love that no other person had ever given her. Well, except for Decker, but she was done with him. Yeah, done. Finished.

"Look, children," she mock scolded, trying not to let the corners of her mouth turn up. "Can you please put down your Mom pom-poms and focus on something I actually care about?"

"And that is?"

April released a heavy sigh, filled her sister in on the events leading up to and including them arriving back at her house, then explained to both of them what had happened after August left them, in her brother's words, pie-eyed and drooling all over each other.

"Tiny"—August rubbed the shadow of scruff growing over his jaw—"I know this looks bad, I do. And if it were any other man, after I kicked his ass, I'd tell you to move on. But it's not. I've met this dude a few times, and I'm telling you, there's an explanation."

"An explanation?" April seethed, the taste of bitterness finally seeping into her words as well as her mind. "There's no explanation, August. It takes two seconds to send a text message. Two. You're saying I'm not worth two motherfucking seconds?"

Ember clutched April's arm, her touch instantly dispelling some of the ire that boiled April's blood. "Come on, April, we both know that men are stupid."

"Helloooo." The way August dragged out the word had both women snickering. "Man sitting right here." August pointed at himself. "You're right, okay, what he did is terrible"—he shot a pointed look at April's older sister—"but Ember, I saw him last night. Hell, I spoke to him. Fucking guy is crazy about her. And not in the 'I own her like she's my favorite pair of underwear' crazy, like that freak she was married to. I strongly believe it had to be something extremely important to pull him away like that."

Fighting back the tears that filled her eyes, April

looked straight ahead and swallowed. Crickets and the sound of rusted metal squeaking above them filled the silence.

"You're right," April muttered. "It had to have been something big. Something so huge that he tossed me aside and ran." She wiped the lone tear that escaped its confines then looked at both of her siblings. "Thing is, I've already been tossed away. I've been told I wasn't enough, and you know what?" Identical crestfallen looks surrounded her. "It sucks. And I don't wanna go through it again. I can't." She looked at her watch. Eight p.m. had come and gone. They'd been out there for an hour, and it was past her son's bedtime. "I need to get Eli home." She swallowed the tennis-ball-sized lump in her throat. "But thanks for talking to me. I love you guys."

She walked back into her parents' house to find a freshly bathed child snuggled up on the sofa in her father's arms.

"We figured it would be easier on you if he was clean and ready for bed," Ellen spoke as she handed April a bag with Eli's soiled clothing. No matter how coarse her mother was to her, she was always marshmallow soft when it came to her grandson.

"Thanks, that was really helpful."

"April, listen—"

"Not now, Mom." Exhaustion ebbed through April's body. "I just can't get into anything with you tonight. You want to cut me down, tell me how much I screw up, or laugh at my foolishness... just do it tomorrow. Because, right now, I don't have it in me to fight back."

Was it guilt that passed over Ellen's face? April wasn't certain, but she knew she was too tired to stick around any longer. After her father tucked a sleeping Elijah into his car seat, they hugged tightly, and she headed home.

◆————————◆————————◆

DECKER SCRUBBED HIS hands over his face and stifled another yawn. He stared out the large plate-glass window in his brother's office and watched the moon make a brief appearance before it was shrouded once again by clouds. Was it really nighttime again?

"It's fucking late, Deck," Ford grumbled, pouring two tumblers of scotch. "Can't believe we've been at it for two fucking days."

Decker accepted the glass and took a sip of the liquid. The scotch was incredible—his brother only drank the best—but fatigue had robbed him of his senses hours before, hence the only thing he knew for sure about the amber liquid was that it was wet. "What a goddamn clusterfuck." Decker gulped his drink as the adrenaline finally began to leave his body.

His brother stood beside him, taking small pulls from his drink. "The police are gone, and those two assholes are recovering in the hospital." Ford's brow arched as a mischievous smirk lifted one side of his mouth. "Maybe the internal bleeding will teach them not to trespass again."

Decker snickered, uncertain if he was appalled at his

brother's callous response or amused by it.

"According to our lawyers, all the legal bullshit that said assholes will try to sue us for is taken care of, and"— Ford's brows snapped together as his voice deepened— "they will not get one fucking penny from us, because you had that site closed down according to legal specifications, and those little fuckers worked pretty goddamn hard to get in. Today was a publicity nightmare, thanks for suiting up and handling the press with me."

Decker drained his glass and looked pointedly at his best friend and business partner. "You know we're in this together, Ford. Fifty-fifty. I'd never let you face anything on your own. That said, this debacle is far from over."

Both men grimaced.

Decker tried to smooth out his tattered clothing before reengaging his brother, who looked equally disastrous. "We should probably head home, shower, and get some sleep before we go back. Mom called the office to say she was keeping Charlie at her house for another night. Thank God for her."

Laughing, Ford pulled out his phone and tapped out a quick text before addressing Decker again. "A shower and sleep sounds perfect. I have a car coming, because neither of us should be driving in this sleep deprived condition." When had his little brother turned into such a responsible man? As they rode the elevator down to the lobby, Decker felt every single one of the hours he'd spent caught up in the work crisis plow into him. Hour by hour ticked backward until he was eye-to-eye, body-to-body with the woman he loved. "Fuck."

"You okay?" Decker felt Ford's steadying grip on his elbow. "You wanna sit down until the car comes?"

Decker reached into his pocket and yanked out his phone. "Give me a second, Ford." Decker knew in his gut even before he pressed send that he had screwed up. He didn't realize how badly until he heard April's voice on the other end of the line.

"Deck, is everything okay?" Her brittle tone told him that things were definitely *not* okay. But he knew that wasn't the question she was asking.

"Yeah, babe, I'm so sorry about Saturday night. Do you remember those guys who kept causing all of the problems on my job site?"

"Yeah."

Decker swallowed. "Well, they broke into the building and caused an accident. They were both badly injured, and Ford and I have spent the whole night and day trying to make things right." Decker saw Ford's questioning expression but brought his attention back to April.

"Okay." The two-syllable word was as flat as paper.

"April, I'm sorry, really—"

"Hey, Deck?" His heart pounded into his ribs as he held the phone closer to his ear in order to hear her quiet words. "That excuse you just gave me, it took less than two minutes."

He heard her shallow breaths and wanted to reach through the phone to hold her. "I know, but that night—"

"No," she interrupted him again. "Saturday when you were in my house, you knew it was a work-related emergency, and you didn't bother to give me even that much information. You just shoved your dick back in your pants and left. Did it even occur to you that I'd be worried? Waiting? Scared? Did you even think to text me just to say that everyone was okay?"

No, those things hadn't crossed his mind, but not for the reasons she probably thought. He, however, didn't have the chance to explain.

"I'm so sorry that those guys caused you and Ford so much trouble. You must be beside yourself worrying about the legalities and the ramifications of that mess." The fact that she even thought about his work situation when she was so upset blew him away. "And thanks for finally getting around to calling me, Deck. I didn't realize it was such a fucking chore." The small sob he heard nearly brought him to his knees. "But now I'm gonna show you how communication really works. I don't want you to contact me again. We're through."

"April, wait. April!" He pulled the phone from his ear and stared at the screen, seeing exactly what he was afraid of. The call had ended. They had ended. "FUCK!"

"Hey, Deck, what the hell just happened?"

With his heart in his throat, Decker explained where he had been and what he had been doing when he received the call two nights before.

"Okay, so there was a work emergency, people were hurt, and you had to leave. Big deal." Ford's nonchalance breathed some semblance of hope into Decker's mind. "She'd have to be a cold-hearted bitch not to understand that." Ford cocked his head. "I thought you said she wasn't anything like Olivia."

"April is *nothing* like Olivia," Decker snarled, the need to defend April an overwhelming urgency. "She wasn't being cold-hearted, Ford. I never told her what was going down. She didn't know it was work related. She didn't know if it was you or Mom. All she knew for a fact was that it wasn't Charlie." As Decker said the words out loud, he realized just how tortured April must have been during the two days she'd waited to hear from him.

"You fucking moron." Ford snickered just as the car pulled up to the front door. Once the two men were inside and buckled up, Ford laid into him. "Let me see if I have this straight—"

"You really don't need to rehash it, Ford. I get it, I'm an asshole," Decker muttered.

"Oh no, I'm totally rehashing, because it ain't often I get opportunities like this. And you, big brother, fucked up royally."

Decker breathed in deep and nodded silently. Yes, yes he did.

"So you finally have April, the woman who's rocked your world since the minute you laid eyes on her, and while I think monogamy should be reserved for swans and antelope, you two haven't been with anyone else, or each other, for that fact, since this whole"—Ford actually appeared to twitch when he uttered the word—"relationship started. Deck, I've met this woman." To Decker's annoyance, Ford's brows wagged comically. "She's smokin'. So you finally have her under you, dick firmly planted in her sweet pus—"

"Ford," Decker snapped, "that's *my* woman. Move

on."

All traces of humor left his brother's face. "Exactly, she was your woman, Deck. Yours. And not only did you answer the phone, which of course I understand because of Charlie, but you bolted without any sort of explanation? Shit, did you even kiss her good-bye?" Decker sat silently as Ford let out a low whistle. "Dude, I'm supposed to be the village asshole, not you."

Blowing out a lungful of air, Decker closed his eyes and let his head fall back on the plush headrest of the limo. "Olivia never wanted to hear about work," he admitted. "In fact, she couldn't stand listening to it. As long as the money came in, all was well in her world." As the memories formed inside him, the words bubbled out like carbonation breaking at the surface. "I know they're not the same, Ford, okay. I know it." His voice cracked with emotion. "Christ, one of the first things she expressed just now was her concern for me, for how worried I must be about the company." The burning sensation he felt in his eyes was from a whole lot more than fatigue. "It's just… I'm so used to keeping that shit locked down. You know?" His brother stared, not acknowledging one way or another, but Decker continued to speak. "Yes, I've discussed BC with April," he quickly catalogued their chats, "and yes, she's always shown interest, but old habits die hard," he finished weakly.

"Old habits die hard?" Ford sighed. "You had me until that last shitty-ass line."

Decker glared at his brother, not finding any humor in the situation.

"Look, the only good part of Olivia was that she gave you Charlie. That little girl is a rock star. But otherwise, you know damn well, while I hate to speak ill of the deceased, the woman was nasty. I've met April. So has Mom. She's good people, Deck."

"I know she is."

Ford shrugged as if the answer was as easy as a simple apology. "Make sure she knows that you're seeing only *her,* and that the past is where it belongs. Buried."

"And how do I do that? What should I do?" "

"Dude, you really have no clue about women do you?" Ford chuckled. "It's all in the flowers. The bigger the better."

Had Decker not been exhausted he would have rolled his eyes instead, he just closed them.

CHAPTER TWENTY

No Whites and No Dents

A FTER RUNNING FIVE miles on the track at the middle school where she worked, April drove home to get a shower before picking Elijah up at day care. It had been months since she'd exercised anywhere other than the gym where she and Decker met, but that afternoon, she couldn't make herself go there. She needed the cardio to burn off the anger, frustration, and hurt that were lodged in her chest, but the thought of seeing him and pretending that she was okay or, even worse, not seeing him and wondering where he was made her stomach twist.

The car was unusually quiet. No music, no chatting on the phone, just the breeze filtering in through the open windows, cooling down her sweat-slickened skin. She didn't need additional noise when her mind was filled with the previous night's heartbreak. Learning, after nearly two full days, that she hadn't been a thought in his mind while he'd occupied almost all of hers would have broken her if she'd let it. The pain felt as real as any wound she'd ever suffered in the past. "Thank God I never told him I love him."

A little voice in her head chastised, *Just because you didn't say it doesn't mean you didn't feel it.*

She swiped the tears that trailed down her cheeks, remembering the way Decker had filled her body with his own, the way he touched her skin, made love to her heart, then just as easily tore at her soul when he left without giving her a second thought.

"I was right to end things." She sniffled. "Better to leave him now than to have him decide to leave me for good later."

Feeling better after her shower—well, at least cleaner—April grabbed her keys and walked out to her car. She felt his presence there waiting for her on her porch but couldn't bring herself to acknowledge him. Not when the pain was still so raw. So instead, she continued the short distance to her car.

"April, we need to talk, please."

Pulling in a shaky breath, she turned to face him. It looked as though she wasn't the only one who hadn't slept in the last two nights. Purple smudges rested under Decker's dark sullen eyes, his hair was rumpled as if he'd run his fingers through it dozens of times while searching for answers, and judging by the tightness of his jaw, he hadn't found them. He wore a tee shirt and shorts, his basic exercise garb, but neither appeared wrinkled or sweat-stained. It took physical effort not to rake her eyes up and down his body, not to reach out and touch the man looking destroyed in front of her, but she stood firm. She kept her distance and reminded herself that *he* left *her*.

"No, Deck, we have nothing to talk about." Once her body thawed from its frozen state, she attempted to walk around him to her car.

"April?" He reached out and wrapped his fingers around her wrist. The warmth of his skin sent tingles up her arm before branching out through her abdomen. "I'm sorry."

When Decker closed his eyes and inhaled deeply, April contemplated tearing her arm free and escaping to her car, but when his lids lifted, the honesty she saw staring back at her kept her rooted in place.

"I can't take back what I did. It was a dick move, but it wasn't intentional, and it won't ever happen again. Olivia... she never wanted to know about work-related stuff, and it pissed her off if work interfered with our personal life. She more than once told me she'd rather not know where I was than to think work was more important than she was."

There was no way April heard him correctly. What woman would feel that way? Her skin felt chilled when Decker released her arm and wrung his hands together.

"After she passed... well, I haven't had to explain my whereabouts to anyone but Charlie in a long time..." His pained eyes met hers as he finished his explanation. "After waiting a lifetime to meet the perfect woman, I found you, and when we finally got the chance to be together... work got in the way." His fists clenched and unclenched as his frustration rose to the surface. "My mind flipped onto auto-pilot, April. *Take care of work and then go home to her.*

Just the way I did with Olivia."

"Just how you did with Olivia?" Icy water thrown in her face wouldn't have appalled her more than being compared in any way to the heinous bitch he'd been married to. "Tell me, Decker," she seethed, "what part of *me*, of *our* relationship has reminded you of your marriage?" His rounded stare and wordless response ratcheted her anger up even more. "You came over here to talk, so talk! When did I ever act like your work wasn't important? Did I shut you down or turn you away when you discussed your jobs or the two men who were giving you a hard time?" Had the volume of her voice not increased, she swore he would have heard the sound of her heart slamming into her ribcage. "The same two men who were the reason for the emergency call on Saturday night. You said you loved me—"

"I do, baby, I'm so in love with you."

As Decker stepped forward, she took a step back. "No, you obviously don't even know me. Reality check, Decker, I would have understood. I would've been supportive, I would've welcomed you back with open arms had you just trusted me." Her throat felt thick as her thoughts churned in her head. "I've been hurt before, and the pain was unimaginable…" She breathed in deep, trying to get enough air in her lungs to say what was on her mind.

Decker's eyes flared. His brows snapped together, and April knew that he understood she was now comparing *him* to her ex-husband.

"I'm nothing like that sorry son of a bitch."

Unwanted tears stung her eyes, but she refused to let

them fall. "Ben left me for another woman, and I couldn't imagine anything ever hurting worse, but I was wrong. I'd rather be left for someone else than just not be important enough to hold on to." Barely keeping her own emotions in check, April quickly shifted her glance away from Decker's, knowing that she would crumble if she saw in his eyes a modicum of the pain she was feeling staring back at her.

"April."

Shit, she didn't need to see his face to hear the agony in his plea.

"It shouldn't have happened, and I'm so fucking sorry, but I promise you"—the pain was masked with surefire determination as his vow landed on her back—"it will *never* happen again."

Keeping her back to him, she nodded once. "I believe you, Decker—"

"You do?" His relief was nearly tangible as he approached her from behind, wrapped his arms around her, and dropped a soft kiss on her head. Being in his embrace felt like visiting one's childhood home after another family had moved in—familiar but temporary, comfortable but no longer safe. "April, oh, honey, thank you."

"No, no, stop." She turned to face him, and bile inched up the back of her throat. Pressing her lips together, she lifted her eyes to his. "I believe you're sorry, Decker. And I also know that it will never happen again, because I'm never gonna let it. I'm done... we're done. I can't do this anymore."

While Decker stood there speechless, she got into her

car and drove away. *Keep it together. Keep it together.* She chanted the words over and over in her head as she forced even breaths in through her nose and out through her mouth. There was no way she'd pick Eli up from day care with red puffy eyes and a runny nose. No, she had to stay strong for her little boy because he was going to suffer enough for both of them. She bit down on the inside of her cheek, and the metallic taste of blood hit the tip of her tongue.

"This is why you didn't date, so Eli wouldn't have to suffer through your breakups," she scolded herself. "Now he too will hurt because you had to be selfish. Fuck." Having to explain to her son why they wouldn't be spending time with their favorite duo made her sick.

As she pulled into the parking lot, April had convinced herself that it would be best for Elijah if she redirected all discussions that geared toward Decker and Charlie for as long as possible, making up excuses for Decker's absence until absolutely necessary. Then she'd tell Eli a portion of the truth. After all, she thought, how much could a four-year-old really understand?

She slapped on a smile, exited her RDX, and entered the building where her son was awaiting her arrival. *I made the right choice*, she reminded herself again as she signed in at the front desk. *Eli's my first and only priority. The last thing he needs is a basket case for a mom.*

✦━━━━━✦━━━━━✦

"**H**EY, ALL, SORRY I'm late," Decker called out as he walked into his mother's house after work to find his brother and daughter sprawled out on the floor in what appeared to be an epic Wii battle of *Mario Kart*. He smacked a loud kiss on Charlie's cheek, her giggles warming him up from the inside out.

"It's okay, Daddy." Her attention never left the television. "Grammy gave me a snack a little while ago so we could wait for you to have dinner. But I'm still hungry." Charlie's hazel eyes widened with excitement as she crossed the finish line before her uncle. "We're having pancakes! Wanna play again, Uncle Ford?"

The hunger that had gnawed in his gut only seconds before fled, leaving an unsettled pang of yearning and loneliness. He could almost taste the surgery strawberry syrup that April and Eli drowned their pancakes in and the way her lips glistened with the pink confection after she'd finished eating. The Tuesday nights the four of them shared at IHOP were some of his favorites, and in the two weeks since she'd left him standing in her driveway, he'd mourned for them as much as everything else. With Charlie and Ford wrapped up in another race, Decker headed into the kitchen, popped open a beer, and watched his mother turn batter into magical discs of love—her words, not his.

"Hello, son."

"Hey, Mom." He leaned down and pressed a kiss on her soft cheek.

Robyn flipped a pancake before shifting her eyes first

to Decker's beer then back to the cooktop. "I know for a fact that your mother taught you better than to serve yourself without asking others if they'd like something."

He fought the urge to grin. "Uh, gee, Mom, would you like something to drink?"

"Why, yes, honey, I'd love a beer. Thank you for asking." She flipped another pancake and mumbled with a smile under her breath, "What a thoughtful man."

He knew her comment was meant to be a joke. After all, he'd always been known as the considerate one of the Brand boys. He was the one who remembered birthdays and special occasions. He was the responsible one who had stepped in when his father died and watched over his mother in the best way a sixteen-year-old boy could. He kept Ford out of trouble and cleaned up after his brother when the trouble wasn't avoided, and when he made a poor choice and married the wrong woman, he had at least been smart enough to make sure a pre-nuptial had been signed, protecting BC in the event anything went wrong— foreshadowing at its finest. Yet when it came to April...

"Sweetie, what's going through that head of yours? I can practically hear the cogs turning." Robyn slid the fluffy cakes out of the pan, turned off the heat, and sat down on the stool at the breakfast bar. Decker took her raised brows as his invitation to join her.

"I've always been thoughtful, Mom." It was a statement not a question.

Placing her hand on her chest, Robyn sighed. "Oh honey, I was just joking before. Of course you're a thoughtful man." His mother's tone was filled with compassion. "You're kind and considerate. I'm blessed to have you for a son, and Charlie couldn't have a better father."

He nodded, believing the things his mother said. Not because he was cocky but because he lived his life each day trying to be the best person he could be—loyal and fair to others, considerate and truthful without intentionally being unkind but also without getting stepped on. That last part was learned throughout his marriage to Olivia and during the time he grieved her passing. However, he still hadn't learned one extremely important lesson, and that may have cost him the woman of his dreams. "Yeah, I may be all of those things, Mom, but—"

"But you fucked things up with the girl." Ford clapped his hands on Decker's shoulders and squeezed before releasing and grabbing a beer from the refrigerator.

Decker tensed as his inner thoughts were verbalized.

"Ford," Robyn barked, "there's no reason to be obnoxious. Your brother knows he screwed up. We've discussed it at least a half a dozen times."

They had. Decker hadn't seen his mom that angry in years as she was the night he called to tell her what had happened with April. Robyn actually drove to his condo to reprimand him about his carelessness in person once Charlie went to sleep. Although once she released the woman's wrath inside of her, she morphed back into Mom-mode and comforted her son and his broken heart.

"He's right, I fucked up with April. She won't so much as return my texts, and today I found out that she put her gym membership on hold indefinitely."

Each day that went by without contact was worse

285

than the day before. Knowing she was out there moving on and not knowing if he even crossed her mind was a form of torture he wouldn't wish on his worst enemy... okay, he wished it on Ben Spears, but that was it.

"I miss her," he rambled. "I understood before why she was upset when I went radio silent for an entire twenty-four, especially the way I left her, but now... after weeks of nothing... I'm going out of my fucking mind. I just want to know she's okay." He looked from his brother to his mom, not expecting information but wishing they had an answer anyway. "I miss Eli. That little boy is ...grrr ... he's something special. You both know me. You know I don't make the same mistakes twice, you know that." He wasn't certain why he was pleading his case to them— maybe because they were the only two who would listen to him. "I just... I don't know."

Robyn reached over and placed her hand on his. "Do you remember the night I had you meet Charlie and me at the IHOP for dinner?" Her question, coming from out of left field, threw him for a loop. Thankfully his mother didn't wait for a reply before continuing to talk. "As you walked me to the door, you said we would discuss how I knew to bring you there for dinner, but that conversation never came to fruition."

"Oookay." With that night going as well as it had, Decker had completely forgotten about his mother's intervention, but now that she mentioned it... "So that wasn't some crazy coincidence then?" Robyn's arched brow made him laugh.

"Do you not know our mother at all?" Ford snorted.

"There are no coincidences with her."

Decker didn't miss the mischievous look Robyn shot at an unsuspecting Ford before she turned her attention back to him. "No, Deck, it wasn't accidental," she admitted. "I happen to play cards at the community center with April's mother, Ellen. Oh, honey, don't make that face. Yes, the woman is definitely... interesting, and I get the impression that she and her daughter don't see eye-to-eye on, well, anything. But I do know that she loves April fiercely." Decker watched as his mother's cheeks flushed, something he'd only seen on very rare occasions. "I wasn't trying to meddle when I told her about the gym you belonged to. After all, she said her daughter had all but locked herself up in a self-made prison for years—her words, not mine. And of course, when we realized that the two of you were not only dating but really hitting it off, Ellen told me that her daughter would 'muck it up' by keeping you at arm's length and using her son as the reason, so I decided to delete that barrier."

Decker's head was spinning. How in the hell had all of that happened under his nose with neither of them the wiser?

Grimacing, his mother looked at him. "On a scale of one to ten, ten being really pissed off, how angry are you?"

Was she insane? Angry? He looked from her to Ford and back. "Mom, I'm a negative twenty. I can't believe you did all of this for me, for us. I... wow. But why?"

"Because, honey, when you first met the *sexy woman* from the gym, you became someone I hadn't seen in years. You were happy, excited, and content. All from just a few words here and there with a *beautiful stranger*. Ellen, bless her heart, said she'd never seen April so confident and happy. What kind of mothers would we be if we knew how to make things better and we didn't?"

"Wow, and I had to screw it up. I'm not sure I'll ever get over her, and knowing how much time you invested —"

"Bro," Ford interrupted, "I thought we discussed this. You're not giving up on April—you're just giving her some space. Trust me, I *know* chicks. She loves you, and she knows you're one of the good ones. Now stop being a pussy and do what needs to be done."

"Ford Marcus Brand," Robyn snapped, "you know I have no problem with language as long at my granddaughter isn't in the room, but *that* word? Ick. It's offensive. Don't forget, I'm still your mother, and punishment can still be dealt."

Ford looked cocksure, as if there was nothing his mother could do at his age that would hurt.

"I made pecan pie for after dinner. Use *that* word again, and you'll not have even a sliver."

His bottom lip curled downward, "Sorry, Mom."

"Hmm." Decker mussed his brother's perfectly styled hair. "Your knowledge of chicks truly is amazing."

Ford flipped him the finger, and their mom flicked Ford with the spatula. The three of them howled with laughter. For Decker, it was the first time in two weeks he'd even cracked a genuine smile, and it felt great. His brother was right; there was no way he was giving up on April, not yet. He couldn't let her go without one hell of a fight, and in the end, if she really was done with him, then he'd respect her wishes.

———————————♦———————————

WITH HER SATCHEL on her desk, April glared at the pile of term papers she'd collected throughout the course of the day. "I'll never learn," she muttered under her breath as she began to shove the reports in her bag.

Each year she swore to her colleagues that she would never give out long assignments again, because while it forced the students to use the skills they'd learned during the year, grading them became a nightmare for her. Not to mention she liked to get the grades back to the students as soon as possible, which meant sending Eli to her sister's for the weekend. It just so happened that her poor planning had the papers due the Thursday before Memorial weekend, so she would work around the clock for the first half of the holiday then spend the second half with her little boy and her family. Eli didn't mind because Ember belonged to a pool club, but just the thought of working Friday night and all day Saturday had her thumping her head against the hard wood desk.

"Ah, there's the pleasant April Maddox I know and love." Rori put her hands in front of April's forehead, protecting it from further blunt force trauma. "Couldn't help yourself, huh? Had to go and give the annual tight-ass term paper?" Rori crouched down and looked April square in the eyes. "You know you're doing this to yourself, right?"

"What exactly am I doing now, Ror?" April sighed. "I give this assignment every year, and I hate it every year. But I think it's important so—"

"Do. Not. Play. Dumb with me, chica. It isn't a good look for you." Her friend stood up and grabbed a chair from one of the pupil's desks, brought it next to April's, and planted herself down. "Do you know what I love about you?"

"My hair?" April deadpanned.

As if she hadn't responded at all, Rori continued to talk. "I love your strength. I love your ability to pick yourself up and move the fuck on. You don't just limp, you soar, and it's amazing to watch. Hell, April, it's inspiring." Rori's eyes flared with admiration. "When that shithead you were married to ripped your life apart, you grieved and then you mended. You're an amazing mother and a wonderful friend…"

"But?" April questioned uneasily.

Rori sucked in a breath. "But that strength has, in some ways, become your weakness. You wear your tenacity like armor, making it practically impossible for people to get through. April, you've mended, yes, but you haven't healed. And that, my sweet friend, is what will bring you down. Sometimes moving on means allowing yourself to actually let go of the hurt from the past. Because holding on to it will block you from finding the happiness you truly do deserve."

The scrape of Rori's chair on the linoleum floor jarred April from her silent state. "I didn't force him to leave me." She wasn't sure if Rori had heard her whispered comment when, after a few seconds, there was no response.

"Who?" Rori finally snapped.

"Either of them." April's voice was loud but shaky. "They both chose to leave on their own. And I refuse to beg anyone to stay with me, Rori. They want out?" She pointed toward the hallway of the empty school building. "There's the fucking door."

Shaking her head, her eyes filled with what looked like sadness instead of anger. Rori placed both palms on April's desk. "That, that right there is what I'm talking about. Listen to yourself. Ben was a cheating, lying asshole, April, and by the sounds of it, he always was. Compare that to Decker. The man made a shitty choice, one bad move in a litany of great ones. Someone finally manages to get past your protective wall, they make a mistake, and you kick them out forever. You kicked him out after he apologized. You. Not him. He came back begging." She pushed off the desk, spun on her heel, and headed for the door. April watched as Rori pivoted just before she exited the room. "Wow, chica, it must be really hard dealing with such flawed people when you're so perfect yourself."

At a complete loss for words, April stood there blinking as her friend left her and the building behind. As if talking about him summoned him, April's cell phone lit up with a text message indicator. While it wasn't the first time he'd attempted contact in the past couple of weeks, seeing Decker's name on the screen in that moment sent butterflies soaring through her belly, but her feelings still felt jumbled. She missed him, that much she was sure of, but was she ready to put aside her fears to let him back in? Was Rori right? Did she hold people to an impossible standard only to toss them away when they failed to meet her bar? She hadn't always been so cynical, but naiveté had gotten her burned.

Decker: *Let's talk*

She needed to sort things out in her own head before adding him, his tender voice, his soft touch, and his playful sense of humor back to the equation. She deleted the text, grabbed her bags, and headed to pick up Eli.

"Mommy, when are Uncle Gust and Aunt Member coming to get me?" Eli scooted off the oversized, upholstered armchair that faced the large window and shuffled over to April.

"Any minute, sweetie," April replied, her eyes focused on the first term paper in the stack.

"Are you sure you can't come with us for ice cream? It'll be fun."

Ugh, she hated missing out on family time, but it was Thursday night. She figured if she made even a small dent in her grading, she'd be able to join her family for dinner on Sunday instead of picking Eli up from her sister's afterward. She looked into her son's big innocent eyes. "Not this time, honey, but definitely next time." She forced a smile before returning to the paper in front of her.

"Mommy, are you okay?"

She recognized the wariness in her son's voice, and

immediately the work she was doing was forgotten as she pushed her chair away from the table and lifted Eli to her lap. "Sure, baby, why?"

While they had had a simple chat regarding the absence of Decker and Charlie—namely that everyone was busy and there wasn't time to see each other—April had done her best to change the subject every time Elijah mentioned them.

"Your face isn't happy again." He touched her cheeks with his tiny hands.

"Again?"

"Uh huh." He nodded short quick nods. "Before, you didn't smile with your *whites*, and then you did!" Her little boy's eyes grew large at whatever memory sparked in his mind. "When Charlie and D-man came around, you showed your whites and your dents. You look pretty when you smile, Mommy."

"I'm smiling right now, Eli." April's stomach knotted at the realization that her four-year-old son had noticed the change in her demeanor.

"No whites and no dents, Mommy. I miss seeing them, so maybe you guys could get un-busy soon, okay?"

"We're here!" Ember called as she and August entered the house. "Who's coming for ice cream?"

"Me," Eli chanted as he hopped off April's lap and ran to his aunt and uncle.

April waved off August's concerned glance and called out her request for a cup of mint chocolate chip ice cream for when they returned.

Sitting alone in her house, trying her hardest to concentrate on the students' reports, her silent thoughts became stifling. They sucked the air from around her until finally she had no choice but to pay them the attention they sought. The past two weeks tumbled through her mind—no, the past few months danced through her memories. While her friends and family members were incredible and supportive, right down to the verbal ass-kicking Rori had given her earlier that day—it was Elijah's simplistic view that finally ripped the blinders off her stubborn eyes.

She'd spent four years *protecting* her child from people she thought would hurt him, leave him, or make him feel unloved; but in the end, it was *she* who'd removed affection and love from his life, and it was she who'd removed it from hers. Eli was right. Decker made her smile, a real smile, one that she felt clear to her bones. While he had screwed up, there was no doubting the agony she'd seen in his eyes when he came to her. He wasn't Ben. He'd learned from his mistakes. Now she needed to prove that she could learn from hers.

But how... how was she going to do it?

Pacing the floors, her mind reeling with decisions, she was startled when the front door opened. "God, that took you no time at all." She swooped Eli into her arms and pressed her face into the top of his head. "Mmm, you smell like waffle cones."

"Tiny, we were gone for two hours." August arched his brow. "You okay?"

Inhaling deeply, April thought for a moment before looking at both of her siblings. "I think I will be"—she smiled—"I really do. Now, let's get Mr. Waffle Cone bathed and ready for bed. Ember, you're still good to have him for the weekend, right?"

"Oh, we have big plans, don't we, E?"

With a loud yawn and a wide smile, Eli reached out, gave kisses to his aunt and uncle, and wrapped his arms around April.

"How about if we wait down here so we can chat after he goes to sleep?" Standing with his muscled arms crossed over his chest, August's presence would intimidate most people, but not April.

"I promise I'll talk to you tomorrow. Let me marinate on my thoughts overnight, and I'll run them past you guys first thing."

"Ahh, look at that, Aug. See that smile?" Ember pointed. "There's some good stuff rolling around in that brain of hers."

"I know," her brother agreed. "That's why I'm scared to leave her alone." He cocked his head to the side, staring as if trying to figure out a puzzle. "Do you have any clue how eff'd up this whole thing could get by morning?"

"Guys," April hissed, not wanting to startle Eli, who was fading fast in her arms, "stop talking about me like I'm some mental patient in need of a rubber room."

"Well..." August chuckled. "If the straitjacket fits..."

April's eyes narrowed, but she felt no anger toward her siblings as the three of them quietly laughed at her expense. "Good night, you two, and thanks for taking this little guy out. While I didn't get much grading done, I actually got a lot accomplished."

CHAPTER TWENTY-ONE

Wonderful and Fabulous. Feel better? Egos stroked?

"**G**ET UP, SLEEPYHEAD. The car's all packed up and ready to go." Decker smiled as he swept away the long tangled hair from Charlie's sweet face and pressed a soft kiss on her sleep-warmed cheek.

She groaned, pulling her blanket over her head.

He couldn't blame her. Hell, the sun had barely risen. "You remember what today is, right?"

As if he'd whispered magic words, Charlie popped up and squealed with delight. "Yes! I forgot for a minute, but now I remember. I can't wait to ride the new waterslide, Daddy. It's gonna be so much fun."

His daughter's enthusiasm was the only reason why he hadn't postponed the trip in favor of pounding on April's door, forcing her to see how right they were to-gether, and seeing the radiant smile on her face reaffirm he'd made the right decision. It wasn't that Charlie would always come first, leaving the woman he loved doomed to a life of second place. It just meant that turns would be taken, choices would be made, and he knew of all people, April understood exactly what that meant.

"All right then, baby doll, go brush your teeth, get dressed, and meet me in the kitchen for a quick breakfast. I'd like to get on the road soon so we can get the entire day in at the park."

His daughter treated him to another brilliant smile before hopping out of her bed.

The cooler on the island was filled with snacks and drinks, in case traffic got heavy, and Charlie's electronic devices were charged and packed in a duffle bag. Yep, he had everything under control. The only thing missing were the two people he'd hoped would be joining them on this year's adventure. His eyes roamed once again over the text icon, and disappointment jabbed his gut. He'd hoped she would respond to his text from the previous evening. According to information his mom gave him, it seemed as though April wasn't faring much better than him. Robyn had told him that April's mom had said April had been unhappy, moody, and sad since their breakup. Something had to give.

His heart thundered when the phone resting in his hand vibrated, but when the screen showed it wasn't April calling, the desire to answer nearly left. "Hey, Mom."

"Decker, the excitement in your greeting makes a mother feel so loved," Robyn teased. "Anyway, honey, I know you're going to be unavailable for the rest of the weekend, so I just wanted to tell you and Charlie-bear to have a great time."

"Oh, thanks, Mom. We will. She loves this weekend."

"No, baby, you both love this weekend. I promise, things will work out the way they're meant to with April, so enjoy the time you have with your little girl, because before you know it, she'll be a grown-up, and these days will be nothing but a memory."

His mother's words didn't fall on deaf ears. He heard what she said, as well as what she didn't say. After all, one never knew how much time they had with their loved ones. Decker made sure his mother had the phone number of the resort he was staying at just in case of an emergency, then they disconnected their call. He and his daughter had some waterslides to conquer, but first they had to navigate the drive.

* * *

DISCOURAGED, APRIL CHECKED her phone again only to see that Decker hadn't returned the text she'd sent him during her lunch break. After a restless night, April had dropped Eli off at day care then three-way-called Ember and August on her way to work. While they both seemed satisfied that she had finally pulled her head out of her ass—their words, not hers—they weren't comfortable with her waiting the entire day to contact Decker.

"Haven't you waited long enough?" Ember whined.

"Games are for children, April," August grunted. "You don't play well, and you lose even worse. Call him now."

April pressed her lips together. The taste of the lime balm, Decker's favorite and the one she'd avoided using since they broke up, sent flutters through her belly. "I'm not playing a game, guys. I just know that if I call him now, he'll want to see me... now." Just the thought of breathing his same air had her heart thumping and her panties dampening. "And we both have a long day ahead of us. I'll text him later and set something up." Excitement poured out of her as she explained what she was going to say to Decker once she got him face to face.

Elation must have beamed from her face, because the moment she entered the teachers' lounge, both Rori and Janie stared at her with slack jaws and curious expressions.

"Uhh, graded a really great paper last night, did ya?" Janie teased.

April's lips curved up as her eyes went from Janie to Rori. "No, not quite." The singsong response only further flummoxed her friends as she lowered her bags to the empty chair and floated over to the only other people standing in the room. "Just so happens I have a best friend who gets pleasure out of punting my ass back onto the Yellow Brick Road when I go too far astray and a kid who's too wise for his age."

"So wait," Rori interrupted, "am I the good guy in this *Wizard of Oz* reference or the bad guy?"

Janie snickered. "Get your panties out of their twist, Ror. It sounded like you were Glinda or maybe a munchkin, but no way were you the nasty green bitch or a flying monkey. Right, April?"

April looked from one friend to the next and blinked... twice. "Are the two of you fucking crazy? Yes, Rori, you're goddamn Glinda. But that has nothing to do with anything, so keep up!"

Rori first filled Janie in on the mini-intervention she'd had with April the day before, only to learn that Janie had been gearing up to stage one of her own.

"I, however, would have included you in my 'Save April' mission." Janie aimed her death glare directly at Rori.

"I'm sorry, Janie." Rori's choked apology came through a tight smile. "There was no time to contact you. Our girl here was talking to herself while slamming her head on her desk. Had I let it go on for too much longer, she'd have turned out like Sloth from the *Goonies* movie." Rori shrugged. "Then we'd have a whole different set of issues to deal with."

"Ladies," April barked, "you're both wonderful and fabulous. Feel better? Egos stroked?" It felt as if it had been ages since the three of them goofed around in such a carefree way, and she hated to end it, but the lounge had begun to fill, meaning the first bell wasn't far behind.

Quickly April explained how even though she'd been missing Decker like crazy, it was Rori's *tough love* that got her thinking about her own imperfections and Elijah's words that made her realize that she wasn't just giving up a man but her own happiness, as well as that of her son.

"I want him back," April repeated the words she'd said to her siblings.

"Why?" Rori asked, not a trace of humor in her tone.

"Because I need him in my life. Because Eli adores him and because we make sense."

Janie closed her eyes. "It's not enough, honey. You know that. That night, before he left, he came to you with his heart. What are you willing to give him in return?"

April knew what her friend was asking. Was she able to give him *everything*?

"April"—Rori's stare was loving but not gentle—"if he came to you *now* offering anything less than everything, I'd ruin him." Rori stepped close to April and tapped her fingers on the left side of April's chest. "Make sure you possess what he needs before you take this thing any further. You've both been hurt enough."

April knew damn well what she had to offer, but as much as she cared for her friends, the first time she admitted those feelings for Decker would be to the man himself. So instead, she nodded solemnly and grabbed her bags as the first bell rang.

April: *Hi*

April: *You're right, we do need to talk. Can we do it today?*

April: *... I miss you.*

There was no way she could wait until the end of the day to contact him. She was surprised she even made it until lunch. The glow that poured from within her faded with each hour that the texts went unanswered, and by the time she was at her sister's house with Eli and his weekend bag in hand, her nerves had practically gnawed through her stomach lining.

"Call him," Ember insisted. "Maybe he's waiting to hear your voice."

Once she arrived home, she grabbed a glass of wine and a blanket from the sofa, wrapped the blanket tightly around her curled up form, and nestled into the chair that had recently found its way back to the small front porch after spending the winter hibernating in the garage. The sun was just dipping into the horizon, highlighting the clouds in a pink glow and painting the sky purple, when she dialed Decker's number.

She left a message explaining that she was ready to talk, ready to work things out, and ready to let go of the things that had held her back before. "Please call me back." She tried to keep the desperation out of her tone, but somehow, she felt she failed in that mission.

After several ineffective attempts at grading term papers, another glass of wine, and the realization that more than just a couple of hours had passed since her call to Decker, April gazed out at the dark sky, taking in the crescent moon, and wondered if possibly she'd actually blown her chance at happiness.

"Tiny, why would you listen to Ember's advice when it comes to men?" The disgusted humor coming from the phone was exactly the reason she called her brother.

"Because I knew you'd tell me to go over to his place naked, August, and that wasn't the advice I was looking for."

Silence met her ear before her brother spoke. "The whole concept makes me nauseous, April, you know that, right? You're my baby sister, for Christ's sake. I don't wanna picture you naked. However, you called me now, which means you want my opinion, so here it is. Decker isn't waiting to hear your damned voice, he needs a grand gesture." August huffed. "Go over to his place with a bottle of his favorite drink, in some skimpy lingerie, and show him just how much you've missed him."

"Oh, really? That is so cliché, August!" Even as she criticized the words, she rummaged through her cabinet, looking for the vodka she knew Decker favored.

"It's cliché for a reason, little sis." August's smile could be heard through the phone. "It works. Women always over think and overanalyze, but you and November aren't too far off when you make fun of us men. We're simple creatures. With fine drink and great sex, in either order, we're as happy as kings. So go polish his scepter… err… okay, that was too far, even for me. I need to go puke."

If her brother didn't sound as if he was ready to lose his dinner, she would have ribbed him for suggesting such lewd actions. However, hearing someone vomit was one of the things that she hated most in the world. So instead she changed the subject. "Hey, it's Friday night. Why are you even home talking to me?"

"It's the twenty-first century, little girl. Who says I'm home? Now, go crown your king… yeah"—he gagged— "still no good. Let's just drop the whole royalty reference, shall we?"

They rang off, and April brought her things inside, took a quick shower, and readied herself to go to Decker's.

It was about ten o'clock when she was ready to leave her house, and while she adored Charlie, she hoped the little girl would be asleep. If not, April's clothing was child friendly, but what was underneath wasn't for public consumption. A tingle ran up her spine. Hopefully there would be a lot of consuming done once she and Decker had talked through their issues.

Pulling in a fortifying breath, April opened her front door. Standing there with one hand up, fisted as if ready to knock, was… Becky Spears.

"And the flying monkeys have arrived," April mumbled as the breath quickly left her lungs.

Gripping the solid door frame tightly, her legs trembled as she stared into the eyes of woman who had slept with her husband. The woman who had shamelessly taken something that didn't belong to her without care, without remorse, and judging by the run-in only a few weeks before, without regret.

April breathed in slowly. The shock of Becky's presence washed over her, and once it was gone, she was able to register the true being who stood at her doorstep. Becky's normally coiffed hair and pristinely applied makeup was a disaster. Black lines of mascara traveled down her cheeks like a river cutting through caked-on cosmetics, leaving banks of blush and foundation on each side.

Standing tall and steady, April stared at her nemesis. "What the hell do you want?"

"April," Becky sobbed, using the back of her hand to wipe at the tears, causing even more of a makeup malfunction. "It's Ben…"

Had he died? While she hated the man, he was her son's biological father, and she'd spent years loving him… she quickly searched deep inside herself and realized that she'd already grieved the loss of Ben Spears the man. If he died, she would only grieve the passing of a young person. "Becky, say what you need to say and then leave." April tapped her nails on the door frame. "I don't have all night."

Sniffling, Becky rubbed her open hand across her rounded belly and looked over April's shoulder into her home. "Um, can I-I have a tissue, please?"

Narrowing her eyes, April stood quietly for a second, suspicious of Becky's every movement, of her mere existence. *What does she want at my house now?*

"Sure." April shut the front door, leaving her uninvited guest on the opposite side, and grabbed a couple of paper towels from the kitchen. *No soft tissues for that home-wrecking whore. I don't care what her problem is.* She opened the door and handed the rough paper to Becky.

"Thank you." She muffled blowing her nose into the first towel and wiped her face with the second. She blanched when she saw the remnants left on the paper. "I must look like a horrible mess."

Was she kidding? Did she expect April to soothe her feelings and play nice? "Becky. Why. Are. You. Here?"

"April, do you think I can come in? I really need to talk to you."

"No." April finally reached the end of her line. Her patience was gone, the time was slipping away, and she needed to get to Decker's house. "You cannot come in my house. It's mine. I know you have difficulty understanding that everything is not yours for the taking, what with my husband being so easily snatched up, but this is my property, my life, and here, *you* are not wanted, so—"

"Ben left me, April." Tears once again streamed down Becky's blotchy face as her body was wracked with hysterical sobs. "He's been cheating on me for months with his secretary. How fucking… cliché."

The world stopped spinning as April listened to the words that poured from Becky's mouth. He'd told her she was too cold, too independent, that she'd gained too much weight, but it wasn't until Becky stated Ben's final excuse for leaving that April, once and for all, absolved herself of any blame in the ultimate demise of her marriage to Ben.

"He… he told me that he still wasn't ready to be a father. That maybe he never would be."

April hadn't realized that during Becky's revelation, they'd both inched toward the porch, but now she was grateful they had, because the iron seat that she'd vacated hours earlier was the perfect spot for her to land on when her knees all but gave out. Becky sat down on the second chair opposite the tiny metal-and-glass table.

"Wow." Her mind was so overloaded, and words were lodged without a means for escape.

"April, I just told you that my husband left me. He's fucking the chippie who works in our office, I'm close to eight months pregnant, and he wants nothing to do with our baby. What should I do? Please, you've gotta give me something more than, 'wow'."

April's eyes sprang open as her jaw dropped wide. "You're kidding, right?" Word blockage no longer an issue, she sucked in a deep cleansing breath to settle the rage boiling within and leaned toward her ex-husband's wife. "*I* don't *gotta* give *you* anything." She kept her tone low, her temper reined in. Because the truth was, Becky didn't even deserve her emotions. "I'm not exactly sure why you decided to come to *my* home when *your* husband left"—Becky opened her mouth, but April lifted her hand to stop the response—"because we are not friends. We are not allies. We are not sisters scorned. You did something horrendous; you carried on an affair with a married man. No, you weren't the one cheating, Becky, he was, but you lacked conscience and morals and values. I was nine months pregnant, and you didn't care. Where in the hell was your sense of sisterhood back then? In fact, I still don't know why you came to me at all. Go to your friends, you mother, hell, go to your damn priest."

"April, I'm sor—"

"Nooo." April shook her head slowly. "I'm not finished. I had my baby more than four years ago. Where were you? Were you on the sidelines coaxing your husband into seeing his son? Were you urging him to have a relationship with his firstborn?" April's brows snapped together in mock confusion. "I can't remember, did you? I do, however, recall perfectly the night you had the audacity to strut your marriage and your baby in front of me. You told me that child in your belly would be Ben's firstborn because my son was a mistake." April snorted. "Good times, huh?"

"I'm sorry, April. I really am," Becky pleaded. "I didn't realize—"

April released a humorless laugh. "What didn't you realize? That the same damn thing *could* happen to you? Or that it *would* happen to you? See, that's the problem, Becky. If we were friends, way back when, I would have warned you that a man who cheats *with* you will have no problem cheating *on* you." April sighed. "But we weren't friends then, and we aren't friends now. Our sons may be half brothers"—April saw the same awe in Becky's eyes at the revelation as she'd felt when she first saw the expectant couple in the restaurant weeks before—"but that still doesn't make us friends. Maybe one day our boys will meet. Who knows, Ben may have left a trail of fatherless children by then." Her heart clenched at the thought of so many little kids wondering where their daddy was and why he'd gone away. She rose from the chair and headed back toward the entrance of her house.

"Oh my God." Becky gasped through her hands. "I never even thought about the fact that my baby already has a big brother."

White-hot fury burned through April's chest. "Hasn't that always been your problem? You've never thought of anyone but yourself. Go away, Becky."

Defeat, while clear in Becky's blue eyes, didn't stop her from calling out to April's retreating form, "April, I just need to know one thing, and then I promise I'll leave you be."

April gazed over at a very pregnant Becky, who stood with her hands wrapped around her belly as if she intended to protect her unborn baby against any battle they may face. Regardless of their warped past, April respected the determination she saw in the other woman's eyes. "Go on, ask."

"How did you do it? How did you move on and take care of your son and yourself on your own? You asked for nothing from that bastard, but look at you." Becky gestured toward the house. "You have it all."

Almost, April thought, *almost*. "That little guy you've already fallen in love with?" April pointed at Becky's stomach. "That's how you do it. You figure your shit out and fast, because your baby didn't ask to be born. He only asks to be loved." She saw a fresh round of tears begin to form in Becky's eyes.

"I'm not like you, April. Ben isn't getting out of this without paying child support. This is his baby, goddamn it."

April had no doubt Becky would make Ben pay, and part of her was glad. That son of a bitch needed to accept responsibility for his actions. "Good-bye, Becky," April called over her shoulder as she walked into her house and closed the door.

Sinking into the oversized armchair, April pulled the blanket over her chilled body. The second Becky's tail-lights disappeared into the night, adrenaline seeped from April's body, releasing an emotional outpouring that no amount of ice cream would be able to pacify. She needed comfort and support, not because she felt weak but because she finally felt strong. Becky's visit, while disturbing, had given her the closure she'd unknowingly waited four years for. April had already known she was in love with Decker before Becky knocked on her door that night, but now armed with the knowledge that her ex-husband was a runner—it wasn't *her,* it was *him*—the last piece of her protective shell crumbled away, leaving her wide open, vulnerable, and ready to finally give all of herself to the one man who truly deserved it.

The problem—it was after midnight, her face, post-crying jag, most likely didn't look much better than Becky's, and Decker still hadn't returned her call. Wiping away the last of her tears, April plucked her phone from her jacket pocket and made one last attempt at contact.

"Decker, it's me," she informed the voice mail, "I'm not giving up on us. This time I made the mistake, and I'm sorry. Please, big guy, call me back."

Still snuggled in her favorite blanket, April climbed the stairs and got into bed. Still dressed in her comfy clothes with the sexy lingerie underneath, she drifted into a dreamless sleep.

CHAPTER TWENTY-TWO

The Young and the Crazy

B ARELY THERE LIGHT forced its way through April's window as the thick grayish clouds held the sun captive behind them. Rainstorms and thoughts of Becky's visit had awakened her several times during the night, and musings of Decker had kept her from effortlessly falling back to sleep.

She grabbed for her phone and called her sister, knowing full well that neither Ember nor Eli would be asleep at eight in the morning on a Saturday. Once she'd spoken to both of them and filled Ember in on her surprise visitor, which left her sister in a speechless state of shock—speechless because April quickly reminded her that Elijah was in the house and all language needed to be G-rated—she hung up and tried calling Decker once again. When the voice mail kicked in, she hung up.

"'Leave a message?' What in the motherfuck!" She screamed to the empty room. "Okay, I get it, I hurt him. But I got hurt too!" April paced. "What the hell am I supposed to do?"

She couldn't just storm over to his condo, pound on his door, and demand he speak to her, because no doubt his daughter would be awake, and that's not the role model she wanted to be. However, she couldn't wait until later that night to try a second attempt at the lingerie seduction because there were too many hours between now and then, and she was through sitting on her ass. August had been right when he said she'd been playing games—she just hadn't realized it. Thinking of games...

She grabbed her phone once again, breathed deep, and swallowed, before slowly dialing the one number she never thought she'd use for advice... ever. "Hi, Mom, um... I need your help."

"Hello, dear. What can I do for you?" While the tone wasn't warm and fuzzy, it also lacked the frosty bite April was used to hearing. It almost sounded like a normal person's voice. *Strange.*

"So you know how I was seeing that guy for a little while?"

"Yes, April, the man from the gym."

April rolled her eyes, awaiting the next comment, the one where her mother would point out how it was she who'd gotten April the membership to the gym in the first place, hence wanting some type of gratitude for the entire relationship. However, the follow-up comment didn't come.

She just asked a simple question with a sincere tone. "What can I do for you, dear?"

With a silent prayer and a sigh, April told her mom

the condensed version of her relationship with Decker. She, of course, left out the part where she texted him first, but she also refrained from telling Ellen that Decker had said he loved her. The last thing April wanted was a lecture about a man who declares his love just before or during *intercourse*. Been there, done that. While Ellen had apparently been right about Ben, April knew in her gut that sex had nothing to do with Decker's feelings.

"Hmm, that's quite a story, little girl."

"Look, Mom..." April strolled into her kitchen and turned on her Keurig. Discussing relationships with her mother before her first cup of coffee was never a good idea. Hell, discussing anything with her mother before coffee was a terrible idea. "I know that you and I don't see things through the same eyes. I'm not sure when it started, and I guess at this point it really doesn't matter, I just need your help—"

"It started with Ben."

The creamer missed the coffee cup, spilling onto the counter, as her mother's response startled April speechless.

"Sure, you were always strong-willed and independent, so we butted heads when you were young, but I loved seeing that fire in your eyes," Ellen continued evenly. "It was when you started pining for and then dating that horse's ass that the fire turned to flickers, and then finally, it burned out. I tried to talk to you about it, but we ended up arguing, and that, April, was my fault. I was the parent, and I acted more like a child than you did."

April stared at her coffee mug, unable to drink a single drop, afraid of choking on the liquid instead of swallowing it. Never in all her life had she heard Ellen Maddox apologize for anything; this was monumental. What did it mean? "Mom—"

"Just wait a second, dear. I acted poorly, but you—you dated that dipshit for years. He was horrible to you, and you allowed it. You, my dear girl, were a moron."

Annnnd there's the mother I've grown to know and tolerate.

"One of the smartest things you ever did was not chase after him for child support and custody when he left you and *your* son," Ellen's voice carried a steely tone as she discussed Ben's defection of her grandson. "Elijah should spend every day of his young life knowing just how wanted and loved he is, and you are doing a pretty damn good job."

Good? "Wait, I'm doing a good job? What the fuck does that mean, Mom?" The whole conversation felt like a roller coaster ride, and she hated roller coasters.

"Well, it's not just important for my grandson to know and feel loved. It's important for him to see how loved his mother is as well. You haven't allowed either of you that opportunity until this man Decker and his daughter came around."

Her mother's words, while for once she didn't believe them to be malicious, made her cringe. Hadn't she come to that same conclusion last night? She hadn't been shielding Elijah; she'd been hiding with him.

"Mom, I think you play bridge at the community center with Decker's mom," April blurted, her mouth moving faster than her mind. She'd meant to ease into it, ask if maybe she knew of the woman and go from there, but instead, she jumped in full throttle. She was once again stopped short when her mother's response shocked her.

"Of course I play bridge with Robyn Brand. How do you think I knew which gym to buy you a membership to?"

April grinned. Some things never changed.

"She's a lovely woman. A bit too involved in her sons' personal lives, but I like her just fine."

Information overload? Sure, the past twenty-four hours had been chaotic, but what she wanted most was still not within her reach. "Do you have Robyn's phone number? I can't get in touch with Decker, and it's important."

Without question, Ellen recited the digits, wished April luck, and disconnected the call.

She began to dial Robyn only to realize she had no idea what she was going to say to the woman. So instead, she drank her lukewarm coffee, took a shower, and made the call when she finally felt comfortable enough not to sound like a fool.

_____

"WAIT, LET ME go where I can hear you better."

April heard the cheering getting quieter in the background as August made his way to a less crowded area. "I'm sorry to bother you while you're at the Phillies game, Aug, but Ember took Eli to the movies, and they won't get out for at least another hour. I don't want her to worry about me if I don't pick up her call."

"Sis, what the hell is going on? When I didn't hear from you last night, I assumed the *royal* plan had worked."

For the third time that day, April told the debacle of the previous night, but this time, she added her conversation with their mother as well as the one she'd had with Decker's mom.

"Holy shit, your life is like an episode of *The Young and the Crazy.* I'm not sure if I should be entertained or exhausted."

"It's *Young and the Restless*, you fool." She giggled.

"Yeah, that too. Just drive carefully and text me when you get there." August's voice rumbled, "I love you, Tiny."

"Love you, too."

With less than an hour of drive time left before getting to the Poconos, April turned her iPod on and thought back to her earlier phone conversation with Robyn.

"April, honey," Robyn Brand had said to her when she called to learn of Decker's whereabouts, "it's lovely to hear from you."

April remembered Decker saying that his mother had taught both he and his brother impeccable phone manners. Clearly the woman led by example.

"What can I help you with?"

Jittery, April had cursed the fifth cup of coffee she'd consumed, not the usual amount for her by that point in the morning. While nerves ate away at whatever stomach lining the coffee hadn't touched, she knew that it was time to pull up her big girl panties and talk woman-to-woman with Decker's mom. "Robyn, I'm sure you've probably heard what went on between Decker and me?"

"Yes, April, I did. And I was really disappointed in my son's behavior."

Had it snowed in Hell, and she just hadn't heard about it? For real, how often did a mother agree to the fact that her son had acted like an ass? Robyn had expressed her disappointment to a practical stranger when April knew damn well that both Decker and his brother were the lights of their mother's eyes.

"No son of mine should ever treat a woman like that," she'd continued. "Not any woman, let alone one that he's crazy about. So believe me, he got an earful. But I don't think that's the reason for your call. Is it?"

Fairy wings and pitchforks tangled in her tummy as Robyn's words settled. Of course April knew Decker cared. She'd believed him when he said he loved her, but hearing it come from his mother was a different type of surreal. That said, if Robyn knew about Decker's role in their breakup, she must also have known about hers.

"No, Robyn, that wasn't why I called. I called because while Decker did screw up, I did too." April drew in a breath and continued to speak. "I was angry, and I know I had the right to be, but I'm not the only one with a nasty past. And I forgot that for a while. Now I'm scared. I'm scared that I've let things go for too long and Decker may have moved on."

"April," Robyn's tone was amused, "why do you think he moved on?"

"Because as embarrassing as this may be to admit, I've been texting and calling him since noon yesterday, and I haven't heard back from him." April heaved a sigh. "After everything that happened, I assume that if he wanted to talk to me, he would have reached out by now."

Robyn snickered. "Oh, honey, you know what they say about assuming?" April felt a lick of embarrassment run up her spine, but it quickly faded with Robyn's next statement. "He and Charlie went to the Poconos this weekend. I think he may have told you about it, right? The indoor water park? Anyway, it's his weekend to unplug from work and the world. His phone is locked in the safe in his room. It may be on, but the ringer is off. Even I am to call the hotel and have him paged in case of an emergency."

As if someone had stuck a thumb drive into her head, memories of Decker inviting her and Eli away with him and Charlie resurfaced. Even as she broke them apart, he still tried to keep them together.

"Shit! Err, I mean... no, I meant shit. Robyn, I'm such an idiot."

"No, honey, you're human. I'll text you the address. I know he'd be happy to see you."

Was she kidding? "Are you kidding? Do you think I should interfere on his time with Charlie?"

Robyn's laugh had been musical. "You're not an interference, April. You were supposed to be there. Drive carefully."

Not thirty minutes later, April had left a message with her sister explaining where she'd be in case Eli needed her, thanked her mother for helping out and also gave her the lodge information in case of an emergency, packed an overnight bag, and headed north to Great Wolf Lodge.

As she pulled her Acura into the massive parking lot, she realized she hadn't called ahead to reserve a room. That would have to wait, because the only thing she could think about was finding Decker and finally being back in his arms.

CHAPTER TWENTY-THREE

A Family-Friendly Establishment

THE WARM, CHLORINATED air blanketed Decker's body and tickled his nose as he and Charlie walked from the arcade back into the water-themed area of the park. It had been a half hour since they ate lunch, and while he didn't ascribe to the waiting-before-swimming rule, he took the waiting-before-water-rides rule quite seriously. There were few things more disgusting than watching a kid vomit their meal down the length of a slide. He'd witnessed said act his first trip to the lodge with Charlie, and the horror and shame that he'd seen in the eyes of both the unfortunate child and his parent was something that Decker never forgot.

"All right, Charlie-bear, time's up. We can go back in the water."

"Yay!" his daughter cheered. "Can I go with Sam and play in the sprinklers?"

The boy standing next to Charlie smiled with a gap where two teeth used to be. Decker still couldn't believe how much he'd grown from the previous year. His eight to Charlie's six had never seemed more pronounced than it did now.

"You'll watch out for my girl, right, Sam?"

"You bet, Mr. Brand." Sam's blue eyes sparkled with the responsibility.

"Daddy, I'm not a baby," Charlie pouted.

"You'll always be my baby." Decker winked. "Now go play before I'm ready for another round of slide races."

Within seconds, the two kids were surrounded by others laughing and splashing and having the time of their lives.

When they'd arrived early the day before, he and Charlie checked into their suite, had a quick snack, and went to the ropes course. It was something she'd been too afraid to try the year before then spent the next twelve months mentally preparing for the challenge. Decker wasn't sure who was more proud of her success: himself or Charlie. Either way, she'd made him promise to do the course once more before the weekend ended.

After they had lunch they went to the resort's version of an enchanted garden. It had been Charlie's favorite part of the trip the previous year, and it seemed to have retained its charm, because his little girl's smile had nearly split her face as her magic wand cast spells and created beauty. The first day of the trip was always his personal favorite, because it was their family time, their time to bond before the other families got there and the trip became more social.

Today, as expected, the other three families had arrived, and both he and Charlie were excited. He'd already caught up with the fathers and sons while the mothers and daughters were at the salon, getting their fingernails painted.

"Well, if it isn't Decker Brand. How are you, my friend?" The attractive woman smiled as she rested her towels on the lounge chairs and looked up to meet his gaze. "Long time, no see."

"Janine the Queen," Decker teased, using the nickname bestowed upon his friend back in their college days, and he chuckled when her eyes narrowed in mock irritation at the old rib. "I'm doing well. And it has been too long. My God, Sam looks like a whole different boy." Decker pointed toward where the children were playing. "Seriously, the kid must have grown four inches since last year."

Janine threw her head back and laughed. "I know. If he keeps it up, he'll tower me by the time he's ten."

Decker smiled as he looked at her from head to toe. The woman was only about five feet tall, so her prediction may not be that unrealistic.

"Gimme a hug, Deck." She stood up on her toes and looped her arms around his neck. "Remember when we all saw each other every day? Man, times have changed."

Happily, he pulled his friend in for a squeeze, remembering the four years the group of them had spent together, a force to be reckoned with. They had an unbreakable bond so many years later. As he dropped a kiss on the top of Janine's head, something moved to his far right, catching his attention. As if pulled by a magnetic force, his entire being shifted when the one woman he'd been dying to see suddenly came into focus, and as luck would have it, it was during the one damn moment he'd had his hands, even platonically, on another female. His body was glued in position, unable to move, speak, or breathe as their eyes locked.

Even from across the vast space, he could feel her heart rate double as her breaths became shallow, or was that his? Her mouth formed a perfect "O," yet to his surprise, April didn't turn away. No, she just stood there in the moist, warm air and stared. He could practically see her rearranging the pieces in her mind, trying to discern what in the hell she was supposed to do next. Was she going to leave? Stay and fight? It didn't matter, because there was no way he was going to let any sort of misunderstanding get in the way. Not ever again.

"Goddamn motherfucking son of a bitch," Decker ground out as the spell finally broke, allowing him to pull away from Janine.

"Uh, Deck, you okay?" Her concern was evident, but there wasn't time for explanations.

"No. Hey, Janine, can you and Michael please watch Charlie? I'll be back as soon as possible. If she asks, I'm fine. I...uh...went to make arrangements for dinner."

"O... okay..."

Anything Janine said after agreeing to look after Charlie fell upon deaf ears, because Decker had already made his way halfway across the watery haven with his mind set solely on making things right between him and April once and for all.

TONE STILL, APRIL took in the scene unfolding before her. After the two-hour drive and prolonged search, she'd finally spotted Decker across the teeming water park, chatting animatedly with a pretty woman just before the two embraced. Her knee-jerk reaction was horror and jealousy, but her gut instantly redirected the thoughts with reminders that Decker loved her. He'd tried to contact her just a couple of days before. There was no way he'd move on that quickly, especially not with Charlie around. *There must be an explanation.*

When their eyes locked, she immediately knew her gut had been correct. Who knew a man could convey so much with a simple stare. There was certainly no misconstruing the foul language that seeped from his clenched jaw as he spoke to the woman before him. While she tried to regain his attention with what appeared to be gentle shakes and soft words, his molten brown gaze bore into April's, rooting her to the ground, holding her captive. Her heart began to race as Decker rounded the woman and quickly stalked in April's direction with fire, hunger, and determination engrained on his beautiful face.

"April."

"Decker."

They spoke simultaneously. His hand snaked out, and the touch of his knuckles as they traced her jawline sent tingles through her body. It had been weeks since she'd felt his touch, and just the small reminder was enough to make her want to beg for more.

"What…what are you doing here?" Curiosity was written over his features, and hope sprinkled like seasoning through his tone. "I mean, Christ, April, I'm so fucking happy you're here, but"—he huffed—"how are you here?"

Unsure if she wanted to laugh or cry at the relief she saw in his face, in his entire being, she settled for both. Hot tears stung her eyes and a smile so broad her cheeks ached spread over her face. She placed her hand over the one he'd left on her cheek, lacing their fingers together. "I drove." She snickered, wiping at a tear that refused to stay put. "I just couldn't stay away any longer. I'm so sorry, Deck," her voice trembled. "*You* may have left, but *I* was the one who ran. It just took me more time to realize what I'd done."

Understanding washed over his features as he stepped closer. The smell of chlorine mixed with his usual cedar essence invaded her senses, making concentrating on her apology nearly impossible.

"Apr—"

"No, wait, let me finish. The night you walked out on me…" She inhaled the chlorinated air deeply, allowing herself to feel the hurt of that night and still be in the present with the man she loved. "You brought back things… emotions, insecurities that I never wanted to feel again. And to be honest, that night, you were one hundred percent in the wrong."

"April, you're right. I know I fucked up," Decker agreed.

"But"—she held up her hand to hold off further inter-

LISA N. PAUL

ruption—"in the days that followed, I screwed up too. You're unlike any man I've ever met, and for me to compare you, even in my own mind, was unfair. You've owned your mistakes, and I honestly believe you when you say you'll never hurt me like that again. I may have been too angry and scared to realize it at the time, but I know it now. I do believe in you, Decker and I believe in us." She lowered his hand from her cheek and pressed her lips into his rough palm. "I'm sorry it took me so long to come to my senses. Can *you* forgive *me*?"

"Beautiful," he murmured, pulling her body flush against his, his warm minty breath tangling with her own, "all is forgiven. I love you, do you understand that?"

She felt the smile on his lips as they touched hers in a quick kiss.

"You've owned a piece of me since we first met, and more of me became yours with each passing day." His second kiss was slower but harder, hungrier. "I wasn't going to give up on you, but I must admit your coming after me"—he grinded his pelvis into her abdomen and whispered in her ear—"turns me on like you wouldn't believe. What? What's got you smiling like the Cheshire Cat, dimples?"

"Oh, your enthusiasm is definitely evident, big guy." April looked around before subtly rubbing her hand over his erection. "This is a family-friendly establishment, Mr. Brand. I think the management would frown on these shenanigans happening out here in public."

"Mmm, you keep touching me like that, Ms. Maddox, and they're gonna need to distribute blindfolds to all the

326

children and half of the adults in this place," he growled as he twined his fingers through her long golden hair finally smashing his lips to hers.

Boneless and vulnerable in his arms, she'd never before felt more cared for, safe, or loved. The sheer happiness that sparkled through her was nearly overwhelming and completely consuming.

"I see you decided to play dirty when you came to find me," he said as he nibbled her bottom lip.

"Hmm?" April cocked her head to the side, confused by the statement but enjoying the happiness that glistened in his eyes.

"Lime lip stuff, beautiful. It's my favorite." Giving her no time to respond, he ate away at her lips until they were once again engaged in a mind-melting kiss.

The harsh sound of a throat being cleared and an unintelligible grumble popped the bubble she and Decker floated upon. Still embraced but no longer lip locked, they caught the disapproving leer of a woman leading four screaming children, who must have been quadruplets, out of the water park.

Decker's eyes widened as both bewilderment and sympathy crossed his handsome features. "No wonder she didn't want to watch us making out." He whistled softly as the door closed behind the frazzled mother and her four unruly kids. "Poor woman probably hasn't had time for a proper kiss in six years."

April chuckled at Decker's comment, his brown eyes warm with affection as he gripped her hand tighter in his. The combination of caring father and hard man was a potent mix that melted April's panties every damn time. "Speaking of a proper kiss…" She playfully batted her eyelashes as a deep laugh rumbled from Decker's chest through hers. "I'd love one of those."

"Oh, babe." The side of his mouth ticked up in his *gotcha* grin. "It would be my greatest fucking pleasure."

It took effort not to close her eyes when his calloused palms cupped her face. The rough texture on her soft skin was tantalizing, arousing, but she wanted—no, needed—to see his face, the look in his eyes just before his lips met hers. Her desire, her love, her commitment stared back with a silent promise to move forward together.

His full lips claimed hers, nibbling as his tongue sought entrance into her mouth. His thumbs stroked her cheekbones as he deepened their kiss. Grateful for the populated area, she knew no one but he heard the quiet whimper that left her throat as he massaged her tongue with his own. She needed this man like she needed fresh air. Where the hell was his room?

"April? You came!"

No, no, I didn't, not yet, her libido screamed before realizing that the little voice came from the girl running toward her and Decker with open arms and a bright smile painted on her beautiful face.

"Daddy"—Charlie's brows pinched with confusion—"you said April and Eli weren't coming."

April's heart lurched as she looked at the misunderstanding playing out between Charlie and Decker. She knew that she was the one who'd created the mess in the first place by not coming on the weekend trip, and she'd made it worse by showing up halfway through without Elijah.

"Charlie, honey"—April got to her knees, not caring that the water from the ground was wicking through the cotton of her jeans—"your dad had no idea that I was coming here today. I didn't want to interrupt your time with him. I just had something really important to tell him." *Gah, how does one explain to a six-year-old that one made a mistake and wants to make things better?* April bit the inside of her mouth, looking for the right words. "I... um—"

"I'm so glad you're here." Charlie lunged her small body at April, giving her no choice but to catch the little girl in a tight embrace. "We've really missed you guys."

———◆———◆———◆———

WHILE HE KNEW the past few weeks had been emotionally disastrous on him, he thought he'd done a decent job of faking happiness around Charlie. Seeing the way her eyes lit up as she curled in April's embrace, he realized that his little girl had been pining for April's return just the same as he had and that made Decker feel wonderful and horrible all at once. He'd had such high hopes of getting April back that he never discussed her complete disappearance with Charlie other than to say she was busy. In retrospect, he'd acted like a pussy. Seeing tiny tears escape from his little girl's eyes made him want to kick his own ass.

"Deck, I'm sorry. I tried to keep her with me, but when she saw you and your friend... well..." Janine snorted. "It would have taken a tranquilizer to hold her back."

Decker roped one arm around his friend's shoulder and puffed out a lungful of air. "It's all good, Janine."

April placed another kiss on Charlie's wet hair before lifting them both up to their feet. He'd seen April's eyes narrow in what could only be described as jealousy when his friend approached, but as soon as he mentioned her name, he watched as her shoulders sagged in visible relief. She knew of Janine and the rest of the group—he'd told her about them when he first mentioned the trip—however, it was sexy as hell to know that his woman felt just as possessive of him as he was of her. That said, he'd never give her a reason to question his faithfulness. After quick introductions, Janine excused herself and went back to the waterslides and her family.

"So, where's Eli?" Charlie questioned, searching the area by the door.

"Oh, well, honey," April hedged, "here's the thing—"

"D-Man!" Elijah squealed as he darted through the door, slipping on the wet stamped concrete and landing flat on his butt.

Decker's breath hitched in his chest as tears welled in the little boy's big hazel eyes. Without thinking, Decker sat on the ground and scooped the startled child, whom he'd grown to adore, into his arms. "Aww, E-Man, are you okay?"

Eli's bottom lip trembled as one large tear rolled down his cheek. Decker did a quick body check and found no torn clothes or blood. He looked up to find April staring down at him, her gaze filled with concern, love, and trust. He was one lucky son of a bitch.

"Hey, buddy," Decker said through a smile to the sweet little boy in his arms, "I've got some bad news."

Eli wiped his eyes and looked up at him with reverence, as if whatever Decker was about to say was the most important thing Eli had ever heard. "What is it?"

"Well, it seems as though when you fell just now... you hit the ground so hard..." Decker pulled in a dramatic breath. "That you split your butt clear in half." He couldn't contain his smile when Eli looked concerned. "Dude, you have a butt crack!"

The sound of Eli's high-pitched laugh would have brought him to his knees had he not already been sitting on his ass.

"Elijah Maddox!"

Decker looked up to find not just Ellen Maddox but also his own mother busting through the entrance of the water park room.

"You can't just run away from us like that. You scared Grandma to death." Sheer panic graced the features of April's mother.

"Mom? What are you guys doing here?" April looked just as confused as he had been just moments before.

"I called her," Robyn said, her lips curling with confidence. "And I'd love to explain, but can we move our conversation to the lobby?" Her gaze met Decker's before traveling to Charlie's. "I can't be in a place like this without wanting to go down the slides, and clearly, I don't have my swimsuit on just yet." She winked at Decker before pulling at the neckline of her shirt.

He knew his mother. The air was thick and humid, and she was probably uncomfortable as hell but didn't want to make a scene.

"I'd love to take this to the lobby. It's hot and sticky in here," Ellen complained, causing April to roll her eyes and Eli to giggle.

Once in the lobby, Charlie and Eli sat together with the crayons and coloring books that magically appeared from Ellen's handbag, quickly getting lost in a world of colors and creations. Decker and April squeezed next to each other on an oversized chair, facing their mothers, who filled the tiny loveseat that faced them.

"This was meant to be a family vacation," Robyn started, "and the four of you are a family."

———◆———◆———

APRIL CHEWED ON the inside of her mouth as she sat snuggled next to her handsome man and listened to Robyn speak. It was true—they had become a family, and it was one that she never wanted to lose.

"After you called me this morning, April, I knew it was time for me to pull out the big guns," Robyn said.

April could feel Decker's eyes on her, burning with love and affection, and it made her burn just as hot.

"Wait, Mom," Decker interrupted. "What the heck are the *big guns*?"

Robyn turned to Ellen and Ellen to Robyn.

"We are of course," Robyn replied. "Doesn't matter how old you get, dear children, sometimes you need your parents to step in and clean your sh... stuff up."

"Well, not all of the time," Ellen clarified before continuing where Robyn stopped. "The two of you were a mess. So we pointed you in the right direction and prayed." Ellen glanced at April. "And when you finally saw past your stubbornness"—she pointed her stare toward Decker—"you guys were already here. So Robyn called me, and we decided to follow April up here with Eli and give you the weekend you deserve."

"And I'll speak for both of us when I say that we're so happy you did, but what I don't understand is, why both of you?" April asked, grateful but still confused. "Mom, aren't you just dropping Elijah off and heading home?"

The way both grandmothers grinned would have been creepy if their reasoning wasn't so damn sweet.

"No, April," Robyn responded. "Your mother and I want you and Deck to have the weekend you all deserve. So we're going to commandeer the suite that Decker and Charlie stayed in last night, and we rented a separate room... for you and Decker to spend the next two nights... alone."

When Robyn winked, April flushed then shot an astounded glare at her mother, who'd spent April's entire life shouting "abstinence makes the heart grow fonder" messages through a megaphone.

"So family time during the day and adult time at night," Decker concluded, his *gotcha* grin draped across his face.

Both mothers nodded, clearly proud of themselves.

April shivered when Decker pulled her tight to his side. "What do ya say, beautiful? Can you handle two whole nights of adult time with me?"

"Big guy, I can handle as many nights as you wanna give me."

Pure unadulterated desire flashed through his chocolate eyes as he leaned in and claimed her mouth. Knowing that she had officially given her heart to the man beside her somehow made her feel stronger, more independent, and more alive.

* * *

S EEING THE LOVE sparkle in her green eyes felt like watching the sun rise over the Atlantic Ocean—breathtaking, enchanting, and unforgettable. He'd finally found the woman who touched his heart, claimed his soul, and healed his spirit. Okay, fine, Ford would say he sounded like a pussy, but he didn't care. April was the woman he'd spend the rest of his life loving, and he couldn't wait to start. Two full days of family time... his family—it couldn't get better than that.

EPILOGUE

"**H**EY, BIG GUY**,**" April called from the first floor of their custom-built single-family home. "Charlie and Eli are arguing over what movies to bring for the car ride up to the Poconos. Can you please get Stella out of her crib and get her dressed?"

"No need to yell, beautiful. We're right here." Decker walked into the family room with their two-year-old daughter, Estella, propped on his hip.

The way he loved Elijah, treated him no differently than he did Charlie, still touched April to the depths of her soul. The look in Decker's eyes the first time Eli had called him Dad was like nothing words could ever describe. However, watching him with Stella, their little baby girl, captivated her. They'd named her Estella after the elderly woman who had fallen off the treadmill at the gym. Each agreed it was in that moment that the true connection between them formed. Each time April thought about the way Decker had fawned over her during her pregnancy, the way he'd held her hand during labor and delivery, and how he'd been there, loving her and their children as though they were the most precious gifts, every minute since had been a blessing.

While she didn't think of her former life often, her ex-husband's words floated through her mind sometimes, making her laugh. He was right. *They* could have never been the fairy tale, because she'd ended up with the best happily ever after any woman could've asked for when she met Decker Brand.

The End

ACKNOWLEDGMENTS

T HIS IS THE part of each book that I love writing the most, but causes the greatest amount of stress. While each story comes from my own mind, every single book is a project that takes a great many people to achieve. I kid you not, if it were only me producing Blocked you would have a hand drawn cover (drawing is NOT a strength of mine...think stick figures), run-on sentences, a word count of approximately two hundred thousand words (to me, everything is important), and this book would have come to you in Word Doc (I can't format). Needless to say, I had help and I am eternally grateful. However, as every author knows, it isn't just those that help with the book that deserve heartfelt gratitude, but those around you who are forced to deal with the everyday craziness of life with a story teller. I'd like to take a moment to thank the people in my world—without them the destination wouldn't be worth the journey.

The first thing anyone sees when they look at a book is the cover. I wanted something sexy, seductive, and... well...silly. As always, the wonderfully talented **Regina Wamba** from Mae I Design and Photography whipped up a cover that had me giggling the moment I saw it. Thank you, Regina, for always giving my words the perfect muse.

When I decided to "try writing something different" I was scared, nervous, and downright anxious that I wouldn't be able to get the thoughts that were so vivid in my mind onto paper without losing my writing voice in the process. Changing genres is scary as hell and going from Erotic Romance to Contemporary Comedy Romance frightened the crap out of me. However, there was one woman who stood by my side from the very first day – megaphone in one hand and pom-pom in the other screaming... "DECKERRRRRRR!!!" **Debi Barnes**, you make one hell of a cheerleader, a great sounding board, an efficient beta reader and a fabulous friend. Thank you for keeping my path lit and cleared even when it would have been easier for me to quit. Blocked would have never been written if not for you.

As I said above, when writing, I tend to think everything is important...EVERYTHING. What I've learned through the process of writing is one of the most important things an author needs is a good beta reader. I was fortunate enough to have several amazing women on my team. Each offered unique insight to my story, and it was through their eyes that I was able to fully see my work. Fleshing out unnecessary words/parts as well as adding to sections that I may have seen clearly in my head but not translated effectively onto paper. Thank you **Joanne Schwehm**, **Debi Barnes**, **Erin Noelle**, **Ilsa Madden-Mills, Jennie Wurtz,** and **Lauren Collins** you ladies are the dream team of Betas!!!!

After all of the writing and re-writing, after the beta reading and the fixing of the most common things, what I heard from each of my beta team was, "You have a ton of grammar issues, but the editor will fix that...right?" My editors are actually superheroes. I mean that, truly. I feel so blessed to have them in my life. **Pamela Snyder**, you have been with me for a while now and I appreciate how you always make time for me. You're steady and calm, kind and caring with my words. Thank you. **Cassie Cox**, you recently came into my life and wow, you're like an encyclopedia of grammatical knowledge. I almost want to come up with questions just to see if you'll have the answers. Thank you for your help. I look forward to working with both of you in the future.

Once my mess of words has become an edited story, I send them to one of the most talented and patient women I know. **Julie Titus** of JT Formatting has been with me since my very first book making the woman a true saint. No matter how many times I've rescheduled (with notice), no matter how many times I've had to change things, no matter how many questions I've had, Julie has kindly answered them without ever showing an ounce of irritation or frustration. See...a saint. I adore you, Julie.

Dave Griffin, you my friend are in Chapter Eighteen. My part is complete. Your turn.

To Edward Galgon and Jasun Romain at Montgomeryville Acura, thank you for helping me out. Believe it or not, you've inspired me more than you know.

Speaking of inspiration, writing is a solitary profession. So many hours are spent in silence with only the tapping of the keys on the laptop for background noise. Without intending to sound rude, unless one is in the field, it's impossible to understand the lifestyle. I have been fortunate, lucky, blessed (you name it) to have found some of the most incredible friends a girl could ever want through this business. While the list is long, there is just a small little group that I can honestly say I wouldn't be able to survive in the writing world without. **Joanne Schwehm, L.b Simmons** and **Ilsa Madden-Mills** you three are my sisters. I can't believe I got through life before meeting you. All of you are different from the other, yet each such an integral part to my life.

Ilsa, you are my sweet southern lady. You're honest and kind and even when you aren't, it still sounds like you are ;). You are one of my favorite people in the world to talk to, because I know how much you truly care about me and whatever nonsense I'm sputtering on about.

L.b, you have been my other half since the start. I feel your happy and your sad. The conversations that we can have through nothing more than emojis will forever crack me up! But NOTHING will ever be better than the time we had a full conversation while we acted out the emojis ;)

Joanne, (the second funniest person I know) seriously? Our relationship is not normal. I fluffing love you. Yes, it's true, if not for you we'd both have ten books written by now, but I wouldn't give up even one of our phone conversations no matter how many books we could have written. There is something so therapeutic about the amount of laughing we do each day. Agree? Thank you for being just as crazy as I am. Thank you for loving my characters as much as I do. Thank you for letting me corrupt you. And thank you for taking Jon and me to Line and Bull, I belong there…for real!! Your family has become mine and I couldn't be happier. I love you.

I'm not sure I've ever laughed as much in my thirty some-odd years as I have since meeting you ladies. Thank you. There aren't enough ways to express my love for you.

To the **Danny's Dolls** – You chicks rock! You show up to play at Happy Hour, you pimp my work, and most importantly, you inspire me to keep working. **Erin Marie Fisher, Heidi Goodwin-Small and Debi Barns,** thank you for corralling the group each week. Happy Hour would be a lot less fun if it was just me sitting by myself. Remember, no matter how hard times get…a Dirty Mind is a terrible thing to waste ;).

Thanks to all of the **bloggers** who have posted and reviewed for me and my books. You have screamed my name and spread my words, my gratitude is unending.

While I may spend way too much time wrapped up in my fictional world, I have to come out sometimes. My real life is crazy busy with kids, family, and day-to-day stuff. But something I have learned over the last few years is that when one keeps themselves locked away behind a computer screen it's easy to lose contact with friends and acquaintances; so thank you **Dara Brecher** and **Roni Jaffe** for never giving up on me. Thank you for texting and calling me even when I suck at getting back to you. You girls are my tether to the real world and not only would I be lost without you, but I'm blessed to have you.

To my husband and sons, I love you. I love you so

hard it's crazy. I know it's hard living with me when I'm writing so thank you for your patience and your understanding. **Jon**, thank you for doing the laundry! You're so good at it I think you should continue to do it all of the time!! Boys, there are so many parts of Eli and Charlie's personalities that I stole from you. Thank you for the inspiration. You both are the best teachers a mom could ever ask for.

Last but certainly far from least, to **You**, my readers, there are not enough words in the English language to properly thank you for all you've done for me. Thank you for putting your faith in me and continuing to read my stories. I appreciate you.

XO,

Lisa N Paul

ABOUT THE AUTHOR

L ISA N. PAUL is a wife, mother, daughter, sister, friend, reader, writer, blogger, and self-proclaimed comedian—just not always in that order. Ever since she was a little girl, she has devoured books. Falling in love with the Sweet Valley High series at a young age drew Lisa to series books and inspired her to write her own. *Thursday Nights*, *Storm Front* and *Breaking to Breath* are the first three books in her Charistown series. *Blocked* is a standalone novel.

When not writing, Lisa can be found eating French fries and Godiva raspberry truffles, or hanging out with her husband and two sons.

Visit her website at http://www.lisanpaul.com

OTHER TITLES BY LISA N. PAUL

THE CHARISTOWN SERIES

www.ingramcontent.com/pod-product-compliance
Lightning Source LLC
Chambersburg PA
CBHW021958260626
47156CB00018B/2082